A TEXAS DESTINY

The SAGA BEGINS

JOE G. BAX

EMERALD
BOOK CO.

Published by Emerald Book Company
Austin, TX
www.gbgpress.com

Distributed by Emerald Book Company

For ordering information or special discounts for bulk purchases, please contact Emerald Book Company at PO Box 91869, Austin, TX 78709, 512.891.6100.

Design and composition by Greenleaf Book Group LLC
Cover design by Greenleaf Book Group LLC

Publisher's Cataloging-In-Publication Data
(Prepared by The Donohue Group, Inc.)

Bax, Joe G.
    A Texas destiny : the saga begins / Joe G. Bax. -- 1st ed.

    p. ; cm.

    ISBN: 978-1-938416-29-3 (hardcover)
    ISBN: 978-1-937110-41-3 (pbk.)

    1. Texas--Colonization--History--19th century--Fiction. 2. Texas--History--To 1846--Fiction. 3. Plantations--Louisiana--19th century--Fiction. 4. Louisiana--Fiction. 5. Texas--Fiction. I. Title.

PS3602.A9 T49 2012
813/.6   2012948258

Part of the Tree Neutral™ program, which offsets the number of trees consumed in the production and printing of this book by taking proactive steps, such as planting trees in direct proportion to the number of trees used: www.treeneutral.com

Printed in the United States of America on acid-free paper

12 13 14 15 16 17   10 9 8 7 6 5 4 3 2 1

First Edition

Dedicated to
Mrs. Marquerite DeGeorge, who taught me how to read;

Fr. John Wick, C.S.B., who taught me how to write;

And to Sr. Mary Brendan O'Donnell, whose quiet trust gave me the confidence this life requires.

CONTENTS

Chapter 1: A Louisiana Childhood. 1

Chapter 2: Fresh Africans. 13

Chapter 3: Rain, Wind and More. .29

Chapter 4: Family Warfare. 43

Chapter 5: Jared Groce 55

Chapter 6: A Visit to Texas 67

Chapter 7: Deep in the Heart of Texas. 81

Chapter 8: Return and Pack. 97

Chapter 9: Texas becomes Home . . . Maybe 115

Chapter 10: Peace at Last. 127

Chapter 11: Horses Away 141

Chapter 12: Whores and Horses .153

Chapter 13: Rack and Romance. .163

Chapter 14: Indians Again 177

Chapter 15: A Change in the Air .187

Chapter 16: Panic and Preparation. 199

Chapter 17: Destiny San Jacinto. .211

Chapter 18: Taking Young Zuber Home 221

Chapter 19: Surprise, Hurt and Disappointment 229

Chapter 20: Houston at Houston. 241

Chapter 21: War Again 249

CHAPTER I

A Louisiana Childhood

"GARVAN FUCHS IS A SONOFABITCH."

Drayton Wilhite was beside himself and of course, if Drayton was upset, his brother Dunwoody would be also. They were separated by all of eleven months. Most folks considered them twins with an elongated gestation period. Drayton, the older, was the talker. There were neighbors who swore they had never heard the voice of Dunwoody. This actually was their good fortune. When Dunwoody did speak, and thank God it was seldom, it was mostly nonsensical gibberish in a high pitch nasal twang. Chills would go down your spine the tone was so irritating. People openly gasped the very first time Dunwoody spoke in their presence. Since I grew up around these two uncles, brothers of my father Abram, I could not recall the shock of hearing Dunwoody. This gave me the great opportunity to watch the horrified expressions of strangers.

"Drayton Wilhite, do not use such language in front of my baby!"

My mother would not tolerate harsh language in our house, a lesson learned well by my father. Regrettably, the baby she was referring to was me. Now twelve, I didn't consider myself a baby. However, I was the only child of Abram and Susannah and probably destined to be my mother's baby forever. In the meantime, Uncle Drayton and Uncle Dunwoody were producing cousins like they were bunnies. Don't hold me to this, but I think Uncle Dunwoody and Aunt Peggy had six young'uns and Drayton and Fanny were not too far behind at four, with a bun in the oven as we speak. Fanny was one of those women who looked pregnant all the time. She seemed to be able to squeeze out a kid and never lose a pound.

"I don't care; the man is a world class son of a bitch without equal!"

"Drayton, I warned you." Susannah was reaching for her rolling pin, which provoked older brother Abram to wade into the fray.

"What has he done this time, Drayton?"

"He is going up on his wharf price again! Double last year! Every damn year he goes up!"

Mother raised her rolling pin shortly after "damn" left his lips.

"Drayton, there are other wharfs." My father had settled down in his chair and was in the process of lighting his pipe. I guess he felt this conversation was going to take awhile. Drayton remained standing. Dunwoody, as usual, stood right behind him and slightly to his right.

"Fuchs' wharf is the closest. I don't see why I should be made to haul my cotton any further than necessary."

"Drayton, you either pay the charge or it becomes necessary to haul it a little further. The fee isn't exorbitant. Pay the man and be done with it." Dad now had his pipe going at its maximum. Smoke was quickly filling the room and now encircled the irritated uncles.

"It is robbery, Abram!"

"Drayton, is your memory that short? Have you forgotten how many times you tried to put the britches on old Fuchs?"

Drayton kicked at the floor recalling the several incidences that my father referenced. In actuality, this whole matter started a long time ago. The Wilhites came to Louisiana as a family. The three boys, there were no sisters, ultimately settled on the river and next to one another. Whatever romance there once was to this arrangement left for other parts once the brothers married. At that time, all three tracts had Mississippi River frontage and each had a wharf. Of course, as was typical for the three, my father's wharf was well-made. Drayton's was passable and Dunwoody's was . . . well, Dunwoody's.

Unbeknownst to anyone, certain pressures, movements and shiftings were going on deep in the earth, not near here, or at least not to anyone's knowledge. But about five years ago, near New Madrid, animals started to act real strange; jitterish at best. The birds simply left the area, as did most insects. Then the earth rumbled, shook and undulated taking on a flexibility that dirt isn't suppose to have. In the process, the granddad of them all, the Mississippi reversed its course. It literally flowed upstream towards the Ohio flooding places that had never been flooded in anyone's memory. When it returned to its usual flow, it rushed South with a vengeance. The velocity was so much greater than its usual muddy meanderings that any weak or soft spot just collapsed and tons of water burst through, taking with it anything in its path. Such a weak spot must have existed just about two miles north of the Wilhite tracts because when it was over, the river bed now ran directly in front of, you guessed it, the plantation of Mr. Garvin Fuchs. We were left with what was now called the False River because it wasn't a river anymore.

I supposed Drayton and Dunwoody expected the Mississippi to return. I had my doubts. I have no idea what my father expected. There are advantages to having the False River around, at least from my point of view. Once the ruckus settled down and the Wilhite family got over not having a wharf—well, they still had a wharf; it just didn't have any use. The former river bed just teamed with all kinds of things. The buzzards and coons cleared out the dead fish in no time. They never had time to even stink. What was left was an amazing assortment of stuff.

Reams Whitworth and I spent weeks dragging out boat anchors, tools, crates and a world of mismatched shoes just to name a few. We pretty much stayed confined to the beds now existing on our parent's land. This avoided any conflict with my cousins who Reams referred to as "the tribe." Gradually, my father started planting the False River, which seemed to grow just about anything. Drayton and Dunwoody could barely get their usual fields planted. Expansion wasn't possible.

"Abram, maybe its time to teach old baldy a good lesson."

Uncle Dunwoody's description was more than just a little bit accurate. Garvin Fuchs was not only bald; he was absolutely hairless. He had no eyebrows, no eyelashes. He didn't even have ear hair, which seemed to cluster by the bushel basket load on most men his age. He was a short, pale fellow, whose face was mostly hidden by a large straw planter's hat. It was a might unsettling to be around old Fuchs. He hiccupped. Not like your normal hiccup, but kind of a long delayed hiccup. Just about the time you forgot that he had just had one, he would hiccup again. He was regular and punctual as can be; he just elongated the space between episodes. Strangely enough, he got along with my father. He detested my two uncles.

"Dunwoody, I don't know what you have in mind, but I suggest you pay the man and get about the business of trying to grow some cotton. The way you two fellows are having young'uns, you are going to need a bumper crop each and every year."

"Oh we may have found another source of income that pays a whole lot better than cotton and ain't near the work."

My father quit puffing on his pipe. He lowered his arm and squinted right at Dunwoody and Drayton. "Well, I am all ears."

"We have been talking to the Lafitte brothers and . . ."

"Stop right there." Abram's complexion was growing red at the mention of Pierre and Jean Lafitte, two privateers that managed to stay just one step ahead of the law of Louisiana, the United States, Cuba and several other countries. "Would this scheme involve the sale of fresh Africans?"

"Now Abram, I am not sure I know what you mean by fresh Africans?"

"Drayton, Dunwoody, the hell you don't!"

I quickly glanced at my mother and her rolling pin, with the mention of hell. She had not moved and seemed as curious as I was to learn of my uncle's plans.

"The Lafittes are privateers. That is a nice word for pirates. They have the authority of some corrupt dictator to sail the Caribbean for cargo. The cargo they are best at seizing are slaves. You can't legally import them anymore so they seize them, take them to New Orleans and turn them in for the bounty money. Then, when the government puts them up for auction, they buy them with the same damn bounty money they just got. Now the slaves are legally in the country and can be sold at a private sale for a huge profit. They are fresh Africans and I don't know what part you two boys want to play in the process, but I want no part of it. You hear?"

Drayton's face was about as red as my father's but he started to reply.

"Abram, I don't see the harm . . ."

"Don't see the harm? My God, I can't believe we were raised by the same parents. Don't see the harm? It's illegal. It is against the law. It is a total fraud. If you two are going to lay down with dogs, you are damn certain to wake up with fleas."

"Abram, they're just a bunch of negroes."

"Don't you ever bring one of them on to my place. I don't want my people to have any contact with them."

"Abram, does this mean we won't pool our hands at harvest?"

"Absolutely! If this is the path you are heading down, you two will go it alone." Abram was now furiously puffing on his pipe.

"Well, can we still use your horses?"

"Dad!" The shock of me even blurting out a word drew the attention and the ire of my two uncles, but I had to do something. Every time they borrowed a horse or mule, the animal came back crippled. My father knew my concern and responded accordingly.

"Drayton, you take horses that are in good flesh and you bring back cripples."

"I must be mistaken, Abram. I thought they were your horses, not Leander's." Drayton shot me a glance that would freeze water.

"They are my horses. But this boy has a way with them and is responsible for their care. I see nothing productive in running one into the ground. And for an absolute certainty, none of my horses are going to be worked by some tribesman right off the boat."

Drayton kicked the floor again. His face was a bright crimson. However, he thought better of pushing the matter any further. Dunwoody was the same blank slate he had been since he arrived. Both said their goodbyes and left. It did not take my mother long to wade into the fray.

"Abram Wilhite, I have had a belly full of your two siblings. I swear to God, they must have been adopted."

"Mother, that same thought has crossed my mind too many times to count."

"It is bad enough that I have to live down the embarrassment of Baptiste, but now your brothers are about to become pirates."

Her reference to Baptiste got my attention. He was the one uncle I dearly loved. A former mountain man who had made it all the way to the Pacific, he entertained Reams and I with tales that seemed to never end. He never repeated one. They went on forever. Plus, he lived in a tree house in the swamp. That alone was unique, that and the Indian squaw he called Big Basket. At every opportunity, Reams and I would slip off to visit him. Most of the time, we had to hide our intentions from my mother. Baptiste Roubleau was her half older brother, and a great embarrassment to a church-going lady like my mother. I don't think being a mountain man, or even living in a tree house bothered her that much. No doubt she would have preferred that he be a preacher. Baptiste was a reminder to her, and I guess everyone else, that my grandmother had an indiscretion with a Frenchman named Roubleau. Baptiste was an "out child." Some folks called them yard children. The point was my grandmother and Mr. Roubleau produced Baptiste without the benefit of Holy Matrimony. It did not seem to bother Baptiste. He appeared perfectly normal, I mean for a mountain man. To listen to my mother, he was almost the devil himself. At any rate, her entire complexion turned absolutely ashen whenever he was around. Reams and I couldn't wait for our next visit to the swamp.

"Now Mother, no rational person holds Baptiste against you, and I hope that no one holds the misdeeds of Drayton and Dunwoody against me."

"Abram, I have grown weary of those two boys and their families. Everything that is ours automatically becomes theirs; except that they take care of nothing. Every single week, you spend one or two days, sometimes more, getting their ox out of the ditch. Think how much further ahead we would be if your efforts went to the benefit of our family. Those two are Wilhites in name only. Your father has got to be turning over in his grave."

I guess I must have blended into the wall. My mother never spoke so frankly with me present. I have heard her say these things, but that was when I was thought to be asleep. Since I slept in the loft, any conversation, in fact, just about any noise, rose up through those planks and just seemed to hover over my sleeping pad.

"You are probably right, but no one around here is being neglected."

"No one but you. Abram, you are becoming an old man long before your time."

Both of my parents moved toward the table. The food was getting cold given the interruption by my uncles. I sensed that the conversation would now change. My parents had a way of communicating without talking when they thought I shouldn't hear something. This posed no obstacle to me. I just made an excuse to go to bed early, then, I could hear everything. In my mother's eyes, I was locked into some level of infancy, despite the fact that I was now a good deal taller than her. What I heard never seemed to be a problem for my father. If we were with a group of men, they just talked. The fact that any boys were within earshot just didn't matter.

Usually, if there was anything left on my plate, I was supposed to scrape it into the slop bucket. It would finally find its way into the hog's trough. Lately, I have had such an appetite that my plate was a lot cleaner than when I got it. Still I had to wait for the adults to finish. My mother said it was good manners. You have to wait for them to start. You have to wait for them to finish. So I wait. It was growing darker. From the table, I could see the lightening bugs now so it had to be pretty late. Finally, my father leaned back, let out a huge belch and complimented my mother on another fine meal.

This was a bit of a stretch. One of the slave women, Momma Mae, had done most of it, but mother insisted on putting it on the table.

The absolute final signal that the meal was over was when dad lit his pipe. Parents are so predictable; all you have to do is watch. I told them that I was going to bed and called for Roy. Roy was my dog, in fact, he was about my age. I wasn't much of a sleeper as a baby. I would sleep for a few minutes and wake up. Then, sleep for a few minutes and wake up. Apparently I was on the verge of exhausting the entire household. Momma Mae took Roy, himself just a pup, and put him in my crib. Puppies sleep. Never seen one that didn't. When Roy would doze off, so would I. Ever since then, Roy has been my constant companion. A lot of women don't want a dog in the house. Since I am only in the house when I sleep or eat, it never became an issue. Plus, I have learned that parents desperately value their sleep.

I used to have to carry Roy up a ladder to the loft. My father took some boards and nailed them to the cross rungs so Roy could get to the loft by himself. A short whistle and he would head upstairs. My parents would head to the other side of the dog trot; that was their sleeping quarters. Unlike most dog trot cabins, my father extended the loft all the way across the entire cabin so you could walk from one chimney to the other. This made for a huge room. For the most part, there was nothing up there other than me and Roy. Some extra blankets and quilts were stored because travelers were always asking to stay the night and they were never refused. Plus, if we had a bad storm, and Louisiana has its share, my father would bring all the slaves in to stay in the loft. Our cabin, with its dovetail joints, was a good bit more secure than some of the slave quarters with saddleback notches.

Roy fell asleep almost instantly. I had a hunch that my parents would continue their discussion of Uncle Drayton and Uncle Dunwoody. Their late night conversations often filled in the gaps when I had questions about something. They did not disappoint me. My mother's opening comment clearly indicated that the issue had some history to it.

"Abram, I am weary of those two fellows and the mischief that they create. Living so close is an absolute bother."

"I understand Mother, but you must recall we were trying to outrun a yellow fever epidemic when we settled here. God knows I never anticipated that they would be permanently affixed to me, us or our lives. There was enough age difference between us that I never really knew them, certainly not their character."

"I don't fault you Abram, but it is time to put some distance between us and them. They are different. They are difficult. Every-one can see it except you."

"I don't understand."

"Abram, you men are amazing. It is so easy for you to miss the forest for the trees."

"I hesitate to ask, but go ahead Mother, explain it to me."

"There are a dozen examples. Have you ever noticed that all of our slaves always take up with the Whitworth Negroes or the Fuchs'? They never take up with their slaves. The reason is simple. Your brothers abuse their people. They are barely fed or clothed. We may own them, but they are not stupid. What little part of their world that they can control, they will. They will never get involved with your brothers' people. You can even sense their hesitancy when you make them help with Drayton's or Dunwoody's harvest. Those boys are mean and brutal."

"Well I am certain they will be even less inclined if those two start trying to work a bunch of fresh Africans."

"Then, Abram, let that be the start. You have made your posi-tion known. Don't waffle—just use this as a way to break from the old pattern."

"Mother, have you ever given some thought that we might find ourselves in need of their help?"

"That will never happen if I am any judge of you. Those two are useless. If we ever need help, there are dozens of neighbors who would help. Plus, it doesn't stop with slaves or Africans. Your son won't step foot on their land."

Now it was really getting interesting. I couldn't stand my uncles because of the way they treated our animals. As for my cousins, they were the most unruly collection of dullards I have ever seen. However, I couldn't wait to hear my father's response.

"I am aware of Leander's attitude towards his uncles. Frankly, I don't blame him. He has a real way with horses. He can break and school one better than anyone I have ever seen. It's a gift and he has it. Between he and Elisabeth, Poppy's girl, we have the best horse flesh in Louisiana. I just haven't figured out how to break the habit."

"That's easy enough. Charge them for the horses they ruin. You handle the sale of all the cotton. Take it out of their share."

"I guess that could be done. I probably need to address this soon. Leander's growing up fast. I don't know that getting paid for a ruint horse is going to make him happy. If he gets a little bigger, he may take the matter up directly with those two."

"What do you think of the cousins?"

"Oh, you mean why doesn't he run with them?"

"Yes."

"Leander is bright. They aren't. I can't imagine what interest he would have in them. Plus, he and Reams are pretty thick. I suspect he prefers his company."

"All this is well and good for now, but Abram, I dearly hope you outlive me because those brothers are going to come for everything you have the day you are gone."

"I've never given that much thought. Let me sleep on that Mother."

Amazing—dad almost got it right. Now I need to find out more about fresh Africans. I glanced at Roy. His front paws were twitching. Puppy dreams I suspect.

CHAPTER 2

Fresh Africans

THINGS SEEMED TO START ALL AT ONCE EVERY MORN-ING. Some rooster would crow and that would initiate movement at every corner of the plantation. Fires would be stoked in the house and in the slave quarters. Water buckets would be emptied into pots. The quiet stirrings of humans of all sizes and colors increased the noise level gradually until you realized everyone was awake and moving.

Momma Mae was in the summer kitchen producing aromas that would be remembered for a lifetime. Even if you weren't hungry when you woke up, the first whiff of her cooking created an appetite. After breakfast, I headed to the barn. This was the province of Poppy. He was in charge of everything that had to be made, built or repaired. I can't think of anything he can't make. All of our wagons were built by him, from the wheels to the tongue. Metal or wood, it made no difference. He built our home. He shoed the horses and the mules. In these parts, you were very likely to be placed in a crib built by Poppy when you were born. It was a certainty that he would build your casket when you died. In either case, the corners would be tightly mitered and the whole affair would have a furniture finish. Poppy was an artist—we just didn't realize it.

His son, Blue, was now apprenticed to him. It is hard for me to recall when Blue really started his training since he is about three years older than me. Blue looked to have inherited his father's talents.

Since Blue was working the bellows, I just waved to him. He nodded and grinned, while wiping sweat from his forehead. My earliest memories are of Blue. We seemed to enjoy many of the same things. But this morning, I needed his sister Elisabeth.

"Morning, Poppy."

"Well, L'ander, how are you?" Poppy had just enough teeth that Leander was shortened to L'ander.

"Oh I am fine, but do you know where Elisabeth is?"

"I 'spec she's in da garden."

Roy and I headed through the barn and out the back door, passing the paddock that held my father's newest stallion. It was not my place to question my father's selection of horse flesh. Having said that, this horse was certainly pretty enough and had balance, but he was spirited. Horses seem to fall into two broad groups. There are those that like you and want to please you. There are those that could care less about you and seem to delight in provoking you. I could only wish my father would have given a little more thought to the purchase of this one –which brings me to Elisabeth. She had a way with critters of all sorts. She just seemed to calm them.

I swear she could stumble over an alligator and it would never bite . . . probably not even move. Since she was only eight, her chores were mostly around the house and gardens. My father didn't like to put anyone in the fields until they were at least twelve. He said life is too short to rob someone of their childhood.

Elisabeth was just the person I needed to help move this stallion into the breeding pen. His proposed mate was a feisty mare named Phoebe, another one of my father's too quick purchases. Phoebe threw beautiful colts and every other one was trainable. They all eventually got trained. It was just a matter of how much of your religion would you lose in the process.

I saw her bonnet bounce up and down a few times. She was hoeing and pulling weeds.

"Elisabeth, you want to take a break from all that fun?"

She turned and smiled. She was just a wisp of a girl. All of Poppy's size went to Blue. Elisabeth was tiny. There was some kind of balance in the animal world. The bigger the animal, the easier it was for her to handle it. Cats gave her a problem, but then a cat has its own mind. But she could lead the biggest mules and horses with no difficulty. I found this out early on and chose to use it ever since.

"Fun. Didn't seem like much fun to me."

"Good, it's time to breed the new stallion to Phoebe. Would you like to make the introductions?"

"Phoebe goin' like him. He so pretty."

I seriously doubted that either one of these two horses were going to take much of a shine to the other. What she saw in this match that could produce something other than bites, kicks and broken fences was beyond me.

"Let me go get a halter and rope and we'll see if we can get him moved over to Phoebe." Roy didn't follow me, but stayed by Elisabeth.

"What chu need dat for? I's just take 'em."

I didn't relish the idea of this stallion running the entire neighborhood trying to breed every mare and knothole in the parish. I just proceeded to the barn for the halter, Elisabeth and Roy now following behind me.

The stallion had been at the fence all morning nickering and trotting up and down. His tail was up. His head held high. He must have sensed that today was special. The moment I entered his paddock, he sprinted for the far corner. Of course he would. There was nothing about him that was easy. I held the lead rope and halter behind my back, thinking that if he couldn't see them, he may forget that he just saw them. He relaxed, or so it seemed, as I got closer. Then, he shot for the gate and for Elisabeth, who stood right in his path. I shouted to her, but there was no need. He stopped right in front of her and followed her with Roy down the lane to Phoebe. I slowly brought up the rear. She opened Phoebe's gate and walked the stallion over to the mare. She had one hand scratching the neck of one horse and the other hand doing the same to the other. No kicks, no bites, no nickering. Then she turned and walked to the gate.

"I think she likes 'em."

I shut the latches, knowing full well that all hell could and probably would break loose after Elisabeth's magic wore off. But it never did.

She was back hoeing, bonnet just a bouncing.

"Thanks Elisabeth."

"Oh, dat nothin'."

She may have thought it was nothing, but it certainly shortened my chores for the morning. This gave me time to get some answers about fresh Africans. Today was wash day. The Negro women of our plantation and of the Whitworth plantation would customarily gather at small branch off the river. It wasn't deep so they could easily wade into it if they needed to. There were three huge kettles. Each was about six feet across. They had once been part of a sugar plantation. A fire would be started under one and the water heated while the clothes soaked in the cold water of a second kettle. Before they were added to the hot kettle, lye soap would be rubbed on the clothes. The clothes from both plantations were mixed together. The women knew what belonged where. Then, using poles they kept them moving. This helped get the clothes cleaned, but also prevented the entire mixture from hardening into an ugly gel. That could happen with lye soap.

Around the kettles were flat logs or logs that had now become flat. Every time the clothes went from one kettle to another, they were poled onto these logs and the women would beat them with flat boards. I could never figure out how this helped, but beat them they did. Rinse them twice and beat them twice. All the while, they would be singing, talking, humming and singing some more. There was no pattern to it. A lull in conversation provoked a song. If they got tired of singing, then they talked. I always enjoyed the singing, except for Effie's. She couldn't carry a tune in a bucket.

Splat, bat, bat, bat, bat.

I could hear them beat those clothes as I approached the branch.

"Good morning, ladies."

My momma told me to always refer to women as ladies. I guess all of them are or are supposed to be. But these ladies chuckled every time I called them ladies. That was something else for me to figure out along the way.

I positioned myself near Momma Mae. She was in charge, gave all the instructions and generally led the singing. However, she would only be here a short time and then she would return to the kitchen. I suspect that the singing brought her here. Without question, she had the best voice. She was always receptive to my curiosity. If she knew the answer, she would tell me. If she didn't know, she told me so and sometimes offered a suggestion to where I could find the answer.

"Momma Mae, I have a question."

" 'Dat don't surprise me. I ain't neber seen you without one." She was carefully polling the hot kettle, fishing for clothes to take out and place on a log. This was fine. She seldom quit working when we talked, whether it be in the kitchen, here or in her quarters.

"What's a fresh African?"

She stopped. In fact, all the women stopped. Six pairs of eyes were focused right on me. Whatever I just asked tripped across something I didn't suspect.

"Oh Lord," Effie moaned. Effie never talked. She tried to sing, but she seldom talked.

"Son, where did you hear dat?"

"Last night my dad got mad at Uncle Drayton and Uncle Dunwoody because they were going to do something with fresh Africans."

Momma Mae tilted her head, "I take it, he agin' it?"

"Oh yes ma'am. He said he wanted no part of it." Six pairs of eyes were still looking directly at me and no one was moving.

"Son, 'dose be negroes right off da boat."

"Off the boat?"

"Yes, right from Africa . . . can't talk, can't farm, can't do nothin'. Dey just been running round wit a sharp stick. Lord, I wants nothin' to do wif 'em."

"My father said if Uncle Drayton was going to use them, that he wouldn't work his people with theirs when it was time to pick the cotton."

"Oh, I's hopin' Massa Whitworth don't get no fresh Africans." Hannah's comment drew a lot of "Amens" from the Whitworth negroes.

"If'n Massa Abram not goin' to use 'em, Massa Whitworth ain't neither."

My father and Ben Whitworth seemed to run their plantations

the same way. They planted at the same time and in the same way. While each was independent of the other, there was much more in common between them than compared to Abram and his own brothers. The fact that these women did the washing together, showed a good deal more cooperation, than had ever existed between Abram and his brothers.

"Son, did you hear when da Africans was comin'?" Momma Mae now returned to polling for clothes.

"No, I don't think. They said something about the Lafittes. Do you know them?"

"Don't know 'em, but heard de ply da swamps. Have camps in 'em and such."

If anyone would know about what was going on in the swamps it would be Uncle Baptiste. Maybe it was time to pay him a visit.

"Leander, son, you tell Momma Mae if you hear any mo' 'bout dese Africans."

"Oh, yes ma'am!"

If she was that concerned, and my father was likewise, I would certainly let her know. So far, all I could figure is that they were directly from Africa and had sharp sticks. There had to be more.

* * *

Roy jumped in right as Reams pushed us off the bank. The old skiff was about twelve feet long and four feet wide. It did not draw much water, which was good. In the dry season, you sometimes had to push it through what was nothing more than a glorified mud puddle. Today the swamp had plenty of water. I always liked the coolness of the swamp. Huge cypress trees surrounded by so many knees, and massive water oaks clad in grey and sometimes green moss, provided all the shade you could want. The sun light broke in among the cracks between trees, limbs and moss.

Roy always rode at the front. He seemed fascinated by the way the skiff parted the lime green duck weed as Reams and I pushed it forward. That lime cover would part as our long poles moved us along, but if you looked towards the rear of the boat, the weed closed in again—no trace of our passing was left. I learned how to get to Baptiste's tree house by looking for certain odd shaped trees, or those that grew at a peculiar angle. The spacing between trees helped as well. You really had to use all of your senses or you could get hopelessly lost. The depth of the swamp was fairly uniform, but every once in awhile your pole would go down much farther than usual. This was a bit troublesome, but the occasional movement of the pole when it hit something at the bottom really got your attention. I wasn't too keen on providing a meal for some hungry 'gator.

"You know they say an alligator can damn near swallow a dog whole."

I knew Reams was just trying to get a rise out of me. When he got bored, he got mischievous. He was smart as a tree full of owls. Thus, he was almost always bored, and therefore, always mischievous.

"Reams, if a 'gator had any sense at all, he would pass up the dog for a chance to haul your big butt down to his den." That was as good a retort as I could come up with on the spot.

"Well, if that 'gator is so smart, he could call some of his buddies and have us all. 'Course your skinny posterior isn't going to go very far."

We were now even, or even until he got bored again.

"Leander, I don't really understand why you're so interested in fresh Africans."

I had filled him in on the conversation between the Wilhite brothers.

"Grown up talk just interests me. You have to wonder how they learned so much."

"Well I suspect it was from running their head into a wall too many times."

"Reams, that may appeal to you, but if I can learn something without the pain, I would prefer it."

Roy was entranced by a squirrel that was keeping up with us by running from branch to branch and leaping from tree to tree. The limbs were heavy with Resurrection fern due to the recent rains. Still he kept up and maintained Roy's attention. As we got closer to Baptiste's, Roy would run back and forth from the front of the skiff to the back, which irritated Reams to no end, and delighted me in the process. For whatever reason, Roy paid absolutely no attention to Reams. He was not used to being ignored by man or dog.

Baptiste's home was on a rise in the middle of the swamp. Rise in the sense that the area was about three to four feet higher than the water level. It would only be a guess, but it had to be at least a couple of acres. It was sort of a reverse oasis in the middle of all this water. To describe it as a tree house was not exactly correct. It was a trees-house. Four large cypress trees were incorporated into his home. The first landing completely encircled one tree. It was about ten feet off the ground and was easily reached by a single flight of stairs. Water barrels and everyday utensils were located at this level, but were quickly moved in the event of a flood. Of course, the stairs were frequently rebuilt. Baptiste now had an extra set, found after he had rebuilt a new set following a storm.

A ladder led to the next level, which was a large platform, triangular in shape that was anchored to three other trees. It was enclosed on two sides and had a canvas sail as the third wall. It was raised and lowered depending on the weather. The top level was reached by means of an interior staircase. Baptiste and Big Basket slept on the top level, but stayed on the second level most of the day. Anything on the first level that had to be brought up to another was handled by a large pulley. Since Big Basket did most of the cooking on the ground, it was either eaten at that level or raised by the pulley.

By now, Roy was beside himself with excitement. Reams was positioned at the front to jump off as we approached land. Just about the time Reams was prepared to jump, Roy would dart from the back of the skiff and leap for land in search of Baptiste. Totally ignoring the careful planning of Reams, Roy would make landfall yards before we would. His sudden lurch would force Reams to readjust his jump, often in midair. Perhaps this was the source of irritation between Roy and Reams. No matter, Roy would quickly find Baptiste while Reams tied off the skiff.

Roy's bark brought Baptiste to the edge of the second deck. He was a large man, but a full gray beard and a massive head of hair made him appear even larger. His face broke into a grin as he called to us. He was a good bit older than my mother, but had every single tooth, a rarity at his age.

"Leander, Reams—so good to see you. Come on up."

Roy beat us up the stairs to the first platform, Baptiste descending the ladder at the same time. Roy planted his front paw on Baptiste's foot. He didn't do this to everyone, but if he liked you, he wanted to touch you. Then, if he really liked you, he would just sit down on your feet. Baptiste stroked his head while we ascended the stairs.

"How are you Uncle Baptiste?"

"Still above ground, which is probably more than I'm due." He adjusted the suspenders that held up his homespun trousers. He wore no shirt during this time of the year. His only ornamentation was a piece of rawhide that passed through a grizzly bear tooth that he wore around his neck. The scars of that encounter could still be seen on his neck and back.

"What is that smell?" Reams couldn't contain himself any longer. I had gotten a whiff of it when we arrived, but let it pass while we exchanged pleasantries.

"Oh, dead birds I suspect. Damn near run off Big Basket. She's been camping out away from the house while I finish them."

"Why do you have dead birds around?" I was thrilled that Reams took the lead. My personal sense of curiosity was a pretty heavy burden, as my family might attest. For Reams to make the inquiries, relieved me of some of the pressure.

"Come on upstairs." Roy had to stay below and given the aroma probably preferred it, while we ascended the ladder to the second floor. This level was pretty large and with the canvas raised, you got the sense of what it would be like in a bird's nest. Even more so today, for there was now a long table covered in birds in various stages of assembly or disassembly.

"Baptiste, you got one of just about every bird!"

"Not really, there are more types than you would think, but I am making a helluva dent in them."

Reams was entranced. His own curiosity had gotten the best of him. "What are you going to do with them?"

"Sell them, or better said, they're all sold. Sold to that fellow Audubon down at St. Francisville. I will sell as many as he wants. I am making a small fortune doing it too."

"Who is Audubon, Baptiste?"

"He is a naturalist."

Now I had never heard that word before and felt it time for me to edge into the conversation.

"What's a naturalist, Uncle Baptiste?"

"He studies nature, birds, fish, flora and fauna, you know." Reams obviously overestimated my knowledge in this area.

"Exactly. He also is an artist and wants to paint every bird we have. It is a damn sight easier to paint a dead one than to try and paint one flying around. I have seen some of his paintings. The man is an artist, no doubt about it. He has an eye for details. With them dead birds, he can turn them around, over, under, upside down until he gets 'em right." Baptiste used a small hawk to illustrate his point.

"I trap them, then dry them out and cart them down to St. Francisville. It is a whole lot easier than hunting bear." His right hand rubbed the tooth hanging around his neck, reflecting upon earlier times.

"You fellows must be hungry. Let me call up Big Basket and see what she has cooking." He reached for an old hollowed out horn and blew into it a couple of times.

He barely finished his last note when I could see her coming towards the treehouse. She was a tiny lady, always clad in deerskin. Her everyday dress was lightly beaded, just a small patch of color on each sleeve. Her Sunday go to church dress had small shells sewn on it and was more ornamented.

Of course, when she and Baptiste did attend church, my mother was absolutely mortified. There sat the "out child" of my grandmother in the Wilhite pew for all the Christian world to see.

Big Basket never talked at church. Around the tree house, her vocabulary was limited to words, or sounds, that started with the letter "h". She might say "hum" or variations thereof, but no real identifiable words. It didn't seem to bother Baptiste. Somehow they communicated. As she approached the house, I noticed that there were now streaks of silver in her braided hair. That seems to happen to grown ups. One day they just quit growing whatever color they had been growing and started growing gray hair.

She was a good cook, but a strange cook. Baptiste tended to roast a lot of meat over a cook fire. Big Basket cooked a lot of stew. It was always tasty, but it was anyone's guess what was in it. Since she didn't talk, there was no way to know. She moved quietly around us as we ate, hardly making a sound. I can't recall Baptiste ever addressing her directly. She busied herself by anticipating his every need.

"Fellows, have you ever heard of a fandango or some call it a rendezvous?"

Reams and I looked at one another, both shaking our heads that we hadn't.

"When I was trapping the Rockies, all us mountain men, that's what they called us, would gather every spring down in the foothills, after the spring thaw. My God, how I looked forward to it. You spent so much time alone. To just see another human, any human was a treat, but to see all your old buddies was a true delight. The first thing I would do was to look for a real good anthill."

"Anthill!" Reams and I were in unison on that point. I was prepared for some ribald tale of debauchery. Neither one of us were ready for an anthill.

"Yup, after being in the same buckskins since early winter, they were oily, dirty and inhabited by more critters than just myself. You got a stick and really stirred up those ants. Got 'em mad. Then you would strip down and drop those buckskins right on the mound. It wouldn't take them long to cart off and eat all the lice, fleas and ticks that had been crawling on your ass all winter." He let out a huge laugh and shook his head. "I guess the ants were as glad to see me as I was to see them."

"There would be more food than you could ever eat. Fellows brought in moose, deer, and buffalo. Now the buffalo gave us a real delicacy, plus a whole lot of fun."

"Delicacy, Uncle Baptiste?"

"Leander, he means something that tastes real good."

I could tell Reams was starting to enjoy the use of his enlarged education.

"Oh, by far and away, the best tasting meal was roasted buffalo intestines. Men would fight over 'em."

I generally have a fairly strong stomach, but the mention of roasted guts, buffalo or otherwise, caused some unnatural stirrings in my own gut. Baptiste was intent on continuing his story.

"You know the damn things are about twenty feet long. So we kind of looped them over a fire until they were done. Then, that was when the fun started. One old boy would get on one end and another would start eating at the other end. The race to the middle was on. They gradually started walking and eating, walking and eating. As they got closer to each other, one old boy would jerk his head. Of course, this would pull a foot or so of intestines right out of the stomach of the fellow on the other end. Needless to say, that didn't feel so great and certainly didn't set well with the fellow who now had to eat the foot of intestines he thought he had finished."

The strange sensations in my stomach seemed to grow, taking on a life of their own.

"Then what happened, Baptiste?" Reams had to ask. I feared the response.

"Oh, finally knives would be drawn."

"What? To kill each other?" Reams shouted.

"Oh no, to cut the intestine; so, it could be finished off by the fellows."

Cold sweat beads had surfaced on my forehead. I prayed that this was the end of this tale or I was probably going to embarrass myself in front of Reams and my favorite uncle.

"So what have you fellows been doing of late? I suppose your dads have pretty much turned their plantations over to you?"

Thank heaven for a change of topic.

"No, sir, we are starting to breed some of the mares. Using dad's new stallion," I offered as a diversion.

"How do you think he'll do, Leander?"

'He'll get 'em bred; what the outcome will be is anyone's guess."

"I don't know why Abram doesn't turn that horse business over to you. You have more talent at it than he does. I know he likes it, but liking it and being good at it are two different things."

"How is your mother?"

"I guess fine. She stays pretty irritated at Uncle Drayton and Uncle Dunwoody."

"Ha, as well she should. Those two peckerwoods don't have an ounce of sense between 'em."

This seemed to be a good place to mine a little more information. I decided to see what Baptiste knew about the Lafittes.

"Uncle Baptiste, have you heard of the Lafitte's?"

"Have I? Of course, you have been crossing some of their trails every time you have come here. I'm surprised you haven't run into them."

"Who are they?"

"Wrong question, Leander. You should ask what are they? They are pirates, pretty plain and simple. They hijack ships, steal the cargo and hide it in the swamps."

"This swamp?" Our apparent close proximity to pirates had my heart racing.

"This swamp and a thousand others. I guess it depends on what kind of cargo and what they plan to do with it. I mean it could be any thing from rum to sugar to people."

"People!"

"Sure, you fellows have to know that you can't bring slaves in anymore. Lafittes will pirate slaves and hide them if they feel it is safe to smuggle them, or they will turn them in for a reward. Of course, then they buy 'em and resell 'em."

"Uncle Baptiste, are these slaves called 'Fresh Africans'?"

"Sure, some people call them that so as not to mix them up with the slaves that were born and raised here. If they were born here, that's no problem. You just can't bring 'em in here anymore."

"My father was real upset 'cause Drayton and Dunwoody were going to use them."

"Your dad wouldn't be nearly as upset as the slaves he owns and slaves your dad owns, Reams. They aren't going to like working with Africans right off the boat."

"Why?"

"They don't know nothin'. No one knows their language. They have been cooped up in the hold of some boat for months. They're as skittish as a deer. Headaches, nothing but headaches for their owner and the other slaves. Of course, if there are any two fools who deserve a headache or two, it would be Drayton and Dunwoody."

"Humph." I guess Big Basket was listening. She seemed to agree with Baptiste's assessment of my two uncles.

CHAPTER 3

Rain, Wind and More

BY EARLY AFTERNOON, A COMPLETE STILLNESS HAD SETTLED OVER THE FIELDS. Stillness of movement and stillness of sound hung in the air, air that now brought no relief from the summer heat. Body temperatures rose, and then rose some more. White faces were crimson. Black faces glistened with sweat. You could see the thunderheads building to the South. They grew to remarkable heights giving some dimension to the blue sky above. When the first rain band blew in, it was a welcomed relief.

However, it was only a momentary respite. The rain stopped and the heat, sun and humidity made the air heavier than before. The next shower was a little longer and heavier and so it went for about an hour. Rain, heat, rain, heat. Then Mother Nature got serious. The rain came with a vengeance. You were instantly soaked to the bone. As odd as it may sound, your body was now chilled—yes, chilled right in the middle of summer.

Since no one could see much further than a few feet, everyone headed home. Blue and I gathered all the harnesses and tack, soaped them and hung them inside the barn. The horses and mules were turned out to rest sore muscles and tired feet. Blue left for the quarters. Roy and I darted for the house. The rain was hard and steady. By the time I finished my chores, the day really hadn't been cut that short. I helped Roy up the stairs to the loft. The heat now tended to work on him a little. By days end, he would be stiff. Once asleep, he didn't move at all. This troubled me, but I preferred not to think about it.

There would be no chance to eavesdrop on the adults tonight. The rain came down harder after dark. It was all you could hear. It was still raining in the morning. I knew what every child in the area knew—Today was a perfect day to tackle the ravine.

We called it the ravine. Some folks might call it a swell, or a branch, maybe a swag. At its source, it was a depression about six feet wide at the edge of a flat field. However, the field was slightly tilted in its direction, probably the result of some glacier eons ago. The field was the watershed for the ravine that sloped directly towards the river. As it approached the river bank, it gradually got narrower and narrower. By the time the water reached the river's edge, it was moving very fast and literally shot off the bank, landing some distance into the river. The entire affair was about three hundred feet long and the drop from the upper end to the lower end was probably eighty to ninety feet. Depending on how much rain we had, a fellow could really get up some speed before you grabbed the rope. Yes, the rope was the most important part. A tight hemp rope was strung between two trees, one on each side of the ravine. You had to grab it or you would be hopelessly adrift in the "mighty Mississip".

I raced to the quarters for Blue, Elisabeth, Little Bob, Randle and anyone else who was game. They all had the same intuition that I had. With the amount of water that had hit the ground, the ravine had to be full and moving fast.

By the time we got there, Reams, Big Charlie and all the folks from the Whitworth plantation were already soaked and lined up for their second try. Even some of Drayton and Dunwoody's offspring were there.

I waited out my turn. Roy chased every one down the ravine from the edge. That is everyone but Reams. His barks mixed in with our own screams and thus added to the excitement. Truthfully, I had never seen so much water. We had received some rain this summer so the ground wasn't totally parched. This created more run off. I eased down to the center of the ravine. The native blue stem grass was bent over towards the river, slick and ready to go. The force of the water almost took my footing away from me, but I sat down and immediately departed for the river.

Without question, it was the fastest ride of my life. All of our butts had made a perfect rut. Once your rear end was in it, there was no stopping you and certainly no need to guide or steer. As the ravine narrowed, I realized that I needed to be very alert. The rope would be coming toward me, or so it seemed, very quickly. Grabbing it, I pulled and inched myself to the edge, greeted by Roy and headed back up the hill.

Tiny Elisabeth was coming down next, with all the personal tranquility she always exhibited. There just was not enough of her for the water to push. Still, she seemed to enjoy the trip. However, behind her was big Charlie. Although I always referred to him as Charles, everyone else called him Big Charlie for a reason. Charles was coming down like a tree. Water was pushing his back, his butt, and coming over his broad shoulders.

I glanced up the hill only to see D.A. cutting in line. D.A. was Uncle Drayton's oldest boy. We all had reached the age that we now knew there was a hierarchy of sorts. Something worked out by the grownups. But when we played, we just played. Everyone took turns. Some of us lived in the quarters; some of us didn't. However, D.A. had apparently figured out that the day to day hierarchy could be used to his benefit. His actual name was David Alan Wilhite. His family called him D.A. This was an unfortunate decision on their part. It played right into the creative juices of my buddy Reams, who became convinced that D.A. stood for "Dumb Ass". He was so certain of his conviction, that he never missed an opportunity to refer to D.A. by his new proper name.

Reams had his hand on D.A.'s shoulder, restraining him from cutting in line. D.A. shook loose and took his cut anyway. It was standard D.A. behavior. In fact, all of my cousins seemed to be of the same temperament; one of the reasons Reams called them 'the tribe."

As I arrived at the starting point, Reams turned to me, "Dumb Ass is up to his same old bullshit."

"Yes, I saw."

"Look there Leander, the jackass has a new trick up his sleeve."

I turned to see D.A. straddle the course in an effort to stop James, the same Whitworth slave that he had cut in front of. James was small and a good deal younger. It would not have been a fair fight if both had been black or both had been white. Why do we have to live so close to these fools? I made a mental note to raise this issue with the grownups.

Reams had splashed into the ravine. Given his cannon ball shape, he was soon upon D.A. who was still straddled over James. Reams had his attention; probably called him something other than his baptismal name. Right before getting to James, Reams raised up both feet and directed them towards D.A.'s private parts. Of course, this made James, D.A. and Reams a collective clump of humanity heading toward the river. Everyone stood in stunned silence as they approached the rope. Fortunately, Big Charlie was there and grabbed D.A. before he hit the river and pulled him from the ravine. James and Reams were then able to snag the rope. D. A. limped home, hunched over and talking to himself.

The rain continued, adding more and more water to propel us all faster. I had worked my way back up to the summit when I heard a scream. Elisabeth was standing next to the rope, pointing at the river and screaming for her brother, Blue. I jumped into the ravine and as luck would have it, cutting in front of James. He would likely never develop a favorable attitude toward Wilhites. I was approaching the rope at a ferocious rate of speed while trying to hear what Elisabeth was hollering. The best I could make out was "Blue's in da riber." This was going to be a new experience. I had never missed the rope. Actually, I couldn't remember any-one ever missing the rope. As I thought about it, I didn't know if Blue could swim. We had been around water all our lives, but I couldn't recall ever seeing Blue swim a lick. The rope passed over my head like a shot. I was truly airborne, the fast moving runoff propelling me far out into the river. As I left the bank, from the corner of my eye I saw a black and white flash. I knew it was Roy. I would have preferred that he not follow me, but at least I knew he could swim. The water was much colder and a great deal mud-dier than usual. Apparently we weren't the only ones getting rain. Up river was getting their share as well. Small pinwheels covered the surface of the water, made as it passed over some submerged object. Hopefully, it was just a snag. I didn't care to happen upon any gators. A snapping turtle would be almost as troublesome. There was more stuff floating downstream that resembled a float-ing Negro than you would ever have imagined. Limbs looked like black limbs. A moss encrusted log was most certainly Blue's head. I was quickly concerned. The river was moving fast and I hadn't spotted Blue.

I glanced toward the bank. Charles and Reams were running parallel to my movement pointing to a spot ahead of me. I swam in that general direction, but being so low in the water, I couldn't see much. Then directly ahead, I saw a log with one large black arm draped over it. I sensed some relief. At least I had found him.

"Blue, Blue," I hollered as loud as I could and his head popped up above the log. I caught the back end and held on. Blue seemed relieved. I moved to his side.

"Blue, are you alright?"

"I'm now."

"Good, let's try to move this log across the river, but at an angle. We can't go straight across."

Blue and I just kicked our way towards the bank at a gradual angle. Reams and Charles had seen us and were making their way.

There was a good sized tree in the bank that had fallen into the river, but was still rooted to the ground. We touched the bank right above it so that it could buffer us from going further down stream. I was exhausted, but caught my breath fairly quickly. Blue stayed in the water.

"You comin' out, Blue? You aren't hurt are you?" Reams extended his hand to help.

"I's can't."

"What do you mean you can't? Are you hurt?" Reams asked again. I sat on the ground still a little winded.

"I's can't," Blue repeated.

"Why the hell not Blue?"

"I's lost my trousers."

His answer provoked laughs from us all. Blue didn't seem amused and seemed even less inclined to move from the river.

"Well Blue, you are going to have to get out sometime or you'll turn into one dark ass wrinkled raisin." The predicament was becoming sport to my buddy Reams.

"Den a raisin I be."

I knew I had to take control before Reams had way too much fun at the expense of a man who nearly drowned.

"Reams, give him your shirt. He can tie it around him."

"Why me?"

"Because you're the only one that has anything on that will come close to fitting Blue."

Reams didn't resist the logic. He handed Blue the shirt and Blue tied it around his waist like an apron.

"You look pretty good Blue. Now if we can just convince everyone to walk in front of you so your big black butt won't be seen, everything will be fine."

Blue's sense of humor had returned and he broke into his usual grin.

"Yelp, yelp, yelp."

I knew instantly that it was Roy and those were cries of pain. He was lost in the under brush somewhere along the bank. But we all moved in the direction of the noise. Charles got to him first. Around his neck was wrapped the unmistakable mottled body of a water moccasin, its fangs sunk deep into Roy's neck. Charles grabbed the snake's tail, yanking it and throwing it into the river, twirling Roy in the process.

Roy just laid there until I got to him. Then, he raised his head slightly looking directly at me. It was the same look I had seen since I was a baby. I picked him up and headed home as fast as I could. Given the size of the moccasin, I doubted I could do much, but you hope for miracles, you can't plan on them. Blue followed close behind me.

"Leander, it's my fault, I's sorry." He repeated this with almost every step. While I assured him that it wasn't, I certainly understood how badly he felt.

I arrived at the barn just as the wind picked up. The rain had never stopped, but now it was coming down sideways. I placed Roy on the ground against the outside wall of the last stall. His eyes were closed, he was hot as could be, but shivered at the same time. I cooled him with a sponge and covered him with a saddle blanket. Given the fact that the bite was so close to his head, there was nothing much I could do. We had horses get bit every so often; but seldom did a snake get a chance to inject much venom. Plus a horse outweighed Roy by a bunch.

Momma Mae brought me dinner; my parents checked on us every so often. At dark, mom brought some candles. No one asked if I was coming in. They knew I wouldn't leave Roy. I watched and hoped, then hoped and prayed.

The spasms and twitching got worse as the night went on. Sometime after midnight, Roy opened his eyes. I continued to stroke his head as I had been all night. I truly believed he knew it was his time, but he didn't want to go. He raised his head, smiled at me and once again became the loving companion he had always been. Some folks don't think dogs have expressions. They do. I suspect some people can't read them; but I could see the pain build in his face. He would lay his head back down, swallow hard and close his eyes until the pain passed or he could gain control of it. Then he would raise his head and look at me again. I wanted him to stay so much, but the lump in my throat told me that wasn't likely. The pain was getting worse. I whispered to him that it was alright to go, only to see him rally again. Each resurgence took more and more of his energy. He rose up again, this time placing his head in my lap and left me forever. We stayed that way for a long while. Reflecting on the fun that I had with this very sweet companion, I almost immediately felt the emptiness, but nothing was going to get any better sitting there.

I stood up. Standing over him, I put my arms under his torso. His head dropped down and his ears tilted forward, just like they had always done. I had seen him in that position countless times. Once again, he was my puppy, the puppy that taught me to sleep.

I finished burying him in a quiet corner of the barn. I could now barely see the house. The wind and rain were blinding. My mother stood in the middle of the dog trot.

"Is he gone Leander?" She softly asked as I made it under cover of the dog trot.

"Yes mama."

"Don't try to replace him son, it can't be done. There will never be another like him, but your next one will be just as precious."

I couldn't respond. It was all too fresh. Dad came out the door with a rope. He looked my way, but probably thought better of talking right then.

"Susannah, I am going to string this rope to the barn. It looks like its getting worse. We may need it to get back and forth. I think its time to get our people out of the quarters and up to the loft."

She nodded.

"Let's get Momma Mae in here and we'll start cooking something . . . at least as long as the chimneys hold up."

I went up to the loft and laid down. As tired as I was, it wasn't time to go to sleep. These storms could present all kinds of problems. I needed to be ready to help if I could. Soon, all the families from the quarters were up in the loft. The men stayed in the dog trot and watched the storm, so I joined them. It had been blowing pretty hard. Usually, there was some break. We all hoped it would come soon. The break would signal the storm was half over.

Poppy sat near my father whittling something. Often it would be a toy that he presented to one of the young'uns. Blue was next to his dad. I thought I should sit down next to him. I eased over and tapped his shoulder.

"I see you're fully clothed now Blue." My poor attempt at humor broke the ice, but didn't distract him from his concerns.

"Leander, is Roy . . ."

"Yes, Blue. I buried him this morning."

"I feel so bad."

"Blue, there is no reason for you to feel bad. You didn't bite him; the moccasin did. Now I know how you feel, but there is no cause for you to feel that way."

"Blue will get you 'nother dog."

"That would be nice Blue, but I don't know if I am quite ready."

" 'den you tell me."

"I will Blue."

I leaned my head against the wall and almost fell dead asleep. But the noise of the wind was a little too loud and I couldn't drop off.

"There's the break." My dad was the first to notice the calming of the storm. Soon, blue sky could be seen; no wind, no rain. I stepped off the dog trot and sunk ankle deep in the mud. We had received a great amount of moisture. The ground was saturated. With the wind calm, you could now hear the strangest sounds from the river. For the most part, it moved quietly, quietly until some tree lost its struggle and crashed into the Mississippi.

The men used this time to bring in some extra firewood from the wood shed. Women emptied the thunder mugs and refilled water barrels. We all knew that the calm was temporary, very temporary. Soon the breezes returned, only this time they came from the opposite direction. The sky darkened again. All of us in the dog trot adjusted our lines of sight. We were now looking in the opposite direction. I had been in the barn with Roy during the initial onset. The strength of the wind now caught me by surprise. The front of our home was shaded by a large water oak. In a single instant, it crashed to the ground, cracking limbs and splashing water in the process. It had fought the good fight for so long; the winds change in direction just uprooted it.

Growing up seemed to come in fits and spurts. I now was looking at a huge branch that had once supported my first swing. It wasn't that long ago, but it seemed so distant. With age came fear. The tree could have easily fallen in the other direction. Its canopy would have done some serious damage had it fallen. Shear luck and random events seemed to play a bigger part in life than I had imagined. I leaned back against the wall, aching for some sleep. There were enough men around that no one would begrudge me a few winks.

"Oh, my God!"

The exclamation came from Poppy, now standing in the middle of the dog trot facing the river. The lightening was pretty steady. The darkness was routinely broken by its brilliance.

"What is it Poppy?" My dad had moved over next to him. Poppy was pointing toward the river. My curiosity moved me to join everyone else now standing at the river side of the cabin's central hall. I saw nothing at first. Then with the next lightening flash, I understood what Poppy had seen.

Everything in the world was floating in the river. If you waited long enough, you were bound to see one of everything. However, I had not expected coffins. Louisiana's water table was pretty high. All the rain had apparently raised it more, pushing Poppy's tightly jointed coffins to the surface. They were now on their maiden voyage to the Gulf of Mexico.

"Oh my God, dat's Aunt Tilley. Oh Lord, oh Lord." Poppy was rubbing his forehead and shaking his head.

Sure enough that was Aunt Tilley's box. She wanted a white coffin. Poppy usually left them natural. Simple process of elimination made that one, good, old Aunt Tilley's. When it was just a matter of an unmarked coffin, you felt bad, but you just figured it was like a burial at sea. Sooner or later it had to sink, didn't it? I didn't see much difference between being consumed by earthworms or consumed by turtles. But when you know who is in the box, and Aunt Tilley wanted a white one, you felt like you ought to do something. But, there was no way you could do anything in this weather.

Poor Poppy looked totally spent. Blue wasn't in much better shape. They knew that they would have to go and find those that had left what were suppose to be their final resting places. How many had already set sail was anyone's guess. The one thing that we all agreed on was that we would make no mention of this to any of the ladies. God only knows what their reaction would be. No one cared to guess. Some things are better left unsaid.

The storm continued through the night. We all ate in shifts. To make it easy, Momma Mae had made a huge pot of stew, which was one of my favorites. It just happened to be easy and feed a lot of folks. Since the women were inside, they went first. At dark, my parents went to their room; everyone grabbed whatever space they needed in the house, or up in the loft. I stayed outside in the dog trot with Blue and Poppy.

"L'ander, how many do you tink dere are?"

I knew Poppy was referring to the now adrift dearly departed.

"I don't know Poppy. I would imagine it can't be that many. Probably, just those buried in the last year or so."

I could see Poppy was mentally counting the number of coffins he had made recently. I figured that Louisiana moisture would probably pretty much rot a coffin and consume a body in about a year, but I had no real way of knowing.

"Blue, we goin' to build a fence around dat graveyard. Yes sir, Poppy ain't goin' to go look for da dead again afin' we get dees back in da ground. Lord, I's never taut' of 'dis. Fence 'em in. Dey may float, but dey ain't going no where."

Blue seemed receptive to the idea, but apprehensive about rehandling a bunch of coffins and corpses. No one knew what kind of shape they would be in.

The rain and the wind stopped about midnight. The sky was now clear as ever and filled with stars. It was anyone's guess what surprises we would find in the morning.

Momma Mae was up first. She always was. She came out and quietly nudged Blue and told him to go get some eggs. She would have sent one of the girls, but no one knew if we still had a hen house or if it was now occupied by something other than chickens. It wasn't. The only loss was some turkey pullets. This was to be expected. Turkeys just didn't have the sense to come in out of the rain.

The fields were too wet to work so my father got some folks repairing tools and making them ready. Further instructions would come after we rode the place. Of course Blue and Poppy headed down river in a wagon to look for coffins. Their best guess was five floaters; this included Aunt Tilley.

His plan was to do a complete loop of the farm. It became very obvious that we would have plenty of firewood. On the east side, the trees that had fallen were pointing west. When we got to the west, they pointed east. These would have come down after the eye had passed. The cotton crop was beaten down pretty badly. With some sunshine, it could rebound, or at least most of it. The livestock seemed to be alright. The horses, mules and cattle were all sharing the high ground, having managed to collectively congregate there during the storm. God only knows about the hogs. They roamed freely, going wherever they wanted. We would not know for a month or so if they survived.

As we approached the turn off to Drayton and Dunwoody's, I held my breath. We had plenty to do on our own place. Their places were generally a wreck without the benefit of a storm.

I prayed that my father didn't want to investigate their situation. It could only cause neglect at home and more abuse of our stock. We didn't turn off. We headed home. Thank heaven for small favors.

Poppy and Blue would eventually find four of the five coffins. Two of them they found right next to one another. What were the chances that would happen? Neighbors down river recognized Poppy's handiwork and brought the other two to them. This left one missing coffin. Yes, it was Aunt Tilley. You know she was a spinster. Maybe she was just overcome with wanderlust.

CHAPTER 4

Family Warfare

HICCUP. THEODORE SKEDADDLED. He was now two years old, a gift from Blue. I had postponed replacing Roy for at least a couple of years. It just didn't seem right to jump up and get another dog. However, Blue pestered me daily. Perhaps he felt a new dog would relieve him of any guilt he still harbored. Ted was a good fit. Not knowing who hung Theodore on the poor dog, I shortened it to Ted. Ted had a far greater affection for Reams than Roy ever had, but he could not abide Garvin Fuchs. The first hiccup sent him to parts unknown.

"Mr. Fuchs, how are you sir?"

"Oh, I am well, Leander."

Fuchs was still an odd duck to look at, plus we were growing in opposite directions. Last summers growth spurt had left me at six feet tall. A generation of wear and tear was just wearing away Garvin Fuchs. A diminutive fellow to begin with, he was getting real close to looking five feet in the eye.

"Is Abram around (hiccup) Leander?"

"No sir, not presently. He should be back this evening. Can I help you?" Fuchs kind of shuffled at the proposal.

"You're about as close to being a man as you'll ever be. I could just take it up (hiccup) with you."

I had no earthly idea what troubled Fuchs, but felt I ought to offer my assistance.

"Mr. Fuchs, if I can do something, I certainly will. If not, I promise to take it up with my father as soon as he returns."

Fuchs nodded. "It isn't my business, but I just came by Drayton's west field (hiccup). One of your horses is in terrible shape, just terrible. I doubt it will make it through the night. (hiccup) Not my business, but those two uncles should be horse whipped. Just pitiful. You do what you think best Leander. Just hate to see an animal abused like that."

He turned to leave. I could barely get out a thank you. The rage just kept growing inside of me. Year after year, we lent horses to Drayton and Dunwoody. Every single year, they wrecked a few to the point that I had to put them down. I was old enough to know that on the frontier you lived close to death. It did not make it any easier, just more familiar.

Ted reappeared as soon as Fuchs had left. He sensed my anger. Dogs always do. I could have waited for my father, but to what end. It was his decision to let his brothers use the horses year after year. If Fuchs felt I was old enough to be told about it, I guessed I was old enough to do something about it. I knew exactly where the west field was. I didn't know what horse, who would be there or what condition the horse would be in when I got there.

I saddled the biggest gelding we had. His temperament and size could be helpful. Ted followed me out the gate and onto the road to Drayton's and Dunwoody's. I say he followed. He would remain in the general vicinity, but felt free to explore every scent and trail that caught his attention. We were about halfway there, when I caught sight of Reams. He was coming directly toward us.

"And where might you be going, old man?"

"To my uncles." The tone of my voice revealed my personal disgust.

"You sound like you are looking forward to it like a poke in the ear with a sharp stick. What's the problem?"

"Mr. Fuchs spotted one of our horses in pretty bad shape. I figured I had better investigate it before they kill another one."

Reams had turned and we were both in a trot toward the west field.

"Leander, Old Fuchs himself isn't exactly a true guardian of horse flesh. If he says it's in bad shape, the damn thing is probably dead already."

"That thought had occurred to me. Reams, I have grown weary of this. Every year, I break and train new horses. Some I break to ride, others to plow. Every year, I put down horses . . . horses that are in their prime, just because they are abused. I am tired of it, just tired . . . I don't know why we keep lending animals to these fools."

"Your dad does it because you make it easy for him to do it."

"What?" I couldn't even come close to figuring out what Reams meant.

"Look Leander, when the tribe started using fresh Africans, your father quit working their fields with them. He stopped because slaves are too damn expensive to injure or abuse. He wasn't going to risk his investment. Now, his horses and mules, that's another thing. You have the most prolific horse operation in the parish."

"Prolific?" Reams' enlarged vocabulary could be a chore at times.

"Each year, you produce more horses and mules than anyone.

Hell, he ought to sell his slaves, except for Elisabeth, who puts you a leg up on most trainers and turn these cotton fields into horse paddocks. Lot more money to be made if he did."

"I still ain't got it. I am doing what he wants me to do."

"Yes, but he doesn't know these animals like you do. They are just another horse and there are more coming next year. So if Drayton, Dunwoody or Dumb Ass . . . by the way, what is it with your family and the letter "D"?"

I could only shake my head. Aunt Fanny apparently had this clever notion that naming all her children with the names that started with D would be so cute. It was beyond me. With now eight little "D's" at home, I was starting to run out of possibilities. I suspect she would start making up new ones that were never heard before because there was no indication that she was going to quit droppin' 'em.

"My point is that you make it easy or at least not so painful for your dad to lose a horse. There would be holy hell to pay if they abused Poppy."

"I get your point. Sorry for being so obtuse."

"Whoa! Now that's a new vocabulary word for Leander Wilhite!"

I smirked. Reams did have a way of motivating me to read and study more. You would never be able to catch up with him. Truth be known, I had been carrying that word around in my head for about three weeks, just waiting for the chance to spring it on him.

We stopped on a low rise overlooking the west field. Cousin D.A. was supervising about ten of their fresh Africans who were slowly hoeing their way across the field. No horse was immediately in sight.

"I see Dumb Ass is in charge. Kinda makes you proud to be a Wilhite, huh?"

Without comment I put the gelding into a lope. I saw the horse laying behind some yaupon brush at the edge of the woods. Emaciated, with his coat caked in salt flecks from his effort to do whatever he was asked, he was at least alive. As I road around him, I saw the proud flesh growing from the whipping wounds across his butt. Glancing down, I saw the problem. These fools continued to use him to plow this heavy alluvian soil after he had lost both his rear shoes. His hooves were cracked and split, one possibly up to the cornet band.

"Leander, this horse is ruint."

"Yes, and it isn't the first one."

D.A. must have seen us and rode over.

"Damn thing just gave out on us," he said with as much authority as his weak little mind could muster.

"The salient point, Dumb Ass, would be whether he gave out before or after he lost his shoes."

D.A. was confused. He wasn't used to talking with anyone of Reams' intelligence.

"Judging from the whip marks, I suspect that some dumb ass kept him in the field ploughing without shoes until he cracked his feet all to hell."

"It wasn't me." D.A. was puffed up and indigent at Reams' suggestion.

"Oh Dumb Ass, I was using "dumb ass" in its general sense, not as your proper name . . . there being more than just a few dumb asses on this place." Reams was sparring with a mental midget and he knew it.

The horse at least acknowledged me. I placed my hand close to his nostrils. He remembered. They all do. I wished I could make him understand that it wasn't my idea to loan him out. The hooves were hopeless. It was best to let him be.

"Reams, I don't know why you're sticking your nose into it. This is family business." D.A. had to be pleased with that retort. I turned towards him.

"D.A. get off your horse."I was getting angrier as I talked.

"What . . ."

"Now! D.A. Come here. Do you see those feet," pointing to the rear of the horse. "Where are the shoes?"

"Dunno."

"You can't plow these fields with an unshoed horse. You see that proud flesh on his rear? It covers deep wounds. Wounds made by a whip with a lot of force behind it."

"It's just a damn horse, Leander."

I had no control, none whatsoever. In a split second, my fist hit the middle of his chest, expelling air that he had just breathed, and any potential air he had thoughts of breathing. D.A. lay wheezing on the ground.

"Quite a grand show, old man. What's the encore?"

Stepping over D.A., who was still in search of his first naturally drawn breath, I loosened the cinch on the buckskin mare D.A. was riding. Once the breast strap was off, I pulled saddle and saddle blanket off and dropped it on the ground. Retrieving my lariat from my horse, I removed the headstall, and placed the loop over its head. I had trained this mare just a few years ago. She would be going home with me and Reams. I seriously doubted that I needed the rope at all. Once we were pointed towards home, she kept slack in the lariat the entire way. Every darky in the field watched us as we left. None went looking for D.A.

Reams and I parted as I turned towards the barn. Evening would soon be upon us and we both had things to do. Blue saw the buckskin as I approached.

"Ain't seen her in awhile."

"You're right about that, but she ain't goin' back to D.A. Could you check her shoes, and let's keep her up close for awhile."

"Leander, I tell you now, all 'dems shoes are loose; saw 'em as you came up."

"I suspected as much." Ted took a good sniff of the buckskin.

"Yell, Ted, she is from here. Just hasn't been around here for awhile."

I went over to the horse trough to splash a little water on my face. I just seemed trapped. If Reams was correct, I wasn't doing anything but encouraging the abuse of the horses we raised.

"You certainly have a far away look about you."

I hadn't heard her approach, but mothers know their children, certainly their moods. I briefly recounted to her everything that had transpired. With every sentence, the rage built inside of me. The memories of so many broken horses and mules returned and returned vividly to my mind. I could recall every wound, every broken bone, cracked hoof and bloody bandage.

"I am sick of it Mother. I don't want to participate in this abuse any longer."

"Leander, you're not abusing these animals."

"The hell I'm not!"

I was a step ahead of her. She did not tolerate harsh language. The open palm of her right hand was headed towards my cheek, but I caught her wrist in midair. My grasp was firm, perhaps even tight. I was looking down into her eyes like I never had before.

"I raise and train animals as instructed by my father so that they can be abused by his brothers and the collection of idiots they are raising. I will not do it anymore; and, if you or my father expect me to, I will leave."

His eyes never left hers. But when he said "leave" something cracked inside her. She knew like only a mother can that her child was now independent of her and her care. He dropped his hand. The utterance of a fleeting cuss word wasn't the issue anymore.

"Son, you can't mean that . . ."

"I mean it with every bone in my body. I want our horses returned now. If Uncle Drayton and Dunwoody are so successful with their fresh Africans project, they can buy others."

"But what would we do with so many horses?"

"Mother, you are assuming that they can make it home. The poor wretch that is in their west field will have to be destroyed."

"But Leander . . ."

"No buts Mother. I don't care to look into the eyes of another emaciated animal that I must kill because they abused it. They do the abusing; I do the training and the killing. You let me worry about what to do with any extra horses."

Leander turned and walked towards the barn to visit with Blue, just as his father rode in. Leander just glanced at his dad. Reams' words still echoed in his head. They were quite an indictment of his father. If accurate, he was no more than a pawn in what D.A. called family business.

Momma Mae rang the bell for dinner. The meal was eaten in silence. I had nothing to say and the grownups weren't going to risk a scene. Afterwards, I checked the buckskin, and wondered if there was any chance the plough horse could be saved. I wanted to think so, but knew better. I stayed in the barn visiting with Blue, mostly about catfish. Tomorrow was Sunday and he looked forward to catching a few. As he talked, his big black feet rubbed up and down on Ted's stomach. The dog was paralyzed with delight. I hated to interrupt his fun, but it was time to call it a day.

Unlike Roy, Ted wasn't welcomed in the house. His spot was in the dog trot on a worn out saddle blanket. My mother took Roy's passing as a chance to clear her house of dogs. Plus, I no longer needed canine companionship to sleep. My parents were already in bed. As best I could tell, my father was retelling his day's events. I could only hope that my mother hadn't told hers.

At the appropriate time, she hit him with my problem with all the subtleness of a sledge hammer.

"Abram, you must stop this insane practice of loaning horses and mules to Drayton and Dunwoody."

"What?" I could almost hear him sit up, but wasn't sure.

"You must bring those animals back tomorrow or our only son is leaving and I'm not so sure I'm not leaving with him."

"What? Have I missed something?"

"Oh yes, Father. I should say you and I both have. We have enjoyed Leander's success with the livestock. We have learned to take his hard work for granted. Oh yes, we have. I've never seen anyone work so hard at raising good solid animals. Even the most rambunctious one of the entire lot is perfectly manageable. Yet every year, you casually take your pick and send them to Drayton's and Dunwoody's for destruction.

"Now, that doesn't happen that often." Father was trying to marshal his defenses.

"It happens more than you will admit. Now we have Fuchs reporting the abuse. I don't like neighbor talk. I've had enough of it over Baptiste. Now your brothers are in bed with the Lafitte's. Where in our wedding vows did I promise to raise your idiot brothers?"

"I don't suppose you did, but . . ."

"It wears on Leander to have to destroy what he worked so hard to make. He is a man now Abram. Taller than you. With his skill, he can most certainly leave and find work and good work at that. You better start to appreciate what you have. Abram, I will not lose my son over your two brothers. Mark my words."

"Mother, let me sleep on it."

"Abram, you sleep on it all you want. Something is going to change and change real soon."

Whatever concern my father had, it did not prevent him from falling fast asleep and rather quickly at that.

The sun was not up when she slipped into the barn. She seldom entered the barn, leaving it to the jurisdiction of the male folk. The fact that she was there and at such and early hour startled Blue beyond comprehension.

He saddled her horse as instructed and assisted her as she got up. It was then that he noticed the two flintlocks in her belt. It wasn't his place to ask and he didn't. The broken plough horse hadn't moved from the place Leander described. She coaxed him up and they slowly headed to Drayton's. The horse's head hung low between his legs. Walking was a painful strain.

Smoke was rising from the chimney. Breakfast was being prepared when she arrived.

"Drayton, come out here," she hollered. The sun was up; even the Drayton clan ought to be in motion.

She did not dismount, but placed herself right in front of the door, which slowly opened.

"Susannah, what brings you here so early in the morning."

There he stood, no shirt, his pants hung low on his waist. She had no idea who his wet nurse was, but they didn't know how to tie off an umbilical cord. He had a fat old belly button that pointed out like a hernia. Tobacco juice drooled down his cheek. My God, what redeeming virtues could Abram have possibly seen in this man? It angered her all the more that such a divide had occurred between her and her son over such a sorry character as Drayton.

"This horse brings me here Drayton," pointing to the lame

plough horse "and every other horse and mule that you and Dunwoody have borrowed from us."

"Ha, well that would sure be just about all of them that we have." She was infuriated that this fool didn't even appreciate the imposition he had created.

"Can't you see the horse is wrecked?" By now Aunt Fanny and her collection of dullards, dummies and dumb asses had assembled on the porch.

"Well, I know Leander had a set to with D.A. Damn near killed the boy and took his horse."

"The boy doesn't look too worse for wear and the horse he took wasn't his in the first place."

"Leander is way too sensitive about those horses. They're just dumb animals."

"Drayton, which one of your dumb animals kept this horse in the field ploughing heavy land without shoes?"

"What do you want me to do, Susannah?"

"Put him down, right here and right now!"

"Now Susannah, don't know if I should do that."

"No, you would prefer to leave him lame along side the road until the season is over, then return him and all the others so that Leander would have to weed through them, destroying those that couldn't be healed. Right, Drayton? Right?"

The second "right" was shouted directly at Drayton. Susannah's horse was getting edgy in the process, when she whirled to the side, pulled one flintlock and put the poor horse out of its misery.

"God damn, Susannah!" Drayton couldn't believe it. Neither could anyone. The shock just hung in the air like gun smoke.

The horse dropped on its front knees, and then slowly rolled over. Everyone there now knew what it felt like to have to put down an animal. Whether they had the heart or soul to understand the emotional drain that it took was subject to some debate.

Drayton started towards Susannah and tried to reach for her horse's reins. Just as quickly, she pulled the second flintlock. Its large bore was aimed squarely at Drayton's forehead.

"You go get every horse and mule that we own. Every single one of them, and have them in our paddock within the hour. All of them. Dunwoody's as well."

She left as quickly as she came. Once out of sight, she broke down in tears. Her body was shaking. Never had she killed anything. The men always did those things. The still bulk of the dead horse would not leave her mind. It just wouldn't go away. Now she understood. The toll on her son had to have been tremendous. If those horses weren't returned in an hour, she would return for Drayton and for Dunwoody. Abram had tolerated this for far too long. Now she had to figure out how to regain the respect of her son. She knew they had lost it.

By the time she reached the barn, she had composed herself. Abram and Leander were in the yard. Abram was the first to call to her.

"Mother, pretty long ride for this early in the morning. We'll be late for church you know."

"Ain't going to church today."

There was no response to that statement.

CHAPTER 5

Jared Groce

RIVER RED WAS ONE OF THOSE WOMEN WHO CAUSED YOUNG CHILDREN TO HAVE NIGHTMARES. She was a tall, thin woman with orange stringy hair. Everyone said that it was red, but it wasn't. It was orange. She was pale complected and freckled. It wasn't so much that her skin seemed translucent; but, you could see her veins. What really made an impression was its texture. It was a continuous collection of very fine bumps, like when a baby gets heat. On her feet, she wore laced-up men's brogans. The only evidence that she might be female was the calico dress that she had on, this day and every other one that I could recall. In her belt, she had a knife that was the envy of every man in the parish.

I assumed the weapon was for her protection, although I could not imagine anyone causing any trouble with this old bird. She ran three large barges back and forth across the river. The number coincided nicely with the number of husbands that she had buried. Just about the time a husband finished the construction of a new barge, some unfortunate event would occur and the simpleton would show up dead. After a couple of dead husbands, you would have thought that the last one would have spent a little more time during the construction phase.

Now 18, my buddy, Reams, had developed a real fondness for girls. As interested as he was in the female form, he could not imagine how any man, and I mean any man, could ever find himself married to River Red. It was just beyond belief. Since there were no known offsprings to any of her unions, Reams started to think that perhaps she did not have the proper portal. We were now spending more and more time together. Our fathers permitted us to run our cow herds together. There was hardly a day that Reams did not muse over some aspect of female portals.

Today River Red was all grins. Smiling did not help her appearance. She had not brushed her teeth since the birth of the nation. Her business was booming. Initially, Reams thought we were being invaded. We kind of were, but not really. On the east side of the river was Mr. Jared Groce, the wealthiest man in Alabama. Groce not only had money, he had a heritage and a successful one at that. He was born in Virginia, the Old Dominion. I had heard Poppy tell many stories about his life back in Virginia, the huge plantations, and the wealth of some planters. Of course, wealth can come and go. Poppy was purchased from President Jefferson during one of his financial embarrassments.

Groce had a business man's mind and was not afraid of a little risk. He left Virginia for South Carolina. After his first wife died, he established Fort Groce in Alabama. You have to figure if someplace was named after someone, he wasn't a common roustabout. With the landing of each barge, the wealth of the man became readily apparent. Mr. Groce and his son, Leonard, came first. Both were riding matching horses in the best condition. I expected that the rest of his party would not be so magnificently mounted. The quality slipped only slightly. Over 50 wagons followed him, manned by the rest of his family and about 90 slaves. It was the damnedest parade I had ever seen. Reams was speechless, and that said it all.

Groce never gave a single order; yet, the organization of the caravan was flawless. The first wagons carried his family and any of his people too small, too old or too infirm to walk or ride. The next group of wagons held the food for the humans and the stock. We only learned this later, after the tarps were removed. His wagons were covered, and covered for wind, rain, sleet or whatever Mother Nature could hurl at them.

The procession went on for hours. Even from our vantage point on a bluff that overlooked the river, we could not see the end of it. Groce had apparently disassembled everything he had at Fort Groce. Wagons moved by with furniture, tools, and supplies. Everything that a man could own, or want to own, passed by us. But the most memorable thing was Groce's people. Except for the men's shirts, all of the slaves wore store-bought clothes. The women's dresses were all made from the same calico material, giving even more uniformity to the sameness of their black faces. Most of the women sang. Those men not occupied with the wagons, herded cattle and horses. On the countenances of each one you could detect an element of pride. It was as if they intended to announce to the world "yes, we may be owned, but we are owned by Jared Groce."

Having wasted most of the day as spectators to the caravan, Reams and I headed home. As we rode towards my house, we were pleasantly surprised by Mr. Groce and his son conversing with my father and mother.

"Leander, Reams, please come and introduce yourselves to Mr. Groce." My father had noticed our arrival and used the break in the conversation to make the proper introductions.

My mother had invited the Groce family to dinner. This was not unusual. She took in every wandering waif and orphan. She might as well feed the wealthiest man in Alabama. Reams was invited, as always. He had long since become addicted to the cooking of Mama Mae. His mother couldn't or wouldn't cook and the Negress that cooked for his family couldn't fry water. Therefore, most of the time, he planned his day so that he would enjoy at least one meal with us.

While the grown-ups visited, we got to know Leonard. Groce's son was about 16, so a couple of years younger than Reams and I. He did not know much about Texas, or exactly where they were headed. He had been away at school when his father called him home. We were all in unanimous agreement that going to Texas certainly justified a quick departure from school, any school. Leonard was an intelligent lad, a cut above most of the young men in our area, including the tribal offspring of Drayton and Dunwoody

In order to seat everyone at the same table, Mama Mae had arranged a series of boards over barrels in the dog trot. Mother had pulled her very best tablecloth from her cedar chest. For reasons unknown to me, she called it her hope chest. Since it was crammed full of stuff, I could not imagine what she was hoping for. The table conversation quickly turned to Texas, and Mr. Groce had become quite a booster of Texas and the quick settlement of its territory.

On a business trip to New Orleans, he had been introduced to Stephen F. Austin. Austin's original plans were to practice law there. However, his father had long been in negotiations with Spain over starting a colony in Texas. Upon his father's sudden death, Stephen stepped in to fulfill his dad's plans and dreams. He described Austin as a man about his age, perhaps a little younger, tall, and slender, with deep set eyes. He considered him a person of good character who could be trusted. Austin was looking for 300 families whose character reflected his own.

"Mr. Wilhite, you must not miss this opportunity. It is a chance to own more land than you could ever acquire in a lifetime. There is nothing more exciting than being on the ground floor of something and watching it grow."

"Oh, there is no question about that." I could see a distant look in my father's eyes, like he was trying to visualize Texas right there at the table. What kind of land are we talking about?"

"Texas is big. There are all kinds of places, however, like you, I intend to grow cotton. The rich bottomland along the Brazos River caught my eye. Assuming we get there within the next month or so, I think we will produce the first cotton crop this next year."

"You certainly are equipped to do just that. But how would a person get selected by, did you say Austin?"

"After such hospitality Mr. Wilhite, I would be amiss if I would not write a letter of recommendation for you. New Orleans would be a quick trip. By the time you put your affairs in order here, I should be well established in Texas and could assist you. Plus I am taking far more slaves than I need, at least initially. The extras can be rented out to get homes built and crops in the ground as quickly as possible."

I could tell my mother had that worried look about her, but knew better than to interrupt her guest.

"It is interesting, Mr. Groce. What does the land cost?"

"Cost, why it costs nothing! Maybe a surveyor's fee, but the land is free. Since you are both a farmer and a herdsman, and by the way my compliments on your horses, haven't seen such horseflesh of your quality since Virginia . . . ."

"The compliment should be directed to my son, Leander. My wife finally convinced me that he was a far better stockman than I am."

"Your horses are quality, Mr. Wilhite, and I like quality. However, to get back to your question, you would qualify for a full league of land. That is more than 4000 acres."

"My word, that would certainly put some distance between me and Drayton and Dunwoody."

This forced a comment from my mother. "Mr. Groce, Drayton and Dunwoody are my husband's less than impressive younger brothers. Abram, I don't know if you intend to haul us off to Texas, but if you do, I would prefer to leave your two brothers here in Louisiana." Mom had seized the moment to get her point across while dad was all lathered up about Texas and 4000 acres.

Groce smiled. "Ha, I have to admit that our relocation to Texas has permitted us to place a little distance between ourselves and certain family members. Do not feel like you are alone."

The meal was over and Mama Mae brought out her best dessert, sweet bread pudding. As a boy, she had to hide it from me. If I saw her making it, I just worried her to death for an early taste. I once finished off her entire dessert before she realized what damage I had done. Reams inhaled his portion, and was looking around to see if anyone was going to leave theirs. A foolish notion for sure.

"There are two requirements of Mexico," said Mr. Groce.

My father inhaled slightly then asked, "well, the land is free, how bad could they be?"

"That depends on your point of view. Mexico does not permit slavery. Yes, I know, but I am bringing 90 slaves with me. They will become indentured servants for life, when we cross the Sabine River. Mexico also is a Catholic country. You will have to become Catholic, Mr. Wilhite."

"That may bother mother here. She relishes Sunday sermons, the longer and the louder, the better for her. Personally, I always preferred the Catholic service. It was short, in Latin so I couldn't understand it and the same every Sunday. Being Catholic is fine by me. It will free up a lot of Sunday."

"Mr. Wilhite, if the truth be known, the Church does not have enough priests to handle the folks in Texas now. They will never be able to service the colonies."

The meal was coming to an end. The men stayed at the table for some serious scratching and farting. The women moved inside to visit. Groce continued to speak of all that Texas had to offer. If Reams and I had a vote, we would have left that evening. However, it was obvious that my father, while interested, wanted to learn a little more before committing to such a move.

The sheer size of the track that you could secure was staggering. The climate and the soil seem to fit the cotton production that we currently had. Just pulling up roots and relocating called for a good deal of thought and even greater planning.

Groce outlined his route to the Brazos River. After crossing the Sabine, there was an area generally referred to as the Red Lands. The name came from the redness of the soil. Ironically, this very area was filling up with Indians, red men, from other parts of the country. Some, such as the Mohawks, had come from as far away as New York. It was their hope, and the hope of several other tribes, to secure land titles from Mexico, just like the Anglos. This confused the Indians that were native to East Texas. While they cultivated the soil and stayed in the same general location, they did not grasp the concept of land ownership. The emigrating tribes had learned their lesson the hard way, with the western movement of whites. If Mexico would recognize their land titles, it would secure their future. So far, Stephen Austin wasn't recruiting any Indians for his colony.

As the conversation wound down, Mr. Groce turned to me. "Leander I have a business proposition for you."

"Sir?" I could not imagine what he had on his mind.

"I would like to trade you a stallion for a stallion. It is always good to introduce some fresh blood into a remuda. Are you interested?"

"Yes sir!" Honestly, nothing could have pleased me more. His horseflesh was superb. The chance to select one of his stallions was a great opportunity. I glanced at my father. He appeared as keen on the idea as I was.

"I will drop by in the morning and make my selection. We will have our horses collected for you to do likewise."

"Mr. Groce, your family is welcome to stay here in the house," offered my father.

"Mr. Wilhite, I do appreciate your offer. But it is my practice always to stay with my people. When we all experience the same discomfort, it is best. I will see you in the morning, Leander."

Reams said that it was time for me to wipe the grin off my face or it would just freeze. Sleep never came to me that evening. I recalled every horse that went passed us. So many beautiful horses, you could not make a bad choice.

I almost beat Mama Mae up. I say almost. I doubt that woman ever slept at all. I inhaled her biscuits, while reporting last night's events to her. She sensed my excitement about the horse trade, and to a lesser extent, about Texas. Mama Mae was a great listener. She took it all in while never making a wasted motion.

"Leander, you give some thought to dat horse. Take your time 'n pick a good un'."

"Oh, yes ma'am. I had better run down Elisabeth. Having two sets of eyes looking would be a big help. Is she back?"

"I 'speck so."

Elisabeth had developed a large reputation for being someone good to have around when a horse is going to foal. It started with Fuchs' mare. She had some problems and he asked my father if Elisabeth could come by. She calmed the mare, got her to relax and the birth happened like it was supposed to. Fuchs was very pleased. He gave Elisabeth a donkey! Yes, a donkey! Like she needed a donkey. Actually it turned out she did; she rode that donkey to every birthing she supervised. However, my father was less than pleased with the form and level of compensation for Elisabeth's services. From then on, he negotiated the pay, which he split with Elisabeth. We all knew Elisabeth could not refuse any critter. Once she took them in, you could forget about ever getting them away from her. Best to head the problem off before it got started. For now, she loved that donkey. Anyway, everyplace should have a donkey. It makes you appreciate your other animals so much more. I found her in the quarters.

"Elisabeth, get that donkey of yours saddled up, we have to go pick a horse."

She smiled, like she already knew everything about it, and, of course, she did. Across the South, there was virtually no delay between information received in the big house and information received in the quarters. Ask any planter anywhere. The slaves knew exactly what was going on, just as soon as the white folks. I could never explain how it happened. Maybe it was just part of being owned by someone that made them good observers of people. At any rate, Elisabeth, while saddling her donkey, a magnificent animal that she prided, told me that she knew which stallion Groce would pick.

"He pick 'da bay," she said convincingly.

"Now, why the bay?"

"He ain't got one. You mens always pick da color first. Da bay ain't da best one, but he'll want da bay."

Groce arrived about the time we were saddled. We headed out to the paddock. Yes, he picked the bay. Elisabeth just smiled. Like I said, they are great observers of people.

We rode out to Groce's encampment. The precision of his organization was impressive. Breakfast was finished. Campfires were
being extinguished. Most of the wagons were packed with their
tarps tied down. They were ready for their next leg to Texas. Groce
took us directly to his remuda and we dismounted.

It was hard not to show my excitement. Christmas had come
again, twice in one year. Elisabeth followed me in amongst the
stock. I noticed a dun that had some potential. She must have taken
note of my fixation with the dun. She poked me square in the back.

"Da gray."

I turned. Elizabeth was now old enough to redden a rag, but in
stature she was petite, almost bird light. She smiled again under her
bonnet.

"Leander, da gray." She nodded in the direction opposite the
dun. I took my time looking through the horses, knowing full well
that when I finally saw the gray I would select him. Elisabeth could
pick the whole package. Her personal quietness attracted animals
of a like temperament. I knew the horse would be balanced, alert
and intelligent. Her selections always were.

The gray stood off from the remuda under a large oak. This surprised me a little. It could be a bad sign. I moved slowly in his direction hoping that he would let me get close enough for him to catch
my scent. I was about 10 feet in front of the gray, when he came to
me. I held my hand over his nostrils. The selection was made. When
the horse picks you, it is best to go with his decision.

Groce again encouraged me to come to Texas. If I did he would
be disappointed if I did not look him up. I promised that I would.

"Elisabeth, do you want to lead him home?"

"No, he's your horse."

"But you picked him."

"I's just help."

He was as docile as could be. I put him in his own paddock while the other stallions called to him. I could not wait to see what kind of colts he would throw.

I waited a couple of days before I rode the gray. It gave him time to settle down, and the smell of his former remuda to leave the area. You always look for holes in a new horse. Sometimes you find them real quick, like when you're thrown off as quickly as you get on. Around the barn and in the paddock, I could not find any. However some horses are entirely different out in an open field.

He saddled easily enough. There was no observable nervousness on his part. A little bit of anxiety on my part, I must confess. If he were going to be tempted to run, it would be in the fields. We headed in that direction. I tried every gait and every lead. Whoever trained Groce's horses knew what they were doing. To test his patience, I stood him under a solitary tree out in the middle of a large expanse of green grass. Most horses would be inclined to inch their way towards the grass. Not the gray.

It could have been a deer, a small one. I saw it moving in the distance through the trees, disappearing then reappearing. But the pace wasn't that of a deer. The gray had passed the patience test, and I was flunking the curiosity test. I put him in a slow lope towards the moving figure.

The woods were getting sparser. As I approached, I saw that it was Big Basket. I hollered to her. She just kept on walking. She had a pack on her back, and a long thin cypress knee as a walking stick.

"Big Basket, are you all right?" For the life of me, I could not imagine where she was going. I had never seen her without Baptiste.

"Is Baptiste all right?"

"Hump." There it was, one of her famous H words.

I rode slightly ahead and dismounted. She would have to tell me something.

"Big Basket, please stop. Is there something wrong? Can I help you?"

"I go home." This was more conversation than I had ever had or heard.

"Go home? What about Baptiste?"

"I got him new woman."

Lord, this was getting confusing. Big Basket did not look well. Her hair had more gray in it than I remembered and it had absolutely no shine.

"Big Basket, home is in the Rockies. Can you make it that far?"

"I can, I must. My people will be there."

She continued walking. Her pace was surprisingly quick. While her stride was short, the speed was exceptional. I really did not know what to do. Indians have an almost mystical attachment to their homelands. I had no doubt she could find it, assuming her health lasted.

"Big Basket, are you sure you want to do this?"

She stopped. She moved her walking stick to her left hand. She grabbed my right hand. Hers was much smaller than mine.

"Leander." She had never said my name. I was not even sure she knew it or could speak it. The shock was just stunning. She said Leander, not one of her usual H words.

Leander, my name is not Big Basket. My name is Latola. Say it."

" Latola."

"Yes, goodbye Leander".

"Goodbye Latola."

CHAPTER 6

A Visit to Texas

THE EBENEZER BAPTIST CHURCH WAS THE PRIDE OF SUSANNAH WILHITE. It stood on the high ground amongst a grove of spreading water oaks and pecan trees. The design was actually more of Poppy's doing than anyone else's. He had recalled similar churches back in Virginia. So the Ebenezer Baptist Church had a slight Episcopalian twist to it. No matter, its whitewashed clapboards gleamed in the filtered sunlight. Since there had not been a recent hurricane, it actually had all of its glass window panes.

Like the exterior, the interior was as white. There was a simple pulpit in front of 20 hard bench seats. Each regularly attending family claimed a bench. Since there was no backrest, by the end of most services your bench had become a part of your anatomy.

Initially things had actually gone fairly well for the church. It had started as nothing more than a flat spot in a yaupon arbor. Its services had been well attended. The elders fought over the chance to ring the large bell that called this flock to worship. Since its services started about a half an hour behind the local Catholic mass, they thought that it would be a subtle reminder of the Reformation. Apparently, it only provoked a greater fervor on the part of the Romans. Their parish was growing and Ebenezer was having a few ups and downs.

For many years, Rev. Joshua Crocker had been the leader of this group of foot washing Baptists. But Joshua met his Jericho in the buxom form of the Widow James.

At the time she caught the attention of the right reverend's eye, she was not yet a widow. She was Annabel James, wife of James James. James James was a rather slow witted fellow. What would you expect? The miracle of this story was that two equally dull people sorted and sifted through all the folks that they knew and found one another, cohabitated, and produced an offspring. Then, miracle of miracles, they both agreed to name the lad James James. How this could happen still astounds me. At any rate, James drowned in his own horse trough, an odd swimming hole at best.

There was no apparent sign of foul play; but, tongues began to wag. Soon the right Reverend was shown the door. Shortly thereafter, the Widow James left the area. One of the traveling merchants told of seeing them running a card game on a riverboat using the widow's ample cleavage to distract the card manipulations of the former Rev. Crocker.

We now had an interim preacher, interim being a word I had never heard before. It was later defined for me by Reams. Wash Hiram had received the calling late in life, very, very late in life. I can only guess he wanted to make up for lost time. His shortest sermon was about two hours, but he had a head cold. Most averaged about three hours. Mother loved him. The men folk wanted to kill him.

Wash wasn't even started real good, when he suddenly stopped and stared at the back of the church. Of course, this caused every other congregant to turn and stare as well. There stood Baptiste Roubleau. Big Basket, or more correctly stated, Latola, was not with him. Uncle Baptiste was accompanied by a black woman dressed like every other black woman that I had seen. He was headed directly for his bench, our bench. My mother had turned bright red when she first caught a glance of the new appendage to her side of the family. Now it seemed that every ounce of blood in her vanished. Her hands were even chalk white. I prepared to catch her in case she fainted dead away. Baptiste nodded to the preacher, who composed himself enough to get back to the business at hand.

I felt bad for I had totally failed to mention Big Basket's departure for the Rockies. Everything that was remotely connected to Baptiste seemed to upset my mother. I suspect that she never knew about half of my visits to his tree house. Perhaps she might have been a little better prepared for someone different, if I had mention that Big Basket was gone. I had to confess that even I wasn't prepared for a Negress. I should've thought. There were not any Indians for Latola to choose from; a slave, and I am guessing that's what she was, would have been about the only option. Baptiste was getting up in years. A conventional wedding was out of the question if the bride had all of her senses.

The good news was that the shock took some of the wind out of old Wash's sails. He pulled up short which pleased the men folk. Mother made directly for the wagon. My father and I sensed it was best not to linger, although lingering around after a sermon seemed to be a distinctly feminine characteristic.

We were still within sight of the Ebenezer Church when my mother turned to my father and said,

"Abram, I cannot live this down. You better go take a look at Texas."

If I had been a betting man, I would have figured that the continuing escapades of Drayton, Dunwoody and the tribe would have provoked such a statement. Uncle Baptiste had not only upset the apple cart; he had wrecked it.

"Mother, I would like to take Leander. Can you manage without us for a spell?"

"Certainly, just be quick about it. I am at my wits end, Abram."

My father often said if mama isn't happy, nobody is happy. He immediately made plans to leave for Texas as soon as possible. Baptiste's new found friend happened at a convenient time; it was the dead of winter. Poppy and Blue could easily keep things going. Ben Whitlock would look in on things. Reams and I had gathered that if Abram returned with a favorable report, both families would head west towards Texas.

My father wanted to travel light. I selected two of our best horses, best in the sense that they were strong and had some endurance. After a great deal of talking, Elisabeth agreed to loan us one of her donkeys. Obvious promises were made concerning the donkey's welfare and maintenance. We could not overload him, had to make sure he was well fed, and generally treat him with a great deal of respect. I came close to abandoning the entire idea, when she finally relented.

We took our warmest clothes. It was only a guess, but we figured the winter would be much like Louisiana's. We didn't get any big cold fronts here, but a little cold front with rain could still be mighty cold. Plus, my father insisted that we travel without benefit of a campfire. He refused to send smoke signals to every Injun and highwayman announcing our arrival and location. Mama Mae had packed enough biscuits and beef jerky to keep us in the saddle for all eternity. Since they were both favorites of mine, I was content to go where ever dad wanted to go . . . until the biscuits and jerky ran out.

The morning we left was clear and cool. Perhaps it was a sign of good luck. I swear my mother hugged me longer and tighter than she did my father. It is a heavy burden being an only child. As I swung into the saddle Mama Mae stepped out of the kitchen with a small bag. She quietly approached the right side of my horse and slipped it into my saddlebag. She patted my knee and returned to the kitchen.

I really did not know what I was supposed to feel, headed to Texas and all. I couldn't sleep at all the night before. Most people say you're just "journey proud." It may have been something but it didn't seem to include pride. If Texas was anything like what Mr. Groce described, I knew for a certainty we would move. Never been anywhere but Louisiana. Everything would be new. New land, new people, a new house. I guess the most important thing for now was to take it all in and not get killed in the process.

"So, Leander, are you going to tell me?" We were about three hours into our travels when my father broke the monotony.

"Sir?"

"Leander, you know. What's in the special sack Mama Mae gave you?"

Sensing that he probably already knew, I thought I might play him along.

"Well sir, it's a secret."

"It is? I just bet I could make a pretty good guess."

"Guess all you want dad. If I told you, we would both know and I don't see any advantage in that."

This brought a smile to his face.

"I can't believe I raised a boy who won't even share one of Mama Mae's sugar cookies."

"Ha, you know I'll share, but they are awfully good aren't they?"

"Yes, they are. I need to make some water. Let's stop for a while and grab a bite to eat. A sugar cookie would make a fine dessert."

We had made good time for several days, had ferried the Sabine River, and were now in Texas. So far, Texas looked pretty much like Louisiana. There wasn't a torrent of travelers, but word had definitely gotten out about Texas and Austin's efforts to bring colonists to it. Whether some of these folks were the type he had in mind remained to be seen. Land is a mighty big lure and it seemed way too tantalizing to some folks.

My father was not overwrought with land fever. In fact, he appeared almost apprehensive. Perhaps he hoped everything Mr. Groce had said was true, but just did not want to get his hopes up. As for me, I was looking forward to Nacogdoches and the Greene Inn. Along the way we had learned that this was an old Spanish town, had been a small fort, but more importantly, it was a place where we could stay for the night.

Dwight Greene was the proprietor of the Inn, which was now filled to the brim each and every night. I could tell that he was doing well because he had actual glass in his windows. I wasn't the only fool who tapped on a pane as if I'd never seen it before in my life. Mr. and Mrs. Greene had the good fortune to have produced seven daughters and, at last, one son. If an innkeeper had a choice, I would think daughters would be preferable. The boy, the youngest sibling, looked to me to have a very bleak future, what with a mother and seven older sisters.

Arriving late in the day, we were shown into the dining room. At one end was a large fireplace. At the other end, there was a pantry and a stairwell that led to the basement. One large, long table filled the room. We stepped over the bench and took a seat before an overturned plate. It was not fly season, but by force of habit, the plates were placed face down. The food didn't really need to be very good. This group of travelers would have inhaled just about anything. Chewing was optional for most. My father paid for the meal and our space.

Space was a loose concept at best. Each bed, and there were nine, was supposed to hold four men regardless of size, or combination of sizes. I had actually looked forward to a night sleep inside and on something softer than the cold ground. However, the pungent aroma of the three dirty, sweaty bodies occupying the first bed I was shown evaporated any notion of sleep. I glanced at my father who seemed to be content as a puppy with his three bedmates. Perhaps my mother had tenderized me to the ways of a traveling man. I took one last breath of reasonably clean air and pushed my way into the bed.

We were fortunate that the Inn did not come under attack. If it had been, we all would've been killed because we never would've heard a thing. My father snored a bit. Not every night and not all night long. This group rattled windowpanes. They were supposed to be asleep, yet, I sensed there was some sort of competitive event going on and I was the only spectator. Just as one fellow would stop, another would pick up the pace as if he were challenging him to return to the battle. Back and forth, all night long. I prayed for a quick death or an early sunrise. I got neither.

I told my father that I was going to skip breakfast. Biscuits and jerky were fine by me. He wanted to visit with a Mexican colonel by the name of Ruiz. He was in town to see what these colonists looked like and to report back to his superiors. My father wanted to pick his brain for some of the specifics of acquiring land and the actual requirements to migrate to Texas.

Having had no sleep, I doubted that I would add much to the conversation. I headed towards the barn, feeling worn and a little lightheaded. The steady, heavy breathing of my bedmates seemed to still be with me, although I was fully awake and moving towards our horses. I recalled Baptiste's tale of using an anthill to eat all the bugs in his buckskins. I had the itchy sensation that I woke up with more than I went to bed with.

I started with the donkey. It took more time to pack and tie our provisions on to him. For the life of me, I could not remember his name. I am sure Elisabeth told me. Every critter she had was named. For now he would just be the donkey, a small but stout gray one with the usual brown cross on his back.

"Good morning Mr. Wilhite."

I'd been holding a biscuit in my mouth while I tied the last knot, so my response was a little tardy.

"Oh, gulp, I'm sorry. Good morning."

Before me, stood the youngest of the Greene daughters.

"I am Rachel Greene. We met briefly last night. Doesn't our breakfast suit you?"

If we had met, I did not recall it. With seven daughters who could count and who could tell?

"Oh no, I am sure your breakfast is just fine. I just needed to get some things done."

Rachel was maybe 12, but I am guessing. She seemed to really have no particular business in the barn. She had now moved just a little closer than I cared for her to be.

"Are you a single man Mr. Wilhite?"

Given the fact that I had always been single, the question hit me with a shock. I've never been anything but single.

"Yes," I responded, trying to hide any confusion.

"If you plan to come to Texas, don't you think it is time for you to take a bride?"

For 12 years of age, she was tripping over a lot of issues that I had never given any thought to and had not planned to think much about for a good while. I figured an honest response was the best response.

"Well, I really hadn't given it much thought. I mean I have no prospects . . ."

"I can provide you with one Mr. Wilhite." Rachel was now standing directly in front of me with a not so sheepish smile on her face.

"You can? Who might that be?"

"Me!"

"Ha." The minute it left my mouth, I begged for it to return. It was just so spontaneous I couldn't help it. Here I stood in a strange barn, before a 12-year-old adolescent girl who had just proposed to tackle me and Texas all at the same time without much in the way of formal introduction. Given the redness of her cheeks and the fire in her eyes, my unfiltered answer was not appreciated.

"You dare laugh at a lady! Mr. Wilhite you are a scoundrel at best. You are totally lacking in manners."

With that she spun around and marched out of the barn, brushing the form of a person I had not seen nor heard. While I stood there gathering my thoughts, the lady spoke.

"Good morning Sir. I am so glad you are here I could use a little assistance."

I was still gathering my wits when I turned slightly to focus on who was now addressing me. The shock caused me to gulp audibly. Now standing before me was a nun! Yes, a nun dressed in her habit. These Texas mornings were moving way too fast. I had left a sleepless bed of strangers, walked about 15 paces to the barn. Before I had totally consumed my biscuit I had been accosted by an innkeeper's daughter with matrimony on her mind; now I was face-to-face with a bride of our Savior. The nun must have sensed my shock.

"Sir, ladies do grow up quickly on the frontier."

"What?"

"I overheard Rachel's proposition, sir."

I seemed to becoming more retarded by the moment. I had already spent more time with the nun than ever before. In fact, more time than I ever wanted. Having been to one or two Catholic masses, I was vaguely aware that Catholics genuflected a lot, but I did not know if I needed to now or what.

"Sir, I am Sister Mary Catherine, I would be forever in your debt if you could help me with this mule. He is very tall, and I need to get this pack on him." She motioned to the corner of the barn.

"He certainly is a tall one. Where are you going with such a large pack?"

"To the Bedais tribe."

"Indians!" For the life of me, I could not imagine this rather frail sister visiting a tribe of Indians, any Indians, by herself. I started to question the wisdom of her trip as I picked up her pack.

"Jesus Christ!" I couldn't believe what I had just said but the heaviness of the pack surprised me. There was no way she could lift it, and I wasn't real sure that I could. Once again I had created my own crisis. Now just what to do or what to say to a nun having uttered such an oath right in front of her. I turned slightly to face my punishment.

She spoke first. "Heavy isn't it?" She smiled.

"Why yes it is. Is this your rock collection?"

"No sir, Bibles".

"These Indians can read?"

"Oh yes, and they love to read biblical stories."

"They are not violent? I mean you're not afraid. I thought . . . ."

"You thought that all Indians were vicious, that they spent their day killing and scalping."

"I guess."

"Sir, I'm sorry I did not catch your name."

"Leander Wilhite, ma'am."

Mr. Wilhite, you need to quickly learn the character of the various tribes that live here in Texas. They are all very different. The Bedais have been Christians for years."

"Christians! The hell you say! Oh God, I am sorry I am not very good at talking with nuns, or apparently any Texas females judging from my encounter with Rachel Greene. I just . . ."

"It is no problem Mr. Wilhite. I assure you I hear worse every day."

"But how did those Indians become Christians?" I was quite certain that my mother would be interested in knowing, she being a rather devout person herself.

"According to the Bedais elders, they say that a lady wearing a cloak the color of the sky visited them frequently. During her visits she told them the stories of the Bible. My order was founded in Spain by Maria de Jesus Agreda. While we will never know, we think she was the lady with the cloak the color of the sky."

"She traveled to Texas from Spain?"

"Actually she never left Spain. She would frequently fall into a deep sleep, almost a coma. When she awoke, she told the priest that she had visited the new world. Some of the Franciscans, who had been here, confirmed her descriptions. They said that they had heard from various tribes that they too had been visited by such a lady."

"When was this, Sister?"

"Around the late 1600s."

"1600s! Why would the Indians even believe her . . . ? That she was from another country."

"Oh, the Bedais believe that humans can take on other forms.

Most often, it is as an owl. When they do this, they can be in other locations at the same time. Most tribes have a common lore that is similar."

"I have a lot to learn about Texas and Indians. You are not afraid?"

"Of the Bedais? Certainly not. But there are tribes to be afraid of. That is why you colonists are being welcomed to Texas." I had just about finished tying down her pack and had managed to work up a good sweat. I sat down on a small bench while she continued.

"Neither Spain or Mexico has ever succeeded in colonizing Texas. The largest established town is San Antonio de Bexar and it is constantly besieged by the Comanches and some Apaches as well. Bexar seems to have a lot of appeal to some colonists. You will travel to there at your peril. The Franciscans tried to convert the Comanches. In order to do so, they built churches that look like forts. Still in the end, most became martyrs."

"So we are to do what Spain and Mexico could not do?" I was having some misgivings about Texas.

"Mexico wants to keep Texas. They know that if they do nothing, the Anglos will eventually take it. Some of the Indians that you have seen around here are tribes displaced by the westward growth of your country. So they have invited you to colonize Texas hoping that you will become more Mexican than Anglo. It concerns some. Have you met Col. Ruiz?"

"I have not; but my father planned to visit with him at breakfast."

"It would be interesting to hear their conversation. The Colonel fears that the Americans will just take over, and transplant their ways and their culture to Texas. I suspect he is correct. I have seen no evidence that the colonists are interested in anything but free land. They circumvent the prohibition against slavery by making the slaves servants for life. There are not enough Colonels or friars in Mexico or Texas to require that you become Catholic. So it would appear that in the end, Texas will become part of your country. Colonel Ruiz knows this, I think."

"So you spend your time converting Indians and not colonists."

"I would love to convert colonists. But making someone become a Catholic is not conversion. It is just the price of a piece of land, nothing more."

I nodded. The little nun certainly had a grasp of things. As I helped her with the mule, I thought one question might be helpful.

"Sister if you were migrating to Texas, . . .well as we are or might, where would you settle?"

"Mr. Wilhite, you're a young man and I hope you have a long life. Do not surrender it easily so that Mexico might have some claim on this country. Stay between the Brazos and the Sabine Rivers. It is an area where there is plenty of good land to be had. Lastly, all Indian tribes are different. If you make friends with those that would have you as a friend, you will learn a lot. Good luck to you Mr. Wilhite. I hope I see you in church some time."

CHAPTER 7

Deep in the Heart of Texas

I DID NOT CARE FOR GUPTON DUBEC. I did not like him the first time I met him. I kept my concerns to myself. He was one of my father's bed mates at the Greene establishment. I had learned long ago not to accept every judgment of my father as prudent or as sound. Too many years of watching his dealings with Drayton and Dunwoody, or far too many bad choices for breeding stock, caused me to be slow in embracing every selection that he made. Gupton Dubec was just another in a long list of questionable acquaintances.

Gupton was older than I, probably in his late 20s. He was light on his feet, slender, almost catlike. Nothing about him added up. I mean everything was beyond the norm. He had recently been a deputy sheriff in some backwoods county in Mississippi. You would think that would have placed him on the correct side of the law. I had my doubts. His departure had been encouraged by an irate husband. Therefore, Texas was no magnet drawing him to it with the usual enticement of free land. To the contrary, Dubec had a past and was being propelled by it to parts unknown. This was the traveling companion that my father so willingly accepted.

We exchanged pleasantries in the barn. Our horses were saddled and ready. The donkey, whose name I still could not recall,
was packed and ready to follow us. If I cared little for Gupton, I
thought even less of his mount. She was a bony, worn-out yellow
mare whose best days were well behind her. There was no pack
animal, donkey, mule or horse. Gupton had a bed roll, a coffee pot,
and a sack of provisions that might have gotten him to the edge of
town. Stated another way, I guessed we would be dividing Momma
Mae's jerky three ways. Was my father completely blind?

Gupton took off his hat and dusted it lightly. I could see that
style was important to him. It was a bowler, useless in the Texas
sun, but stylish. It went with his brocade vest. Yes, this was going
to be an interesting trip, assuming that Gupton and the bar of soap
he was riding could keep up. My father was still bent on getting
through the Redlands as quickly as possible.

We were told that the El Camino Real, the Kings Highway, was
well marked and readily identifiable. First of all, it was no highway;
it was not even a road. If a pig trail was immediately adjacent to
it, you would be as likely to follow the pig trail as you would the
best effort of Spain to provide a road. As far as being well marked,
I failed to discern a single mark of any sort. This did not bother
Gupton. For all intents, he was just a passenger. He did not really
bother to even look for a mark.

The best we could do was to try and follow whatever signs earlier travelers left. Of course, some of them had the same difficulty
I was experiencing. We retraced their missteps as we retraced our
own. Pine needles littered the floor of the thicket to such an extent
that, except for Gupton's constant talking, all three of us could
travel without making a sound. No clicking of horseshoes. No ping
of metal against stone.

Initially, this was different, to the point that it intrigued me.

Then, I realized that if we could travel so quietly, so could everyone else. The good Sister had quieted my fears about the Indians in this part of Texas. However, every highway man in Arkansas plied their trade in the Redlands. Judging from the color of what soil did appear between the leaves and the needles, we were still in the Redlands. The silence of the deep forests became unsettling to me, but not apparently to Gupton.

I had led the way the entire day. This meant that I caught all the spider webs, and they were abundant. The trees were so close together that these little critters could jump back and forth from limb to tree with ease. I finally cut a small pine limb and held it over my horses head so that it caught most, but not all, of the silk. Gupton was amused. So far I had found nothing positive about Mr. Dubec, whose appetite for Momma Mae's biscuits and jerky exceeded even my own. Such an irritation.

The sun was setting. I picked a camp spot that I thought was suitable. I later learned that it was a selection typical of a white man. We always look for a small clearing in the forest. The surrounding trees would act as a wind break. They could possibly hide us from view, assuming we did not do something to call attention to ourselves, like light a fire. Indians did the exact opposite. They got far out on the prairie so they could see you coming. This gave them time to skedaddle. We gave away that opportunity by selecting an encircled trap.

I hobbled our horses. Gupton did not hobble his. I hoped the old mare would run off during the night. But knowing my good-natured father, I would have to share my horse if the mare wasn't there in the morning. Abram explained to Gupton, again, that we would not be having any campfires, that we would never have a campfire while traveling in Texas and that if he wanted a campfire, he needed to move several miles away from us. He also needed to provide us

with an address of his next of kin. Gupton saw no humor in this
at all. At nightfall, the quiet of the thicket erupted with noise and
sounds of all kinds of hoots, growls and howls. They could not be
seen, but the woods were full of nocturnal creatures, and they were
painfully aware that we were present.

I wasn't a coffee drinker, so I did not mess with it nor did I need
it to get started. Of course, Gupton explained to us that he was
absolutely useless without several cups in the morning. It was difficult for me to grasp how he could be more useless than he already
was. Saddled and ready, I moved out and onto the Kings Highway,
such that it was. Abram and Gupton could catch up once they finished their conversation. I had the nameless donkey and the biscuits. In short order, they caught up, both complaining about a lack
of breakfast. Since I saddled one horse and the donkey, I suggested
that they could wait until we stopped for lunch . . . If we stopped
for lunch.

Gupton's banter today seemed to focus on San Antonio de Bexar,
which I gathered was generally referred to as Bexar. All that I knew
of it was Sister Catherine's warning that you traveled to Bexar at
your peril. Gupton thought it would be a great place for a sporting man such as himself. So I had now confirmed that Gupton was
probably one of the few traveling these trails that had no interest
in Texas land. Dark eyed señoritas, whiskey and card games drew
his attention. I wondered just how he thought he would get started.
If he sold this yellow sack of bones upon his arrival, he would not
have much of a grubstake to start a new career as a gambler. Perhaps his saddle bags were full of gold . . . I doubted it.

We had been following some wagon tracks for quite some time.
The forest was not as thick as it had been. With more ground
exposed, the wheels could make deeper imprints. They could not
be too far ahead of us. The monotony of watching the tracks was

becoming downright hypnotic. Even Gupton was now dozing in the saddle.

The scream broke the quiet, shocking all of us out of our naps. My dad and Gupton spurred their horses. The sound was definitely feminine. I hurried along with the donkey. It did not take any time at all for Abram to ride up on the wagon. Two small girls were holding each other against a large tree, watched over by a teenage boy who was still mounted. The girl's eyes told Abram that the source of the scream was on the other side of the wagon. Wheeling his horse around, he came upon a grizzled man on top of a lady and amidst a pile of petticoats. Abram hollered for the man to stop. When he didn't, he got off his horse and had almost made it to him when the shot blew off the top of the man's head. He collapsed instantly, a bloody mess on top of Isabel Lee. This resulted in an even louder scream than the first one. Abram pulled the body off the lady. I had stopped by the teenage boy who seemed totally expressionless. It was as if he was completely detached from the events.

Gupton dismounted while my dad tried to comfort Mrs. Lee. Gupton approached the teenager, his pistol still smoking.

"Who are you?" Gupton was looking into the most vacant pair of eyes he had ever seen. There was no response.

"Well, who is he then?"

"Paw." At least we all thought he said Paw. Judging from their filthy condition, they were probably some highway men, most likely from Arkansas territory.

"Gupton, I do not think you're going to get a lot of information out of him."

Gupton nodded to my father, he motioned for the boy to get down and stand behind the wagon. He wasn't armed. Neither one had much in the way of equipment, bed rolls or anything else. Either they had some pack animals hidden, or they planned on relieving Mrs. Lee of more than her virtue.

It was decided to tie the rapist onto his horse and send him away with the nonsensical son. Sooner or later he and his horse would find home. Gupton didn't mind shooting the fellow, but a burial was far too much work. I wasn't volunteering either. It was decided that we would stop our travels to stay with Mrs. Lee and her two daughters.

I could not help but reflect on our visit to Texas, at least so far. Back in Louisiana I considered myself to be an adult; I think most people saw me in the same light. My mother would be the exception; in her eyes, I was locked into some state of infancy. As mature as I thought I was, Texas was hurling a whole new collection of experiences at me. I had never seen a female assaulted by anyone. I had never been a witness to a shooting; and, most certainly, never been this close to a corpse. I had tied all kinds of things onto a horse, a mule or a donkey with some degree of success. Tying a dead body to a horse was a challenging project. I only hoped that the knots held until the boy got Paw home. Given the total lack of emotion exhibited by the fellow, if Paw dropped off along the way, I sensed that would be his permanent resting place. Dubec and my father handled Mrs. Lee and her daughters. I was at a total loss for what to do. It seemed that Mr. Lee had recently gone to his heavenly reward. It had been his desire to come to Texas to preach and to convert sinners. Mrs. Lee thought she should try to carry out his intentions. I wasn't sure what she thought she could do. The good nun was the only female that I had ever run into that was in the business of sinner conversion. Crossing the Redlands with two small girls did not seem terribly prudent.

It was decided that my father would accompany them back to Nacogdoches and then catch up with us. This was a great relief to me. I feared that I would be selected as the escort. My conversational skills would have been severely taxed in short order.

Gupton and I decided to stay put for the rest of the day. We could rest the horses and my father should be able to catch up with us by the next evening. A small creek ran nearby. All of the creek beds in Texas seem to have a good stand of pecan, walnut and hickory nut trees. Berries were not in season, but the nuts would give us something to eat while we traveled. So nutting we went. It did not take long for us to gather a good-sized sack of various types.

I had replayed the day's events over and over in my mind, wondering what I would've done had I been alone and happened upon Mrs. Lee. Dubec did not hesitate. His approach was one fluid motion resulting in the quick death of Mrs. Lee's attacker. But how did he know what to do? What if he acted in error? I seriously doubted that I would have been so certain. As we returned to our camp I thought it fair to make inquiry of the former deputy.

"Mr. Dubec, you acted quickly earlier today. Had you run into similar situations before? I mean when you were a deputy?"

Dubec settled down in a nest of pine needles under a large bull pine. For a talkative sort, he did not respond as quickly as I expected.

"Never ran into someone in the middle of a rape; assaults, robberies, shootings and just about every other form of theft, but never a rape."

"But you seemed so quick, so certain, what if . . ."

Gupton smiled, "what if I were flat wrong? What if the guy was Mr. Lee and her scream was just some domestic spat in progress?"

"Well, yes, a man would be dead because you were wrong."

"Leander, we all knew more facts than you think. Think about it. We're in the middle of a thicket, in the middle of the Redlands. This area attracts an evil sort. The good folks try to get through it as quickly as possible. Hell, your dad will not even start a campfire and we're three armed men. The scream I heard didn't sound like it came from anyone related to the attacker. Plus I saw the two girls huddled together with that vacant looking nit wit standing guard. It seemed like shooting the bastard was the proper recourse."

I was reflecting on a statement when Gupton continued to make his point.

"Look Leander, life out here on the frontier is not going to come with a lot of instructions. Many times, if I had hesitated I would be dead. To hesitate is the riskiest thing you can do. Go with your gut and you will be right more often than not. Doubt will find you dead. Texas is going to attract a lot of folks of all stripes. I haven't seen a whole lot of law around and if there is some, they will be Mexican. I do not have much confidence in Mexicans of any sort. Your own confidence in yourself will be what saves you. Don't hesitate."

I had a new outlook towards Mr. Gupton Dubec. My sense told me that his advice had probably been tested before. It had some balance to it. So far Texas was different.

My father returned that next evening and brought with him a change in the weather, a big change. We left the Redlands in the middle of a thunderstorm that seem to hover over us for days. The pine forest was no more. The terrain was rolling. Thus, we crossed creek after creek after creek. A description of one would fit them all. By now, their banks were swollen. The line of debris told you the water level was a good bit higher than usual. Cottonwood, hackberry, elm and pecan trees clustered at the edges of each creek bank. As usual I was in the lead, clearing spider webs as I rode. Even though we were all wet to the bone, the first splash into moving water was always a cold shock. The so-called Kings Highway was itself a moving mud puddle. I chose to travel to its side and not turn up any more mud than need be.

Our destination was Jared Groce's place. We were told that it was on the Brazos River, another moving body of water that we had not yet met. It meant nothing to us, except I remembered the good nun's warning to stay on this side of the Brazos. The humor of the Indians in the area west of the Brazos seemed to change from good to ornery. One drizzly afternoon we saw a wagon approaching. A black man and woman hailed us as we got closer. I recognized the dress material of the woman as that worn by the slaves owned by Groce. I spoke first.

"Hello, we're looking for Mr. Groce. Can you direct us to him?"

I expected the man to answer, but the woman was quick to respond.

"Massa Groce bees back on da' riber, 'bout 2 miles dat way," pointing in the direction from which they came.

I thanked them and encouraged by the news and the close proximity, we hastened along. I couldn't help but wonder what kind of a dent 90 slaves could make in this wilderness called Texas. Our pace quickened almost subconsciously.

The first sound came as a shock. We had heard plenty of noises over the past few weeks from every critter along the way. The first discernible human sound brought a smile to our faces. It was the heavy sound of an ax hitting a very solid tree. It was almost immediately followed by the crack of limbs hitting other limbs and ending with a thud. We slowed our pace straining to locate the woodsman before the fall of the next tree.

Coming over a slight rise, we saw the ax man and further in the distance were about 20 slave quarters, uniformly aligned into rows. Each was identical, with two doors, no windows and a chimney at each end. The lane between the rows had been filled with the bark removed from the logs that now were the walls of the homes. This made a compacted yard of sorts that reduced the amount of mud you would normally have expected. Seeing this, we looped around the backside of the houses and continued down the slope towards the river.

Off in the distance rose the unfinished structure that would be Groce's home. The second floor and the roof were framed, but not closed. Our presence was quickly noticed and Jared Groce himself was soon riding in our direction, waving as he came. It was comforting to see a familiar face so far from home.

My father made the necessary introductions and Groce welcomed us to his home. Our horses were taken by one of the slaves I remembered from his trip through Louisiana. After a quick meal, Groce had to show us his part of Texas. As a special treat, he had the stallion that he had gotten from me saddled, another old friend from Louisiana.

Groce had made quite a dent in the wilderness. By dividing his slaves into specialized teams, he had moved forward on all fronts. Along the Brazos River, he had cleared about 50 acres of good bottomland. He was bent on producing a cotton crop this year. While he wasn't sure of the quantity or quality, a crop was a certainty. Given the amount of construction that was ongoing, many of the slave women spent their time hunting and fishing to supplement the stores that he had brought with him. Groce said that he had plenty, but was not inclined to exhaust them and then start looking for some replacement.

His remuda, always of interest to me, seemed more impressive now than when I first saw them. The winter grasses, and some rest following the trek from Alabama, had put some weight on them, even the draft horses. We rode over to a cleared area adjacent to where the trees were being felled. Several men were trying to reassemble the contents of about three wagons. We were told that, if they could figure out how to put everything back together, it would, hopefully, resemble a saw mill and a planer. Judging from his statement, I sensed he had some doubt about the success of this endeavor.

We stayed a couple of days with the Groce family. Mr. Groce shared every possible bit of information with my father. Should we, and hopefully the Whitworths, choose to migrate, Groce offered to rent slaves to assist with the construction of our houses and out buildings. The saw mill, if assembled by that time, would also be available for finished lumber. Our next step was to meet with the Empresario Stephen Austin at San Felipe.

Gupton Dubec had little interest in meeting Austin or acquiring land. However, since it was generally in the direction of San Antonio de Bexar, he would continue to consume Momma Mae's biscuits and jerky a little more.

I had never heard the word Empresario. I assumed it was Spanish. Not having a clue to its meaning or origin, I had even less preconception as to what an Empresario should look like. Austin did not look like what I did not know he would look like . . . That is if I had any idea in the first place. His office and home was a standard dog trot, which gave me no clue about the man. When we arrived he was not home. We sat down in the open center hallway on a log bench. In short order, Austin rode up and greeted us.

He was a good bit younger than I expected. Dark curly hair accented deep set dark eyes. If that sounds hard, it is not meant to for the effect was to create almost delicate features. He was no backwoodsman. His manners and gentility were unexpected.

He had a quiet confidence that came with his conviction towards Texas and the colonization effort that he was responsible for. Mr.

Groce must have mentioned us to him at some point. He seemed to know our name, or at least, the possibility that we might be headed in this direction. We, Austin, my father and I were soon poring over maps of his colony. Dubec was napping. Whenever my father seem to focus on an area west of the Brazos River, I tried to return the conversation to areas east of the Brazos, recalling the advice of Sister Catherine. That was not difficult. The facilities of Jared Groce were on the east side and even Abram could not ignore that kind of help.

My father, for the cost of the survey, could get one league and one labor, which equaled 4621 acres. There was some discussion about me, an 18-year-old single man. I sensed that Austin and my father left this issue open. 4000 acres was a pretty piece. How anyone could handle that was beyond comprehension. For his commitment to Texas, Groce had been granted 10 leagues. For all I knew, we may have been still standing on Groce's land. The size and distances just did not match up with what I was used to back home in Louisiana.

The next day was to be our last at Groce's. We needed to find our place soon and get back to mother in Louisiana before both forgot about us. Groce and I rode through his horses before breakfast. It created some strong feelings within me. I would have been happy just to remain with Groce and manage his herd of horses. However, my father did show a good bit of confidence in me. Our efforts were showing some success. Perhaps Groce and I could work to our mutual benefit in the future.

After breakfast, my father and Dubec totally took my legs out from under me. I had assumed that Dubec would head for Bexar, card games and senoritas. Thus, we could get about the business at hand, which was to find a spot suitable for our future. For reasons unknown to me, we were fording the Brazos with Dubec. In other words, we would be traveling on the west side of the river until again we found the Kings Highway, assuming that it was findable. Dubec would then head west to San Antonio and we . . . Well I guessed we would sooner or later try to find a spot to light. The whole concept disgusted me. Once again my father had made a gross error in judgment. Ignoring the fact that we never should have taken up with this fellow in the first place, we would now be on the west side of the river. If, by chance, my father found a place that he liked, we would always be a river away from everyone and everywhere. I would be remiss if I failed to mention the need to feed Mr. Dubec some more biscuits and jerky.

I took the lead and headed north. My father and Gupton brought up the rear. I had the donkey. They would have to keep up with me or at least with the donkey. I stayed out of earshot almost the entire day. As it got dark, my father inquired if I intended to stop for the evening. I said "sure." It wasn't a particularly good place, but I was really too irritated to care.

The next morning was clear and cold. There was no wind, just cold, which was better than wet and cold. Gupton unpacked a coffee pot and built a fire. On the one hand this showed more industry than I had ever seen coming from Mr. Dubec. On the other hand, we had cold camped all the way through Texas. I inquired what had changed.

"Well Leander, we are out of the Redlands and I am headed to Bexar. So I kind of thought this is my part of the journey now."

Yeah, his journey and our biscuits! I looked at my father whose perplexed look revealed little to me in the way of explanation. I packed the donkey, saddled my horse and prepared for another day of talk. I was growing to love silence more than I had ever known. Dubec finished his coffee with more slurps and "aws" than I had ever heard.

We were moving out of the river bottom toward the upward slope of a grassy prairie. The winter frost had turn the grass stand golden in the sunlight. What little breeze that there was drifted lightly across it, slightly bending the tips of the stand as we made our way. Initially I saw nothing but my horse must've picked up a scent as he snorted. The days had been so uneventful that I paid it no mind. Then my father spoke in a very low voice.

"Gupton looks like that campfire wasn't such a good idea."

When he said that, we all looked at the ridge above us and slightly to our right. They wasted no time. The moment we took notice, they descended down the slope. Six, maybe seven, I did not have time to count.

"Make for the river Leander. Drop the donkey."

I was prepared to make for the river. Dropping the donkey was another matter. So many things were moving through my head at once. Sister Catherine said the Indians west of the Brazos were different. We were damn sure west of the Brazos and these boys didn't look real happy. The donkey had all of Momma Mae's biscuits and jerky, plus what would I tell Elisabeth. After the Indians ate the biscuits and jerky, they were most certainly going to eat the donkey, whatever his name was.

When the first arrow passed me by, I no longer had any doubt about the donkey. I spurred my horse. We were all about 10 feet apart and headed down the slope as fast as we could go. But Gupton's horse had little wind and was falling behind quickly. I had never raced an Indian pony; but dad and I were well mounted. We could probably outrun their horses. Could we outrun their arrows? The thunder of the hooves now drowned out the whoops of the braves chasing us. I did not like the eagerness of the sounds; but the speed of our horses gave me some confidence. They were lathered, but steadily pulling away. Dubec was now 20 to 30 yards behind us.

Three of the braves were trying to corral the donkey. I could see under my armpit that the donkey was not cooperating. Donkeys can whirl on you. He had just caught one brave in the middle of his chest with a well-placed rear hoof. Dubec's horse was slowing even as he whipped her to give him speed. Then, Dubec sat straight up in the saddle and then fell forward. His horse, her head now held low, slowed. I saw him fall to the ground. I did not slow down a bit. My father and I were still on a direct run to the river. When I looked again, the rest of the braves were on foot around the torso of Gupton Dubec. One pulled his knife and then with a single motion, held up the grisly scalp of Dubec. I could not hear it, but I could easily imagine the bloodcurdling yelp.

We hit the river. The cold water cooled the horses as they swam. We moved with the current. They were strong animals, but no need to tax them any more than necessary. Once on the other side, we kept them in an easy lope for a while. Neither of us spoke a word. I can only assume that my father saw what I had seen. That evening, we camped out in the open—Indian style. We did not want any more surprises. The horses remain saddled, bridled and un-hobbled. We agreed to sleep in shifts, but I didn't sleep at all. I doubt that my father did.

At daybreak, we were about to break camp, except there was no camp to break. Then we heard the familiar heehaw of . . . . Ulysses. Yes Ulysses! He didn't have any biscuits and all the jerky was gone, but he would be going home with us.

CHAPTER 8

Return and Pack

I WOULD NOT FEEL ITS WELCOMED WARMTH MUCH LONGER. Twilight was fast upon us. I had enjoyed the sun's heat on my back this very cold and windy day. We were both bone weary, but close enough to home to not even consider stopping for the evening. The horses and Ulysses were familiar with the road and could find their way from this point. My father and I dozed in our saddles. I say dozed. The stomach noises we both made were clearly audible to each of us.

Except for the meal at the Greene Inn, we had not had much to eat since leaving the Brazos River bottom. While in Nacogdoches, I caught up with the good nun. I told her that everything she had told me had turned out to be exactly correct. Of course, I studiously avoided running into Rachel Greene. We stayed but one evening. My father was anxious to get home. Texas fever was working its magic on him. As for me, I was just anxious to get home. My father's endurance had impressed me. He was actually more alert than I; sleep could not come too soon for me.

The steady rocking back and forth in my saddle caused me to drift off every so often. The motion reflected what little mental thought processes still filled my mind. Without a doubt, we would be moving to Texas. Mom had pretty much given her approval in advance. You had to wonder if she would be so eager when she learned the tale of the trip. Leaving behind the embarrassment of Baptiste was quite a motivation for her; that said a rape and a scalping could give her pause for reflection.

The word Texas, so recently new, was now wrapped in layer after layer of enticements. The sheer size of the land was intoxicating. From what I could see, the soil was fertile, certainly as fertile as ours, and we managed pretty well. But Texas was rough, untamed and even with a steady influx of like-minded folks; it would be some time before we would have the support of a community of neighbors. I guessed it came down to a single question. Did you have enough confidence in yourself and your ability to survive, to take a gamble for so much land? My father appeared to have answered in the affirmative. I was not so sure.

Louisiana had been my only home. Our place was comfortable. The neighbors, except for the "tribe", were generally nice, or, at least, you knew their quirks. This spirit of adventure enthralled in Texas could prove to be a bust, even deadly. Would the Whitworths go as well? I suspected they would. But, would my dad's ne'er-do-well brothers follow us? Since I viewed them as parasites, I suspected that Drayton and Dunwoody would follow, their existence depended on it. Texas without uncle Baptiste, but with Drayton and Dunwoody would be the worst of all possibilities. If that happened, I personally would prefer to move back to Louisiana and live with Baptiste. It would be better than dealing with the "tribe."

"Jesus, Ulysses stop it!"

Elisabeth's donkey had picked up the scent of home and had been fighting his halter and lead rope for the past couple miles.

"Dad, just stop for a minute. I'm going to cut him loose and let him trot on home. He has about worn me out."

Dad smiled, "Leander, don't you think he is as anxious as we are to get home. After all, he came fairly close to having feathers braided in his mane."

Ulysses took off. We were only about a mile away. He headed right for the quarters. When we got there, everyone was awake and standing outside. Ulysses heehawed and kicked, then grinned like only a donkey does. He did this repeatedly until Elisabeth woke up and hugged him. Then, he calmed down to just small heehaws and snorts.

Dad spoke first. "Elisabeth, he certainly seems glad to see you. I would too if I'd come as close as he had to becoming Injun property."

Elisabeth cut a glance in my direction that was chilling. You had to wonder how my father could get so old and still be so loose with his tongue. I mean he did not need to say a thing.

There were hugs and back slaps all around. I swear my mother hugged me more than she did my father. I hadn't shaved since we left, hoping that a beard might wean her of my permanent state of infancy. I might as well shave. I took the horses to unsaddle them and make my way to bed. My father, I could tell, was ready to recount the entire trip for anyone inclined to listen.

The crow of the first rooster brought us all to attention. In an odd way, it was a welcomed sound, one that I had not heard for a while. The hunger pains reminded me that I was very close to Momma Mae and a breakfast that I had missed. Still groggy and tired, I wandered into her kitchen.

"Good mornin' Leander."

I did not answer. I just grinned and gave her a big hug, lifting her off the ground as I did.

"You and Massa Abram had a big 'venture in Texas."

"Oh, you heard?"

"Heard, your father just finished da' story. I'd never gone to sleep . . . . Just start breakfast."

"Where is my traveling companion?" I really expected to see him wolfing down a breakfast we had both discussed about every morning since we left.

"Gone to da Whitworths."

"Oh, I suspect that he has to give them a report."

I eased over to the table. As I sat down, she placed a platter, not a plate, a platter of eggs, grits, biscuits and ham, before me. The aroma was downright intoxicating.

"I must be in heaven."

"You goin' to think heben when you see all da' work you have to do. Your father gave us a list of things to get ready. Suspect he wants to leave as soon as he can. Journey proud, I tell you . . . Journey proud."

My father's enthusiasm was his burden for now. I focused entirely on Momma Mae's breakfast. I was confident that there would be plenty of time to prepare for our return trek to Texas.

"Leander."

"Yes ma'am." I looked up at Momma Mae who seemed unusually quiet. I had not previously noticed in my rush to fill a very empty stomach

"You might look in on Poppy."

Just the way she said it sent a shiver down my spine. Poppy was the heart and soul of our little community. With so many talents, he was involved in every aspect of just about everyone's life.

"Is there a problem?" I almost held my breath for her answer.

"He took ill after you left. Still tries to do his chores, but he ain't well. Not by any way. No sir."

My appetite left me and I headed towards Poppy's cabin. I guessed that no one told my father last night. Too many stories to be told, no one would have interrupted him.

Poppy's cabin was the very last one, the highest on the rise behind our house. I knocked and entered. Elisabeth and Blue were still eating breakfast. Poppy was sitting in his rocker. I would recognize his rocker anywhere. He had made dozens identical to it.

"Good morning Poppy, Blue, Elisabeth. Poppy, Momma Mae says you are not feeling well?"

I hoped that my face did not reveal my shock. Poppy had lost a lot of weight. His eyes were sunken. You could see the fever in them.

"Dat old woman dud ent know nothin'."

"Judging from your looks she knows something. Poppy, I can tell you don't feel well. What is it?"

Elisabeth seized the opportunity to tell her side of the story.

He got cold and ain't done nothin' for it. Let it get bad. Stubborn. Taken potions from dat old woman dat Fuchs owns. Ain't helpin' any. No help at all."

"Poppy, you stay inside and rest. I will call for the doctor and . . . ."

"L'ander, got no time to be idle . . . Gots to get you ready for Texas."

"Poppy, Texas ain't going anywhere. We need to get you well first."

"Told you, told you. You needed a doctor." Elisabeth wanted to make certain her father remained in his place and right now that was resting in his rocker.

Blue and I left for the barn.

"Blue, Poppy looks terrible, how long has he been this way?"

"'bout since you left, Leander. He won't slow down. Said he had to keep things going while you and Massa Abram gone. Ain't nothin' been done. It's winter, but Poppy kept pushin', worse at night. Don't like da sound of dat cough . . . Got some rattle to it. Don't like dat sound." Blue showed every bit as much concern as Elisabeth had. I headed for the doctor. At Poppy's age, he could easily get down and not get back up. As you would expect, the doctor was not home but would head our way sometime after lunch. I proceeded to check the cow herd and the horses.

The calving season had started and started in a big way, either that or I had been gone longer than I thought. I rode quietly through the herd. This wet winter was starting to wear on the cows. Most were still in fairly good flesh; but with calf birth and the walk to Texas in the near future, I had to wonder how many would live to see their new home. Mentally, I made notes of who I thought were stout enough to keep. Some of the older ones probably should be sold here, or butchered.

"I've already made my cuts. What are yours?"

I had not seen or heard Reams come up from behind me; not a good sign for someone who had just experienced Texas.

"What are my what?"

"Come on, old man. Some of these girls won't make it out of the parish much less to the Sabine. Going to have to sell them and stick with the stronger ones. I figure we sell any sixes or older. The fives and younger ought to handle the trip even if they haven't calved."

"We leave? I take it you folks are going along?"

"Hell yes. I am made for Texas!"

"Reams, just how do you know you're made for Texas? You haven't even seen it."

"But I have investigated Texas, old man. While you and your dad were eating biscuits and sunning yourself on horseback, we went to New Orleans to make the arrangements."

"Arrangements?" I obviously had missed a step or my father failed to mention something.

"Leander, sometimes you are as dumb as a sack of rocks. You can't just pack biscuits and move lock, stock and barrel to Texas. Hell, it isn't even part of the United States. You have to make arrangements. You know, with banks and dry goods stores. Texas doesn't have any of that."

"So you chose New Orleans because . . ."

"Because Austin's business relationships are in New Orleans. He was a lawyer there you know."

Actually I did not know that. It never came up. Now I was utterly frustrated that I could actually meet the man and Reams could stay home and know more about him than I did.

"You seem a little uninformed Leander."

"Reams, I've got a few things on my mind, why don't you just fill me in, and I think keeping the fives and under makes sense. Do you think we can sell the sixes and older?"

"Not a problem, already been working on it, old man. But we will have to get moving. Get them sorted and divided between us and I think we can sell them pretty easy. Now while you were on your grand tour, my dad and I established a banking relationship in New Orleans. You know so that the bank could handle the note payments."

"Notes?"

"We got to sell our places. Ain't going to get all cash. So there will be notes."

"Who's going to buy them?"

"Fuchs, Garvin himself. He is really interested in your place. I think it's a way to get back at those towers of intelligence, Drayton and Dunwoody."

"Yes, I've met them." The mere mention of my uncles caused a momentary heartburn.

"Anyway, the lawyers draw notes. Fuchs pays the bank and our dads can draw on the funds when they need to. Of course, they won't need much to get their league and labor. That you get for the cost of the survey. And, old man, Austin is going to let you and I have one third of a league and a labor since we are single men. You are still single, aren't you?"

I did not respond but just cut him a glance. To respond to every one of Reams' jokes is to encourage him, and he does not need a lot of encouragement.

Reams continued, "Any way, the way your dad talked, we will need to get packing."

Without question, it made sense to leave now and try to get established quick enough to get a crop in the ground. But Poppy weighed on my mind.

"What do you know about Poppy? He looks terrible."

"Leander, he kept going like a house afire . . . Couldn't slow him down. Hell, there wasn't that much to do, but he repaired every wagon, implement and harness he could find. I think he just got down. This damned weather hasn't been much help. He has been relying on some potions from that old woman of Fuchs'. I doubt they are doing him much good."

"No doubt. I have the doctor calling on him."

"Yeah, our saw bones. I am not so sure Poppy isn't better off with the potions. He is up in years. Maybe he fears the trip."

"Fears the trip?" I had not given that any thought. I guessed the spirit of Texas had infected us all, but maybe not. Maybe some folks would prefer to stay here.

"On another note, old man, I believe there is a business opportunity for us in New Orleans."

Now this I had to hear. Reams could sniff out any form of money if it were in the vicinity. However, you had to be careful. Some of his ventures turned out to be a bust. "And what might that be?"

"I gather the speed of your horses is what permits you to be here talking to me."

My stomach did a flip-flop. I saw a mental image of Gupton Dubec's scalping and his last moments. Reams must have sensed my discomfort.

"Sorry, what I mean is that I thought Injun ponies were pretty fast and you seemed to have out run them."

"No one was chasing them. Maybe they weren't as motivated as we were, Reams."

"Perhaps, but I met a fellow, William Tunstell Lowe."

"Who?"

"William Tunstell Lowe, do you know him?"

"No, and with that name I doubt that I would forget him. What does he do?"

"He promotes horse races. I mean some real quality horse races. Good horses, running with clipped shoes. They turn in some times. Lots of heavy wagers. I think we could make a buck or two."

"My horses I suppose?" I already knew the answer.

"Leander, you have the best bloodlines around. It's damn sure worth a shot."

"I suppose, but Texas . . ."

"Oh hell yes, we have to get to Texas first, but then a return trip to New Orleans would be a nice diversion.

"Diversion?"

"Vacation to you, Leander."

"We started this conversation with your announcement that you were made for Texas."

"And rightly I am".

"How do you know?" Honestly I had my doubts. Texas seemed like a lot of hard work. Reams wouldn't shirk but he didn't go looking for it.

"Down in New Orleans, those guys promoting Texas say that the Sabbath never crosses the Sabine."

"Ha, I get it. If there's no churchgoing in Texas you're the right guy."

"You bet I am."

"Let's get these cattle sorted tomorrow. That will be one chore out of the way. All your wagons in good order?"

"I told you Poppy has us ready to go. Extra wheels and tongues. It's like he wants to get rid of us."

"I better check on him. I will see you in the morning."

It seemed that I needed to pick up the pace. We were going to Texas and going soon. I headed for the horse pasture. Reams' idea of horse racing probably had as much to do with whore chasing as it did with horse racing. He had become quite a sporting man and New Orleans was the perfect place for whoring and wenching. That said, as I rode through the remuda, there were some young horses that could poke a hole in a cloud if you turn them loose. We hadn't seen any colts out of Jared Groce's stallion, and horse racing might be something we ought to take a look at. I wasn't sure that I knew what I needed to know about clipped horse shoes, but I was certain we could find someone who could give us some pointers. Maybe William Tunstell Lowe. What a name.

My loop around the place uncovered nothing out of the ordinary. In fact, everything seemed in good shape. As I rode up to the house, which never looked right after that storm blew down my swing tree, I wondered what our home would look like in Texas. I guessed about the same. Everyone seemed to favor a dog trot. I dismounted and walked to the barn. Elisabeth was inside.

"Did the Doctor come?"

"Yes, and left a potion."

"Medicine, Elisabeth. A potion is what he has been taking that hasn't done him any good."

"Well, he took it and went to sleep."

"Well, what have we here?" I couldn't resist a grin. In the corner of the barn was Ted, his brow furrowed and a perplexed look on his face. He wanted to come to me but, at his feet, biting his tail and encircling him, were six Ted look-alikes.

"It's called responsibility Ted, get used to it."

"When did this happen, Elisabeth?"

"'bout two, maybe three weeks ago. Six boys not one girl." Elisabeth seemed a little put out that Ted only sired boys, but, I suspected that she would get over it.

"Good looking pups. They will love Texas."

"You take better care of him dan dat donkey."

"Elisabeth, Ulysses got home in one piece."

"Hum."

I headed for the kitchen before I got too deep into the care and custody of donkeys.

* * *

The interior of Poppy's cabin was now lit only by the red embers of the fireplace. The potion, as Elisabeth called it, left by the Doctor, provided Poppy with some rest. He had slept most of the day. It did nothing for the rattle and a cough that seem to descend deeper and deeper into his chest with each passing hour. Blue had moved his cot next to his father's; Elisabeth rested at his feet. Both were exhausted; yet, they drifted in and out of sleep worried over the steady deterioration of their father.

Poppy turned his head slightly in Blue's direction.

Blue, y'all dare?"

"Yes sur". Blue awoke out of his light sleep immediately ready to do whatever Poppy asked.

"Blue, you knows dat part of da millstone back da barn?"

Blue was confused but knew the stone. It had been leaning against the barn forever.

"Yes sur."

"Son, when I go, I want you to chisel my name on it, put it on my grave . . ."

"Now Poppy you . . ."

"Son, I knows I don't have long. Listen to me. I wants someone to knows I've been here, not dropped in a hole and forgot. Pick a place, under a tree. Someplace cool and use dat stone."

"But Poppy you . . . ."

"Son, I ain't goin' to Texas . . . Never make it."

Poppy coughed again. The rattle was chilling. Blue knew what it meant.

"Blue, you take care of your sis. She's a sweet girl."

"Yes sur." Blue could hardly speak. The lump in his throat seemed to grow and grow.

"Blue, you take care of L'ander. He'll be a good man. Goin' to be somebody. But you need to help. Keep a lookout for him. White folks gets in a rush. We got da time to watch. Think things out. Dat will help L'ander. Goin' to be somebody. Member he went in dat riber for you. No one else did, just L'ander. Take care Elisabeth."

Blue looked at his sister exhausted at the foot of Poppy's bed. He thought to wake her, but did not want to interrupt whatever Poppy had to say.

Poppy swallowed hard and turned his head away slightly. He was now in that twilight between the here and the other side. One deep breath and he was gone. Blue's sobs woke his sister.

The coffin maker for so many had made his own. Blue found it in Poppy's shop. The attention to detail, the precision of the cuts, reflected the experience of his lifetime. The selection of the wood was different. Most of Poppy's coffins were pine. Sometimes someone wanted oak. Poppy selected pecan, just plain, old horse pecan wood found along every creek and river bed. It gave the coffin a unique look. It was naturally distressed with a black grain going throughout its honey colored wood.

Word got out immediately. Blue was prepared to load the coffin onto one of the field wagons to be pulled by a single draft horse. Leander and Reams told Blue to go comfort his sister. They selected four matching bay horses as the team to carry Poppy. They loaded the coffin onto a buck board wagon trimmed in black. Poppy and Elisabeth rode with Abram and Susannah. The gravesite was under a huge willow oak in the curve of the Lane leading from the house onto the main road. The semi circle remnant of the old millstone was Poppy's headstone, as requested.

The hustle of Texas left little time for grieving. That was probably best. Too much idle time gives way too much grief.

* * *

The Sunday service at the Ebenezer Church was to be followed by a church social . . . sort of a collective sendoff and farewell to the Wilhites and the Whitworths. As a result, the services were well attended. Folks who had not darkened the door of this church or any other for years were in attendance. This resulted in an unusually long service. I guess the thought was to seize the moment. While the sinners were captured by their hunger for the feast to follow, the preacher did his best to bring the back sliders to redemption. I had my doubts about the strategy. After a few seconds short of eternity, the service ended and everyone moved outdoors where tables and long boards had been placed to hold the fixin's that the women had prepared.

Reams and I were eating ourselves through each table, a table at a time. The food was absolutely wonderful and we were on a great pace to reach the dessert table ahead of everyone else.

"No, you can't! You just can't!"

The collective conversations were brought to an abrupt halt with my mother's shout of shock. I turned in her direction, along with everyone else. She was standing directly in front of uncle Drayton and uncle Dunwoody. This could not be good. Out of the corner of my eye, I saw my father hastily moving towards them. We may have been on church ground, but she saw no reason to lower her voice. My father had just arrived when she continued.

"Abram, you cannot let this happen, you just can't. Will we never have any peace?"

My father was obviously a step behind.

"What is it, Mother?"

Of course, the entire world was now interested in what could have provoked such an outburst from Susannah Wilhite, pillar of the Ebenezer Baptist Church.

"They are going to Texas!" Directing her index finger in the direction of my two uncles, who just happened to be standing in the general direction of Texas. It took a moment for my father to gather his thoughts. The news was news to me and provided me with a sinking feeling. Just as I had imagined, we were leaving Louisiana to avoid my favorite uncle Baptiste, and we were soon to be ensconced in Texas with the "tribe". The thought of Baptiste cause me to survey the crowd. He was not at the service and did not show for the social. I would've thought he would have come. As I turned, Reams moved over behind me. He touched my shoulder and said, "You know Leander, family is one of life's great rewards."

Before I could fashion a response, my father finally gathered his wits.

"Boys, is this true? Are you going to Texas?"

"It would have been nice of you if you would've included our places in your deal with Fuchs." Drayton kicked the ground for reasons known to him alone.

There was an audible murmur from the crowd that could best be described as a resounding "who would want them."

My father deflected the comment with a question.

"Who have you sold your places to?"

"Rezan Bowie. Drayton seemed proud that he had negotiated the deal with one of the Bowie brothers.

"Jesus, Drayton, you'll never get paid. Those Bowies have clouded more land titles in Louisiana and Arkansas than just about anyone. Why . . ."

"Why do you care, Abram? Good God! The problem isn't the sale of their places. The problem is that they are coming to Texas. Will we never be rid of them! Mind your wit's Abram." Susannah was fuming.

"Now look here, Missy." Drayton had his dander up and wasn't exactly pleased with the rather frosty reception he was getting from my mother. "Texas is a big place and you can't keep us out of there."

Susannah was now crimson.

"Drayton Wilhite, you do whatever you please but expect no help from us. No help. You have been a parasite your entire life, just a parasite. When we leave you won't be part of our group. No sir, you won't."

"That is just fine, Missy, we have some business to attend to before we leave . . . It'll help us along the way."

Drayton and Dunwoody left. My parents said a few goodbyes, but really I viewed it more as a relocation of the fight. I was confident that my father was just beginning to get a piece of my mother's mind. I saw no reason to follow them. Reams and I returned to the dessert table. The afternoon warmed nicely. Folks sprawled all over the church grounds. Bits and pieces of various conversations return to Drayton and Dunwoody, and the Bowies, as well. The huge amount of food was cause for a nap. I woke before Reams. When he finally came to, I told him that I thought I would like to ride out to uncle Baptiste to say goodbye. It nagged me that he wasn't here. Perhaps he had gotten wind of my mother's true motivation to depart for Texas and thought best not to attend. Even so, for a mountain man, he was a fairly regular church goer.

The skiff wasn't where it was supposed to be. Odd, but it just meant that we would have to loop around and take the one route that could be traveled on horseback. It still went through the swamp, but was manageable. As we approached the tree house, I called out to Baptiste. There was no response. In fact the entire swamp seemed unusually quiet. I looked at Reams who shrugged his shoulders. We ground tied the horses. Since we came by horseback, we approached the tree house from the rear. When we came around front, a few of the barrels on the first landing were turned over. The skiff had been there and was gone. You could see the footprints. A piece of calico was on a branch near the landing. We both called for Baptiste again, but there was no answer.

"Reams, I don't like the looks of this. Let's go up and see if he is there . . . Could be he's sick. I don't know."

The second and third levels seemed untouched.

"What do you think, Leander?" Reams was as puzzled as I was.

"It seems like there was a ruckus downstairs. It would take a little effort to turn over those barrels. I don't think it was an animal."

"What about that cloth on the tree?"

"Reams, I would think that might be part of the colored ladies dress. Someone didn't want to get into that skiff that is for sure."

Reams and I left, probably as confused and as concerned as we could be. A place acquires the sense of a person. This place didn't seem to be part of uncle Baptiste's world anymore.

I would've mentioned it to my father when I got home, but my mother and he were having quite a row. Given our anticipated departure, I thought it best to look for another opportunity. My gut told me that I might not see Baptiste again.

We left at sunrise. No one had to walk. We had plenty of horses and mules. Elisabeth and Ulysses led those animals that we had to herd. We had combined all the cows and hogs into one grand bunch. However, with all of us on horseback they stayed in a single group. The womenfolk were handling most of the wagons. My father and Mr. Whitworth took the lead. When we reached the large willow oak in the lane where Poppy was buried, they took off their hats, as did everyone else. Poppy's wagons, his wheels, his yokes and tongues were going to take us to Texas. Poppy was staying in Louisiana.

CHAPTER 9

Texas becomes Home .... Maybe

THE JOURNEY TO TEXAS WAS EVERYTHING I THOUGHT IT WOULD BE. Basically, we crossed the Sabine and fell into a moving mud puddle. The King's Highway was now a wide ribbon with the footing and consistency of thick glue. The color of the mud might change. But, wherever we were, it was everywhere. Once we left the Redlands, it became a soft gray. You could not get away from it. It was in your eggs in the morning. By lunch time you had enough on your hands that everything you ate was gritty. I wondered if I would have any teeth left by the time we got to the Brazos.

Each evening, I took my knife and scraped the caked mud from my pants and boots. The exercise left nice little piles of East Texas dirt throughout Central Texas. The only break in the monotonous soup of filth was the dogwoods and redbud trees that were now in bloom. You could not ignore them. The shock of bright white dogwood flowers against the green background of pine or the pink red buds quietly giving color where color was not expected. They were the only milepost along the El Camino Real. Texas was quite a magnet. Judging from the roads width, many earlier caravans had abandoned the muddy road bed for its shoulders only to create a much wider and muddier road.

My father took his leave of our little band to call on Jared Groce. I was to lead the way to the new Wilhite and Whitworth properties. My father planned on renting some of Groce's slaves to help with the building of homes, barns and cabins and, hopefully, get some crops in the ground.

When we hit the Brazos, I headed us north. My memory was that our land was about a day and a half's ride to a bend in the river. Of course, we were moving a good bit slower than I had traveled on horseback, but I felt confident that I would find the general locale. My father had paid the surveyor during our first trip. What I did not know was how these tracts of land were to be laid out. Stephen Austin had placed restrictions on the amount of river frontage a settler could have and that was no more than a mile. Since a league and a labor were more than 7 square miles, the tract had to be rectangular. Some poor fools thought that they would hog as much river frontage as possible. Austin made short work of their effort by refusing to recognize their claims.

Our fathers had decided that Reams and my land would be placed between the lands that they claimed. This wasn't explained. I assumed the parents wanted to hem us in so that they could keep an eye on us. I am confident this crossed my mother's mind.

When we arrived, we camped on our tract, keeping the same routine we had followed the entire trip. As weary as we were, the excitement of the place invigorated sore muscles and most everyone had to take a look see. Since I had seen it before, I stayed with the livestock until everyone had their "gander".

We decided to keep the herds together until things settled. I would manage the horses. Reams would manage the cattle. The pleasant surprise was the hogs. Blue came to me totally befuddled. We left Louisiana with a combined total of 50 hogs and arrived in the Brazos bottom with 76. Apparently, lost or abandoned hogs just fell in line behind Elisabeth and Ulysses as we traveled. Some of them looked pretty fair. Since we all were pleased that we arrived with the original 50, the excess was divided among our people as their own. Elisabeth was reminded that they were for eating. She did not need any more pets.

In fairly short order, we had identified a clear drift line along the river. This gave us some idea of its width at flood stage, which was actually fairly uniform throughout our tracts. Thus, possible home sites were marked well back from the drift line. It was obvious that the Brazos could flow some water. In places, the drift line was 10 to 15 feet above the ground.

The womenfolk, namely my mother and Mrs. Whitworth, had spent a good deal of the time discussing the need to name their respective places. Some of the large plantations in Louisiana had names. It seemed an odd idea. You were not going to have a conversation with a plantation. It would not respond to your call; so what was the point? It didn't need to have a point. The women wanted to name their homes and name them they would. In a burst of logic unusual for their sex, they did think it best to actually see the land before they finalized a name.

Abram and Blue were the ones who actually picked the home site. They had selected several. Some were obvious losers from the get-go. This gave my mother the chance to reject them, which kind of directed her to the site that they really wanted. It sat on a high point on a wide sloping hill. The drainage would be good. The circumference of the summit would easily handle our home, the quarters, a barn and other outbuildings. A grove of Cedar Elms would be preserved to shade the house and to act as a wind break. This was a slight problem. My mother had decided that the home should be called Catalpa. Cedar elm did not fit her fancy. True enough, there were Catalpa trees around, just not immediately noticeable at the home side. She seemed to be able to justify the connection. Catalpa it would be.

When Abram rendezvoused with us, he brought six slaves with him, all rented from Jared Groce. They were Hiram, Major, Wash, Coleman, Mack and old Squire. The first three were combined with half of our people and would start breaking the land for gardens and for cotton. The second three would work with the remainder of our folks to build the homes, the quarters and the outbuildings. My father and Mr. Whitworth thought that this would be beneficial. Our people could learn how to best handle the Texas soil, and generally what worked here. The work was staged. As we finished something at Catalpa, they would move, as a team, and repeat the same effort at Oak Ridge, the name Mrs. Whitworth assigned to her home. The rental for the extra slaves was split between the two families. Likewise, Jared Groce split some of the rental income he received with his slaves. If they saved enough, they could buy their freedom.

If I should live to be 100, I am confident that at no time will I ever be as tired and as worn out as I would be during the next several months. Regardless of the weather, I would lie down at night caked in my own sweat; limbs limp from work, and a head that ached with both physical and mental fatigue. I think the extra help encouraged Abram to be a little more grandiose than if it had only been our people trying to raise the plantation out of the ground. The home was to be a two-story dog trot, with four actual rooms on the first floor. This was beyond me. There were only the three of us and frankly, I was quite happy in our old loft. Our part of Texas had no rock to speak of and the foundation usually called for some kind of stone. What we did have was an abundance of bois d'arc trees. The wood was hard as hell. If you could cut it green, you had just a short time before it became rock hard. Blue insisted that we use it to support the foundation. Holes were dug and bois d'arc logs set in a fashion so that the sill would be 2 feet above ground. The general thought was that you had to be 18 inches above ground to avoid the wood eating bugs. Blue was never one to tempt fate. It would have to be at least 2 feet. Then, he used the same wood as the sill. The good Lord has not made a bug that could eat bois d'arc wood. Insect destruction would not be a concern.

The sills were notched on the underside to fit over the pillars, acting as a cradle for the sill. Blue then cut the sleepers for the floor beams. For this, he chose pine. We had plenty and it was a good deal easier to work with than bois d'arc. The sleepers had a hole bored into them and they were pegged to the sill.

Each day, after I finished my chores with the livestock, I joined the crew to help with whatever construction project they were working on that day. Blue had certainly inherited the talents of Poppy. I had some concern that we would not be able to manage without Poppy as he had built everything and did it to perfection. Blue had the same abilities and work ethic.

* * *

We had been cutting trees now for about two months. They were positioned near or at least kind of close to the foundations of the structure that they would ultimately become. In front of what was to be our home, the home of the Whitworth's and the respective slave quarters, was a mountain of shingles. They were all finely cut, and 14 to 18 inches long. Old Squire, who apparently did not need to, or want to sleep, had negotiated a deal with my father that he would cut shingles after the day's end for pay. Old Squire did not intend to remain a slave all his life. To the contrary, old Squire aspired to gain his freedom so that he could acquire his own plot of land. If the number of shingles cut was any indication of his diligence, Squire would be a freeman soon.

As for me, I dreaded this day like no other. There was something thrilling about dropping a big, old pine tree. The crack of the limbs at the top, followed by that ground moving thud was reward enough for the effort. Today, we would start hewing logs and building the walls. Our sleeping arrangements did little to nothing to refresh our spirit or reinvigorate aching muscles. The women folk slept in wagons, most of the contents, except for mother's hope chest, had been removed or rearranged and covered with tarps. The canvas of the wagons gave them some protection from the wind and rain.

The men folk tried to sleep under the wagons. This was utter folly. First, if it did rain, and it seemed to do so frequently, the water ran off the canvas in sheets falling right at the edge of the wagon. Depending on the slope of the ground, it would often run under the wagon, in other words, under me. We repositioned the wagons every time this happened and had yet failed to direct the runoff away from our beds.

Even a dry evening provided little chance for a sound sleep. My bunk mates were Blue and Wash. Both were terrific snorers and they snored in unison. I had taken to the hills, literally, on more than one occasion. My absence was apparently not notice. Simply stated, we were now prepared to erect "Catalpa" and I was desperate for a good night's sleep.

While Momma Mae finished breakfast, I surveyed the logs scattered around on site. Each log would be hewed to a uniform thickness, probably 6 to 8 inches thick. Blue and Abram would work that out between them. The tops and bottoms of the logs would be left round. This morning Blue appeared somewhat anxious and was busily digging through every toolbox and crate that we had.

"I knows I'd brung it, I knows it."

"Brought what, Blue?" He did not seem to care to respond; finally he stopped his digging. "Poppy's go by . . . Gots to hab it."

"Go by?" I thought he might be looking for some kind tool Poppy had.

"Gots to hab it, Leander . . . . Makes good notches."

After turning over every crate that might remotely hold "Poppy's go by," Blue inhaled completely and pulled it out, and grinned "dare it be. Oh Lord, I's glad to see you."

What he held, I later figured out, was a pattern for a dove tail notch. Poppies notches were so tight they made a log cabin into a piece of furniture. If the notch fit snugly, no pegs were needed. The cut itself pulled the logs toward the inside of the house.

The logs were started. By picking logs of a similar diameter, there were times when we could hew the entire wall at one time, instead of a log at a time. It was good to see the progress. Getting the walls up seemed to go so fast compared to the other parts of the process. The roof rafters and shingling took forever as did the chinking. Fortunately, the women were in charge of the chinking. Red clay was the best. We had both red and gray. Mostly they got mixed together, along with lime and sand. The recipe was 100 pounds of clay, some sand and three shovels full of lime. Add a little water and start chinking. It really wasn't difficult. Women's small hands worked far better than man's. The most important thing was not to let the chinking bulge out because it catches rain and rots the logs. The chinking had to be indented. With both Blue and Abram supervising, it was done right.

* * *

The breeze was light but cool. It felt good to be doing something other than building a house. I had been slowly working my way through the horses. My entire body ached with fatigue. With little effort at all, I could have fallen asleep in the saddle. I noticed his familiar form approaching, although even Reams was a good deal slimmer than he was when he left Louisiana. Louisiana, it seemed like that was eons ago.

"I bring you greetings from the Oak Ridge plantation old man." He punctuated the statement with his biggest grin. I smiled in return; the fatigue seemed to ease a little.

"The whole plantation, or just the house?"

"Leander, you must know that the women folk name the entirety. The house is their sanctuary; but, make no mistake, the name applies to the whole kettle of fish."

"I see. I guess I'm not completely up on things of this nature."

"Is the house finished, Leander?" We had now moved to the shade of a pin oak.

"Has been for some time. The quarters are finished too. Now Abram has his sights set on the barn."

"Barn! Doesn't that fellow ever relax?" He has gone like a house afire since we got here. Hell, I had to adjust my suspenders, I suspect his pants are about to fall completely off."

"Reams, I have noticed that you seem to be missing some of your baby fat."

"Touché, old man. What kind of barn is he hankering for? No doubt, something slightly larger than Noah's Ark."

"Let's ride over that ridge and you can see the frame."

"Jesus Christ! Leander, I guess Noah's Ark was a good guess."

"I really don't understand him anymore. He has driven us all like a man possessed. We are worn out. He keeps going. More plans every day. I am grateful he left for Jared Groce's for a couple of days. He took old Squire and two wagons. They're going to bring back some milled lumber for the barn and part of the house, I guess. I don't know. I can hardly keep up with him."

"He and old Squire you say. We have a ton of shingles left over. Squire cut the same deal with my father that he did with yours."

"Well Reams I suspect his freedom is quite a motivator."

"So Abram has been gone a couple of days you say. Then he probably doesn't know the good news." We had now drifted back to the shade of the tree.

"What news?"

"They had quite a row downriver. Austin found a couple of fellows who were trying to block up about 10 miles of the Brazos . . . you know, not the 1 mile he permits. Plus, evidently they did not impress our Empresario, and he told them he would not honor any claim of theirs. Needless to say, this did not set well. One of fellows was a big talker and let his mouth sink any chances of colonizing in Texas. The other fella did not say much. Sound familiar?"

I stopped dead in my tracks. "Are you sure?"

"Come on Leander, you had to know the poor bastards would follow you. They can't make it in this world without your dad."

The shock was just too much to take on top of my own exhaustion. A thousand questions. Where were they now? What was my mother to do? Why can't we get away from these bastards?

"You look ill, Leander. Let's get off these horses before you fall off." We moved to a shady spot. I dropped the reins and sat down. I had not had a passing thought about Drayton or Dunwoody in months. Now the tranquility of their absence was shattered. So much confusion, so much confusion.

"Reams, I don't know what to think. What will my dad do?"

"Oh, I can tell you that old man. He will do whatever your mother tells him to do. These women folk did not leave hearth and home to get drug across Texas for the chance to enjoy the same collection of hangers on that they knew and loved in Louisiana. Oh, hell no. If I were Drayton, I would not get within rifle range of Susannah Wilhite. But I ain't Drayton and he ain't smart enough to avoid trouble."

"Do you think they know where we are?"

"Hell yes. There aren't that many of us here. All he would have to do is ask around. Probably will run flat into your dad at Groce's. Everybody seems to light there at some point."

I was physically nauseous. My worst nightmare, we ran from my favorite uncle right into the two I detested.

"Leander, if I'm any judge at all, those wonderful Wilhite brothers don't have a lot of options. They and their tribes, along with their collection of Africans, are going to have to light somewhere. My guess is they will try to tug on your dad's heartstrings for some kind of start. Get him to give them some land or support them until they get on their feet, or . . ."

"Get on their feet! My God, they have never gotten on their feet ever, ever."

"Look, I hate to be the bearer of bad news, but you need to be alert. They may be here already and you just don't know it. It takes a little while to ride this place. Austin isn't going to let them in as colonists, but he hasn't got anyone that can bounce them out. You need to be vigilant, Leander."

I moved towards my horse. My legs seemed to wobble. Was it the fatigue or the news? Who could tell, I must do a little riding. Reams and I parted and I started a slow loop that would take me to the areas that they might come to first. He was right. They could already be here. As I rode, I couldn't decide if I should tell my mother the news, or wait until my father returned. Being an only child made keeping secrets difficult. Plus, my mother had an advantage. She could read me like a book. As I drifted around the southern perimeter of Catalpa, I drifted towards telling her. Nothing would be gained by hiding it.

It was close to dusk when I got home. The breeze was steady but colder. The evenings were a good bit cooler now. She and Momma Mae were sitting in Poppy's rockers in the dog trot dipping snuff. The peace was to be soon broken.

"Did you have some trouble, Leander? You're a little late." Her punctuality did not always conform to the realities of agrarian life. Breached births, hailstorms, or contrary horses just did not fit in her orderly world. She was about neatness and cleanliness, not dirty and irregularity. I had no chance but to hit it straight away.

"I've been riding the South approach."

"Looking for your father I guess? I really don't expect him for a few more days."

"Wrong Wilhite, mom."

She paused, a little confused. "Just who would you be looking for, Leander?"

"Reams tells me Drayton and Dunwoody might be in Texas."

I saw her look once before. I was a great deal younger and had fallen out of my swing tree and broken my arm. She had turned white as a Lily. Once again she was almost chalk like. But, it did not last long. Her color came back, moving immediately passed her usual pinkness and into various shades of red.

"Leander, tell me what you know right now!"

"Reams said they tried to block up a good deal of river frontage."

"This river, Leander?"

"Yes ma'am, as I understand it. Austin wouldn't have it. He isn't going to recognize them as colonists."

"Austin wanted a better sort. Those two are a far cry from that. Go on Leander."

"Reams suggested that I keep a lookout for them. I mean where are they to go? Reams thinks that they will try to soft soap dad . . ."

"They can try, but they cannot soft soap me." Momma Mae cut a slight smile at me. I recalled her concern about Drayton and Dunwoody's fresh African trade. No one wanted to see those two again, certainly not me. However, where would they go? Who would want to deal with them at all?

"Leander, this is a big place. You cannot ride it every day. Divide it up, but get it ridden by someone every other day. I know we all have chores. Those two brothers are a pestilence of biblical proportions. The minute they set foot on Catalpa, I want to know about it. Her rocking had increased measurably. Thank Heaven Poppy had put some balance in his rockers or she would've gone over backwards by now.

"Go get your dinner, I know you are hungry. I've got some thinking to do."

CHAPTER 10

Peace at Last

SUSANNAH TOOK AS DEEP A BREATH AS SHE COULD POSSIBLY INHALE. It would be her last breath of fresh air before she opened the door to what had now become a sweat lodge. It was anyone's guess when Abram and old Squire really got back to Catalpa. Momma Mae, always the first to stir, noticed the two wagons. To her shock, both men were shivering in their seats, too weak, too feverish to step down. Most likely, they had been sick for a couple of days. The horses found their way home with little assistance from either man.

When Susannah saw her husband, she knew what it was immediately. Her memory of its symptoms was as fresh as it was when her father caught it. She had both men placed in the backroom and ordered everyone else out. No one was to enter the room, only Susannah. By accident, this room was well suited for its purpose. It had no windows. She and Abram could not decide exactly what its purpose was to be. They had built so many more rooms in the Texas house, that they had no idea what to do with them all. It was easier not to cut in windows. They could be added later. Without windows, there was no draft to chill the men now wet with fever.

As she opened the door, she was hit with the heat of the room and the stench of urine, sweat and bile. The only comfort she could provide the men was to sponge bathe them, a chore that gave only temporary relief. It kept them slightly clean, at least for a while. When the last phase commenced, nothing, and no one, would be able to keep them clean.

She suspected that old Squire had contracted the disease first. When he arrived, he was almost without his senses. Abram could at least speak. Old Squire was in the middle of such a fever that you could barely hear him breathing. His black forehead glistened with sweat. Yesterday, just like Susannah's father, old Squire rallied. He was alert and seemed to improve a good deal. Susannah knew the black vomit would start today. It always did. A short respite, then an agonizing death. Yellow fever was so predictable.

She left the door slightly ajar, just enough to let a narrow band of light into the room. The men lay on pads of horsehair on opposite walls. Normally, she would have looked towards her husband first. Today she knew to look towards old Squire. So predictable. The quilt that covered him no longer showed its pattern of colors. It was completely black with vomit.

Her glance moved from the darkened quilt to old Squire's face. His gaze was fixed on somewhere off in the eternity. She had known he would leave them soon and soon it was. Abram was asleep. His breathing was deep and steady. She had to be at his bedside when he rallied. There was so much to do and not much time.

She arranged the quilt to cover old Squire. She had not known him long; however, she admired his industrious nature. There was no extra meat on his bones. He had not been a tall man, but had long hands that could handle any tool. She was aware of his agreement with Abram and Mr. Whitworth to earn extra money for splitting shingles. He made it look so easy and the shingles were so uniform. He was someone who required so little of life and probably got very little in return. He died like he was born. He never got to buy his freedom.

She reached for the edge of the horsehair pad. It was damp with all of the fluids a body can produce. It made the pulling all the more difficult, but she had to get him out of the room and into the dog trot.

"Mae," she hollered once she got him moved. Susannah was the only one who ever called her by her name without "Mama" in front of it. Momma Mae came quickly, seeing the covered body she stopped, the shock soaked in as she slowed her pace. Susannah answered before she could ask.

"It's old Squire, Mae, could you get Blue?"

"Oh yes, ma'am."

Susannah sat down to catch her breath. The fresh air tasted almost sweet compared to the stench of the room. She figured Abram was probably a half day behind old Squire, but that was only a guess. She had almost dozed off when Blue appeared.

"Blue, I never thought about needing a cemetery so soon. We just got here, but . . ."

"Massa Abram?"

"No Blue, old Squire."

"I'll finds some place, don't chu worry about dat."

The way he said it, Susannah knew Blue was thinking of some place different for Squire. The slaves and the white folks always had different cemeteries in Louisiana. She never saw the point. Weren't the good folks all supposed to end up in the same place?

"Blue, don't handle this body without some gloves. Find a nice place for us all. You understand Blue?"

"You sure?"

"Yes, Blue, you and Poppy were always in charge of the burials. No need in spreading us all over the plantation." Blue left to get the wagon. Riding Catalpa on the lookout for Drayton and Dunwoody had given him an idea of at least a couple of places that might be suitable. One place, in particular, reminded him of a burial plot back in Louisiana.

Susannah left the door cracked. She laid down next to it in the dog trot. She had to be ready. Abram should rally soon. She did not know how long she had slept. A chill woke her. It was near dusk. She quietly entered the room. To her shock, Abram was awake.

"Mother, how long have I been sleeping?"

"Several days, Abram, several days."

Abram rubbed his eyes and his head.

"Whew, what is that smell?"

"Dear husband, that smell is you. You and old Squire."

Abram glanced towards the opposite wall. He remembered that Squire had been sleeping there.

"Where is he?"

Susannah knew there would be no way to sugarcoat the news of the situation that now confronted the Wilhite family. With every bit of strength she could possibly gather, she had to tell her husband that he had little time left. Neither one of them could enjoy the luxury of grief or regret. If they cared one bit for Leander, they must move forward and do so quickly.

"Abram, you and old Squire have yellow fever. I knew it the moment you arrived or when we found you. Squire died last night." There, she had out; now, she would have to move the conversation to other matters as quickly as possible.

Abram seem to inhale, and then just held his breath for a moment.

"I know better than to ask you if you're sure. We have both seen enough of it. I feel pretty good, weak but pretty good. This must be the respite before the worse."

Susannah nodded, doing everything she could not to let the tears come. If they started, she knew they would come in torrents.

"Odd isn't it, mother? This same fever drove us to Louisiana. We come to Texas and it finds us again."

"Abram, you don't have long and there are things we have to do."

"Things?"

"Abram, Drayton and Dunwoody are here in Texas. I will not dig up the past. There is no time. Austin has refused to accept them as colonists. Without question, they will come here. Without you, they will take this place as sure as I am standing before you."

"Susannah, you are every bit a match for those two . . ."

"Abram, I won't be here either. I will not let them take this place from Leander. I will not. I will not let you avoid reality. They are despicable. Austin could see it, why can't you?"

"Mother, what are you telling me. My thinking is a little slow."

"Dear husband, you and I will both be dead in a matter of days. I suspect that I am just a few days behind you. Drayton and Dunwoody may already be on Catalpa. We have been riding it, but it is a big place. Our only child will soon be without either of us. I want to give him Catalpa right now and have Austin acknowledge his ownership. At least that way he will have legal title. That won't protect him, if they decide to take the law into their own hands; but if that happens, I swear I will haunt those two until the end of time."

"You are sure you have it? I am so sorry Susannah, so sorry."

"It couldn't be helped Abram. I couldn't risk exposing the others. We have traveled a long piece of road together. It is best that we leave this world together."

"What do we do next?"

Susannah pulled a letter from her apron. She had composed it a couple of days ago. In it she tells Stephen Austin that they both would soon die of yellow fever. It expressed their collective desire to immediately give Catalpa to their only child, Leander, while they were alive. Their position would not change, even if, by some miracle, one of them survived. Susannah could not resist expressing her fear of Drayton and Dunwoody and the likelihood that they would try to take advantage of the situation. Abram and Susannah signed and dated the letter.

Susannah called for Leander. She placed the letter in a leather pouch. Although he asked to see his father, Susannah continued to refuse to let anyone in the sick room.

* * *

My mother handed me the saddlebags that held the pouch I was to deliver to Stephen Austin. Momma Mae had packed one bag full of biscuits and jerky. Once again, I asked to see my father. This time she told me there wasn't any time. I must go. She avoided any eye contact. Everything about this trip told me something was terribly wrong. She had given me one instruction. Get the pouch to Austin as quickly as I could. As I approached the corral, Blue stepped out of the darkness, the reins of a saddled horse in his hand.

"I's pick da big sorrel. He gets you dare."

"Yes Blue, good choice. He'll do just fine." Blue probably knew more about what was going on than I did. The black folks always knew what was going on in the big house. I suspected he knew what was in the pouch. Thoughts swirled in my head. Should I really be leaving at this time? Would my father be alive when I return or would he follow old Squire? Nothing but questions, no answers.

"Blue, if Drayton or Dunwoody show up while I'm gone, you get to Oak Ridge. Tell Reams or his father. They must come. They have to!"

"Yes, sur."

I had heard it. Blue knew I had, but I couldn't look at him. He had said "Sir." I had always been Leander. Blue knew something was about the change. I dreaded it, but they always know. Those in the quarters always know.

Texas was so big and vacant. I doubted my ability to find San Felipe. I knew to hug the river and head south. What trails there were had been old hog paths and a few Indian wanderings. Hopefully, something would remind me of Austin's locale. The sorrel was quick enough and had the strength to get me there. With a saddle bag full of biscuits, I would find it sooner or later.

By nightfall, I had built up such a level of anxiety, that I felt it pointless to try and sleep. I rested the horse for a while. The moon was full, so I thought I would walk him rather than try to sleep. He was a mature horse, once pointed in a direction he would pretty much stay on that course. Any extra time I could make brought me home that much sooner.

By midday, the terrain had flattened. I was out of the rolling hills. San Felipe had to be nearby.

It actually came upon me by surprise. I had been following a beaten path near the Brazos, when it just appeared amongst a grove of scrub oak trees. This was probably the same path my father and I took when we left San Felipe months ago. Things always look different in reverse.

San Felipe was not much, just a few houses and buildings scattered about. Austin's home was the very typical log dog trot. At least it had windows. Whoever cut his shingles did not have the skill of old Squire. Austin's were quite irregular; Squire's had precision.

I entered the center hall; a man came out of one room. He was not Austin, or not as I remembered Austin.

"Good day sir. Can I help you?"

"I am Leander Wilhite." I examined his facial expression for some reaction to the Wllhite name. It was a tragedy that we would have traveled so far and still be haunted by the likes of Drayton and Dunwoody. At least he was honest enough to bring it up directly.

"Wilhite you say? There were some Wilhites here recently."

"Yes sir. I am sure you are referring to my father's two brothers. I assure you that is where any likeness ends. I have made some fast tracks to get here and I fear my two uncles may be headed to our home in my absence. Wherever they go, trouble is close behind."

"Son, you know them better than I, but I suspect your judgment is quite accurate. I am Samuel Williams, Mr. Austin's assistant and secretary. How can I help you?"

"Actually you can't. My mother wants me to deliver something directly to Mr. Austin."

"He is down near Columbia . . . . Should be back in a day or so. I handle all correspondence, legal documents and the like. What does it concern?"

"I don't know."

Williams was a little puzzled. "You don't know?"

"My father is gravely ill, I fear. Having his brothers nearby is of no comfort to my mother, I assure you. I guess I'll just camp nearby until Austin returns."

"Camp, I think not. Make yourself at home here. You may sleep in his quarters, half of Texas has. Of course, if someone else shows up, you will have to share the bed. We desperately need a hotel, but no one has taken a mind to start one, yet. Are you sure I can't expedite things? If it involves any kind of document, Austin will turn it over to me. My Spanish is much better than his."

"Spanish!"

"Why yes, amigo. It may come as a surprise to you and most everyone else, I suspect. You are in Mexico. Fortunately, I spent a good deal of time down in Buenos Aires with my uncle. I did not think this Spanish stuff would ever come in handy, but it certainly has."

"Sir, I could only guess at what my mother intends and I have never been very good at guessing. I reckon I best wait."

It is funny what will wake you. Sometimes it's a change in the temperature. Often it is a noise. Today it was the faintest breeze that blew across the covers when he opened the door. I recalled him instantly, and was quite embarrassed to be found asleep in his quarters. Leaping from the bed, I tried to make a quick apology that only brought a smile to his face. He put me at ease immediately.

"Mr. Wilhite, it is good to see you. Texas needs as much youth as it can get. Mr. Williams tells me you have something for me . . . I understand from your mother."

"Yes sir." I was now on my feet retrieving the pouch entrusted to me. Perhaps now I would learn its contents, but that was no certainty.

Austin opened the pouch and commenced to read what looked to be a letter. The sunlight on the page passed through the paper. From the opposite side I could tell there was a good deal written on it. While he read, I did everything I could to try and glean some hint of its contents from his face. Unfortunately, I could discern nothing.

"I am so sorry about your parent's, Mr. Wilhite." I glanced at the letter now in his hand.

"I don't understand, Mr. Austin?"

"The fever is almost always fatal. I have lost many friends and relatives to it. It has visited New Orleans so often, my former home, that they call the city, America's Cemetery."

"But, it is my dad who is sick sir."

"I am sorry. I forgot that they did not share its contents with you. Mr. Wilhite, both of your parents have yellow fever. They have instructed me to transfer their league and labor to you, which I am happy to do. Son, I can only offer you my deepest sympathies and friendship. You must feel free to call upon me for any assistance that you might need. Texas needs men like you. This is a terrible blow to a family so new to the colony. I hope you can look past your loss and judge objectively the wonderful future that awaits you and Texas as well. You may want to read the letter yourself. Let me give you a moment alone. Please give the letter to Mr. Williams. We have to have it for our records. I will instruct him to make the necessary changes to place the land title into your name."

He handed me the letter. I think I read it. I recalled she could not look at me. I had to hurry. Perhaps, one of them might have survived. I stepped across the dog trot. Mr. Williams was folding whatever documents I needed. He placed them in the pouch and exchanged it for the letter. He was groping for something to say.

Finally he said, "I am sorry. When the dust settles, if you have any questions about the documents come see me. They are in Spanish you know."

I nodded and headed for the corral. Austin had saddled my horse.

"Mr. Wilhite, your mother is concerned about your uncles. The land is yours. I will not recognize those two men as colonists, now or ever. If you have any trouble, please send for me. Godspeed, Mr. Wllhite."

I thanked him as best I could with such an enormous lump in my throat.

* * *

Abram's rally was longer than Susannah expected. With all of her heart she wanted to believe that maybe it was over. Maybe he would survive this most terrible disease. However, her head told her otherwise. His appetite was good. While her strength sustained her, she carried food to him as frequently as he wanted it. Men are so odd, she thought. There really was some anatomical connection between their stomach and their heart. He was so appreciative.

She could see the warmth of the fever coming back into his face. The rally would soon be over. The evening breezes and coolness perhaps would postpone the inevitable. He must've sensed it as well. He turned towards her.

"Susannah, do you think Leander has made it to San Felipe. I have no sense of time."

"Yes, I am sure he has made it there by now."

"Mother, I am so sorry to bring this on you. You don't deserve it and your husband caused it."

Susannah did not have the time to think about her own growing pain and weakness. One patient at a time was all that she could handle.

"Abram, we have been together a long time. To follow close behind is just fine with me."

"I have thought of so many memories, old times. There were some good times, wasn't there?"

"Why sure, Abram."

"I don't feel that I have been the best husband. You could have done so much better. I think I didn't measure up to what you could have had, or deserved."

"Husband, I have had the good grace to have been married to the most kindhearted man in all of Christendom who gave me a beautiful son. Now what more could I have asked for?"

Abram smiled, coughed, and then, wiped the sweat beads that were now starting to gather on his forehead.

"Mother, you know that you are given to exaggeration."

Susannah smiled but watched the redness return to his face and neck.

"Susannah, you must leave me now."

"I shall do no such thing."

"You must! If you have any respect for me, you must go. I want you to remember me as I was, not as I soon will be. We both know what comes next. I will be gone by morning. Please Susannah, leave me now before it starts. I will go quickly. I promise."

"Abram, you ask so much."

"Susannah please, I can't hold it back much longer. You must."

His eyes were closed with pain. She saw the tear pool at the corner of his eye and run down his red cheek.

"I love you Abram. We will meet again soon."

*　*　*

As soon as the room was ready, Susannah laid down on another horse hair pad. She had no desire to prolong things. In truth, she was much further along than even she thought.

It felt like the next day, but it probably wasn't. She could have been there maybe three days, when the door opened. It maddened her. Her instructions were to leave her alone. She could manage. When she opened her eyes, there he stood almost as she had predicted. He was as dirty as ever, more unkempt than usual, with the same drool of tobacco juice easing down his chin and falling onto his shirt.

"Well, Missy, you don't look so well."

Susannah gathered her senses. "It would be a lie to say it is good to see you, but I expected you. Here to express your condolences for your dead brother, Drayton?"

"Yes, I heard. It would seem you're going to need some help to take care of all this land. We have had our differences but I suspect we could reach an understanding."

"Drayton, I have all the help I need. Leander is quite capable."

"Leander, yes, Leander. Susannah, there is only one Leander and there are a whole lot of us.

Susannah's temperature was rising fast and it was not the fever.

"I haven't seen your shadow. Where is Dunwoody?"

"With the horses. Old baby brother seems to be developing a streak of independence. He didn't want to call upon you folks. Prefers to head home, but I told him with so much Wilhite land here for the taking, we just couldn't pass it up."

In a whisper Susannah said, "Drayton."

"Susannah, I can't hear you." Drayton was clearly frustrated.

"Come closer, Drayton." She whispered it again.

"I don't know that I should, you look mighty poor."

Once again she whispered "Drayton." This time he moved to her bedside.

"Drayton . . . ."

He bent over slightly in order to hear her better.

"Drayton, I would trade my soul to stop you. You will get this land over my dead body."

BOOM! The bullet tore through the quilt and sunk deep into Drayton's chest.

The concussion knocked Drayton backward. He landed part in and part out of the room. The shot brought Momma Mae from the backside of the house arriving slightly before Dunwoody entered the dog trot from the front. Momma Mae jumped over Drayton's twitching torso. Susannah's bed covers were afire, ignited by the shot. She jerked the covers off causing Susannah's fever wracked body to chill and shiver.

" Susannah, are you all right?"

Momma Mae was almost at her wits end. The blankets were still on fire but mostly now smoldering in the dog trot. She pulled off her apron and tried to tuck it in around Susannah.

"Are you all right?"

"Mae, I have never felt better. Peace at last."

* * *

I pushed the sorrel beyond all limits. I was on Catalpa land. The sweat and lather poured off of the horse. I prayed that if the horse collapsed, I could jump free of his falling body. One more rise and then it would be a downward sprint home. I crested the hill and stopped. Before me were three graves. I was too late.

CHAPTER 11

Horses Away

SUSANNAH GAVE CATALPA ITS NAME. Abram built its home; but, Leander turned it into a plantation, the likes of which, could not have been envisioned by his parents. The milled lumber brought by Abram and old Squire was used to complete the barn, and what a barn it made. Adjacent to the barn was the shop of Blue, containing all the tools and bellows a smithy required. Since Blue was much more than a blacksmith, the shop actually had two separate sections. One was for the metalwork, and related activities. The other section, Blue used to make furniture, wheels and tongues, and the occasional tombstone.

As anticipated, the cemetery became Blue's exclusive jurisdiction. He erected a handsome fence around the perimeter, causing Reams some concern. He felt that its size suggested either a famine or a plague. All Wilhite graves were individually surrounded by a wrought iron enclosure. No more bodies would set sail for parts unknown.

The most unique structure at Catalpa was the summer kitchen of

Momma Mae. This part of Texas had no real outcrops of rock or stone. Yet, prudence required that a kitchen, particularly one that handled as many meals as this one, be constructed of stone. Gradually, a source was found north of Austin's colony. It wasn't the best rock, but it did not burn. The kitchen sat behind and separate from the house. Included within its structure was a room for Momma Mae. She and her family still lived in the quarters, but, the additional room gave her a chance to rest between her chores.

Catalpa was now well over 6000 acres, given Leander's original grant and his inheritance. Cotton was the principal crop, or as everyone called it, the cash crop. Cattle and horses demanded about the same attention as cotton. Both herds were widely sought after by neighbors interested in improving their own livestock. However, Leander was slow to sell breeding stock to just anyone. His experiences with Drayton and Dunwoody made him cautious. He came to rely upon the impressions of Elisabeth, whose judgment of people was just about as good as her opinion of livestock.

If Leander had a mentor, it would have been Jared Groce. He was free with his counsel and Leander was glad to accept it. They continued to improve their respective remudas, with Leander gaining a slight edge in the area of horseflesh. As additional slaves were needed, Leander first sought out any that Groce might sell. Since there was a regular commerce between the two plantations, it made for an easy transition. Both slaves and Masters knew they would be seeing one another regularly. Leander had become a member of the planter class, now owning more than 20 Negroes.

Texas continued to grow and Catalpa became a way station for many immigrant families. Leander, used to the loft of his Louisiana childhood home, made the second floor his quarters. In his room, he moved his mother's hope chest. Not that he intended to use it; he just wanted it near him.

Having it upstairs provided some protection from the house-guests that frequented the first floor. They became so numerous that Blue had to build beds for all the rooms. Better said, all the rooms but the one where his parents died. This room Leander locked. Like his mother, he never refused lodging to anyone. However he never felt that it was his duty to entertain the travelers. Momma Mae took care of their needs and the meals. Leander stayed in the saddle pretty much all day. More often than not, he took his meals with her in her kitchen.

Now 26, he found that his guests that had daughters of marrying age tended to stay longer than those who did not. Hospitality was one thing; matrimony was something else.

* * *

"Blue, just where is the dullest man in the country this morning?"

Reams always seem to burst into a place. Most people kind of eased into a room. Although they had known one another all their lives, Blue was always caught off guard by Reams. He never got used to his entrances. Even so, he knew who Reams was seeking. He had heard him lecture Leander about all work and no play making Jack a dull boy. If it worked in the opposite direction, Reams had to be downright brilliant.

Blue let the horse's hind leg down easy; it slid off his knee, down his leg to the ground. He needed to reshape the horseshoe anyway.

"Spec he's down wit da horses," pointing in the proper direction with the reverse end of his shoeing hammer.

"Blue, if I was to kidnap our mutual friend, do you think you and Momma Mae could hold this place together for a month or so?"

Blue knew Reams wasn't likely to be able to kidnap Leander, not if he did not want to be kidnapped. Leander seldom left Catalpa. An occasional visit to Mr. Groce's place was about the only time he left home. That is not to say he was a hermit. To the contrary, Catalpa seemed to attract folks. Travelers frequently stopped for a night or so. Then, there were the horse and cattle buyers. The cotton business had its fair share of brokers and dealers; and, the locals had an endless list of requests that they thought Leander ought to weigh in on. Usually it was some pet project of their own choosing. Monaville, the name now given to the community, saw Leander as someone who would not shirk responsibility. Apparently, the virtue was rare. There was plenty of the opposite kind around.

"I believe we could." Blue smiled. He seriously doubted that Leander would leave for any extended period. Frankly, he liked having him around. Blue wasn't the type to look for a lot of spice in life. He liked things steady and even. It gave him time to do his best work. Leander was predictable. Blue could read him, like he could read the temperament of a draft horse. Steady. Some would say monotonous. To Blue, it was comfort. Skittish horses always caused trouble. Fortunately, a skittish horse did not stay at Catalpa very long. Even so, Reams and Leander had grown up together. They had spent some part of most days together. If anyone could get him to leave for a spell, it would be Reams. Blue was curious to observe the outcome of his effort.

* * *

Reams could not have been more delighted. He and his extremely dull friend had Monaville behind them, and they were pointed in the direction of New Orleans. He was almost lightheaded with excitement. In tow was one of Leander's fastest horses; although the one Leander was riding was no plug. None of Leander's horses were.

He could almost count the money. William Tunstell Lowe would finally see what he had been bragging about for so long. Moreover, he had a belly full of Momma Mae's biscuits and a saddlebag filled with the same. Life could not get any better.

As for Leander, Reams could tell he had that look of discomfort. The look you had when you put on a new pair of boots. Yes, they were new, but you preferred the comfort of the old ones. Reams was bent on forcing Leander to have a good time. His hope was that he could convince Leander to join in on some serious whoring and wenching; but that could be a step too far. He might have to go it alone. Getting Leander to have fun was downright hard work.

The entire first day, Reams just knew his friend was going to turn tail and race back to Catalpa. By the middle of the second day, he sensed some relaxing of Leander's typical stiffness. Perhaps, he might enjoy the trip after all. The terrain had changed. The rolling hills of Austin's colony were behind them. They were on the flat grasslands of the Texas Gulf Coast. This area grew grass that, in some cases, came up to the withers of their horses. The area intrigued Leander.

"A man could run all the cattle he wanted to around here and never run out of forage."

Reams was not the herdsman that Leander was, but the prospects did look inviting.

"It would appear that way, but I would like to see it done by someone else first before I jump off into that."

"And you tell me I'm the conservative one."

"Dull, Leander, dull doesn't mean conservative. Really old man, our weather has been fairly predictable the past few years. If the pattern changed and we caught a drought, ... It takes some kind of water to grow grass this high."

Leander nodded. All the same, he wanted to see what kind of marketing opportunities there were in New Orleans. It seemed odd that so many settlers darted right through this area and headed for the Brazos River bottom. Cotton, cotton, and cotton was all anyone talked about. A cash crop true enough, but the grass was here and free for the taking.

"Reams, you have been making these trips to New Orleans fairly frequently. What does this grass looked like during other times of the year?"

"Oh, I don't know. It has a pretty long growing season, but can get mushy during a wet winter. Probably best to get the calves to market before the winter rains started. Leander, my butt is sore as hell. Why don't we call it a day and head for that little ravine with that clump of trees."

"Trees?" Leander had never forgotten the lesson from his first trip to Texas.

"I'd rather be under some leaves in case it rains." Leander thought better of it, but knew not to argue with his buddy. They hobbled the horses that really did not show much interest in grazing. They had been clipping the tops of the tall bluestem grass all day.

Leander's boot made sudden and swift contact with Reams' butt. "Wake up!"

"Wake up, we've got to go." He repeated.

Reams rolled over. It seemed like he had just dropped off to sleep. They had put in two long days. A few extra winks couldn't hurt.

The boot was a little more direct. "Now, Reams, the horses are gone."

"Gone!" Leander wasn't much of a gabber. If he said they were gone; it meant gone, as in stolen, not gone as in wandered off.

"Oh hell, which way?"

"It looks like back west. Maybe there are two of them, not a big crowd. Get up. Leave the saddles, and grab the rifles and saddle-bags, let's go."

Those were the words he feared. You had to be a damn fool to steal a horse from Leander Wilhite. They were family, not horses. Reams knew this wasn't going to be a stroll. This was going to be a forced march on the double quick. If they didn't catch up with the thieves soon, he would see parts of Texas he had never seen before.

"I know better than to try and talk you out of it."

Leander didn't even acknowledge the comment. He could track them like a bird dog. The tall grass of the Texas Gulf Coast just laid down pointing in the direction of their departure. Leander figured they got about a three hour head start. That reinforced his guess that the thieves were injuns. They probably trailed them to their camp. He had known better than to settle in that wooded ravine. Such a stupid white man's choice! Indians would sit up and watch all night. Then, they would make their move before dawn, when it was darkest.

Reams was getting pretty tired. He hoped by engaging Leander in some conversation, that perhaps Leander might ease up on the pace. They came to a pile of horse apples; Leander stopped, bent down and squeezed them.

"Jesus, Leander, was that really necessary. I suppose you're going to tell me which horse left that handy clue."

"Actually Reams, judging from some of the corn bits left in it, it most likely was one of my horses. We're gaining on them. It was still pretty warm."

"For the love of Pete, I never guessed you knew so much about horse shit, but if anybody does, I suspect it would be you. Still think there is just two?"

Leander stood up, dusted his hand on his pants leg and put his glove back on. Adjusting his gear, he said, "Pretty confident it's two injuns. Their horses are unshod. The hooves are small. I think they are injun ponies. We will wake them in the morning."

"Morning! Great God Almighty! We're going to walk all night?"

Leander turned again, "Reams, no one is twisting your arm. You can stay right here; but me and the biscuits are going to get our horses back." With that he fell right back into a steady pace.

What a boring day. Reams was following his dull friend across a monotonous field of tall grass. He was tired, sweaty and itchy. Dew wet grass just made him scratch. By midday, the breezes had given out. The grass dried, but it was everywhere. More irritating than the conditions, was the fact that none of this seemed to bother Leander, not even the mosquitoes. By evening, the breezes had picked back up. Leander had handed out some jerky and biscuits, giving Reams enough energy to keep pace. As the sun began to set, Leander outlined his plan.

"Reams, I can't really tell how far behind them we are. We must be ready. We could come upon them at any time, certainly before dawn. They will camp out in the open and could easily spot us. Do you have that pepper box pistol loaded?"

"Yes, and my shotgun." Reams was a little put out at the question. He had not walked all this way to shake hands with a horse thief.

"Good, I hope to catch them asleep. If so, we will make our move at first light. Don't want to kill'em, but if they make any kind of move, send them to their maker."

This actually was a little surprising to Reams. He had recalled how upset Leander had been when his horses had been abused by his uncles. It never occurred to him that Leander would blow anyone to kingdom come over a horse. His tone was direct. His friend would not hesitate. Reams hoped that these thieves would have the good sense to not test his friend.

The Texas night was clear. The moon was about half full. It and the stars provided enough light to follow the trail of trampled grass. Once they got over their initial fatigue at their usual bedtime, the walk actually became very pleasant. What might await them could quickly change that.

Leander held up his hand and knelt. Looking over his friends shoulder, Reams could see five horses grazing ahead. The count was right. Two were fairly small. They had to be the injun ponies. The conformation of the other three looked for all the world like theirs. Leander moved steadily to the North so that the coastal breezes would not be blowing their own scent towards the horses. Once in position, he knelt on one knee. Reams did the same.

It was still very dark. The Moon had traveled across the sky and was well into the western side of the horizon when one of the thieves got up from his bed roll and walked towards them. The hearts of the two trackers now beat in their throats. Leander had been right. They were injuns, or at least this one was. He looked to be in his late teens, maybe his early 20s. He needed to make some water and then he returned to his sleeping spot.

Leander looked at Reams and pointed at his boots. This Indian had no moccasins on; he must've felt that he had not been followed, or was far enough ahead to relax. Reams nodded. He got the point. Of course, he was bemused that these two braves hadn't thought that two white men would care so much about their horses that they would go so far on foot. Texas Indians did not travel far on foot, not anymore.

The transition to daybreak always comes on rather suddenly. It is pitch dark and then without warning, it is gray and clear. Leander gave the sign. Quietly, they moved closer, slightly crouched until they came to the encampment. Leander pointed to Reams and then to the sleeping form farthest away. Reams moved accordingly.

Leander pulled his pistol and held it in one hand. He lifted his long knife from his boot, and then kicked the sleeping Indian.

His brown eyes open immediately to the large bore of Leander's pistol. He started to rise up, but Leander's boot was now on his throat. Reams' prey was sleeping on his side, and turned quickly into the quiet form now standing next to him.

"Is this a good day to die for you chaps?" Leander's eyes were focused directly on the eyes of the Indian fully expecting him to run. The tension of the Indian left him. He was caught and he was not willing to trade his life for these horses. Not today. Leander took a step back.

"Reams, gather their bows and knives. I don't see any firearms." Reams gathered the items.

"Get the horses, all of them." This wasn't hard. They had left the harnesses on the three stolen horses and had a tie rope of rawhide around the necks of their ponies. In no time, he had their two horses ready to mount with the other three ready to follow.

"Reams, take their moccasins."

"What?"

"Take their moccasins." Reams juggled the reins and his rifle, placing the moccasins inside his jacket.

Leander, never looking towards his friend, now spoke to the Indian before him.

"Get up," without looking at him, he motioned for the second Indian to get up as well.

"What do they call you?"

The Indian clearly understood the question and keenly appreciated that the face before him was prepared to kill him where he stood.

"I am called Long Feather."

"Long Feather." With a swift arching motion Leander's knife

moved over the head of the thief cutting in half the single feather stuck in his hair. "Your feather is not so long now."

Leander studied the young brave. Thoughts were moving through his head rather rapidly. They really had not experienced any problem with the Indians around Catalpa. In fact, a Kicka-poo family lived on part of the plantation at various times of the year. The patriarch of that family had used Leander to teach his boys how to track. Every time Leander left his home, he would see red youngsters trailing behind him in the distance. Even they had now stopped; another vote for his dullness and predictability, he guessed. He really wanted to find out more about the young man standing quietly before him. Yet, the thought of losing his horses, to anyone, clouded his objectivity. He cooled his anger. They were not his uncles. They were probably just trying to show their own skills to their tribesmen. Leander raised his knife, placing the point right under the braves' Adam's apple. The young man did not move. He returned Leander's intense stare in kind.

"If you want horses, I will trade with you. If you ever steal my horses, I will open you up and watch you die." His blade drop down the young man's chest leaving a faint line of blood bubbles. Leander turned and mounted his horse and left as quickly as he had arrived.

Dawn was well on its way to becoming morning when Leander turned to his buddy. "Do you want those injun ponies?"

"Not especially."

"Then cut them loose. Those two are going to have enough explaining to do when they return without their moccasins."

CHAPTER 12

Whores and Horses

"HELLO THE HOUSE."

The draw had been quiet, steady and constant. Sort of like gravity. Since crossing the Sabine, it was unspoken, but obvious. Neither friend wanted to admit it; however, when they entered the Louisiana swamp, it was readily apparent to both of them. Perhaps, it was nothing more than the remembrances of their boyhood. It could have been the nagging, almost aching curiosity associated with their departure eight years ago. Whatever the reason, whatever the attraction, Reams and Leander now stood before the tree house of Baptiste Roubleau.

They expected to find nothing, no one, or, something and Roubleau. The range of possibilities seemed infinite and each possibility had been thoroughly discussed as they made their way down familiar, old trails. Their horses seemed as curious as they were. They were not Louisiana bred. Constant wet feet, and a continuous, tree canopy were new and, actually refreshing.

It looked much like they remembered it. In fact, it looked occupied, when, to their pleasure and surprise, a shock of white hair and beard leaned over the second level banister. It was not the round, fleshy head, they remembered. Now it was narrow, slightly more wrinkled. It belonged to a much thinner Roubleau. It took a moment for them to mentally adjust to the passage of time and its impact on their old friend. Once he spoke, there was no doubt.

"Boys! Leander, Reams, what a surprise!"

With surprising agility Baptiste descended the stairs and was shaking their hands and hugging them. He was delighted to see them, probably, delighted to see anyone. There was no evidence that there was anyone else around. No female companion of any stripe or color appeared.

The conversation skipped and darted from any number of subjects, some pleasant, some not. He had heard of the deaths of Susannah and Abram. Later, he learned of Drayton's demise. Texas fascinated him, but he was now truly a swamp person and here he would live out his days. After dinner, fish and some other nondescript meat, the fellows waded into what Baptiste had been doing these past few years.

"Leander, do you like Texas?"

The question caught him a little off guard, but he responded quickly.

"Yes sir, I expect I do."

"Good, that makes me feel so much better. I knew I had something to do with Susannah's haste to leave Louisiana. It nagged at me that, well, maybe you folks were jumping out of the frying pan and into the fire on my account. I am sorely relieved that you like it."

It was still a little odd to be sitting next to such a shrunken Baptiste. His muscle tone had left him. His bare feet revealed the chiseled, discolored toenails of a much older man.

Reams decided to start the conversation. "Baptiste, is that why you did not come to the church social?"

"Pretty much, just did not seem appropriate. Anyway, after that the real excitement started, ha, boy I'll say."

Reams and Leander exchanged glances. They knew they were in for one hell of a tale like only Roubleau could spin.

"Long about dusk, Leander's favorite uncles showed up here in the skiff. You know, Drayton and Dunwoody. I thought it odd. Neither had ever been here before; now wait, maybe one time. Anyway, they hollered for me so I went to meet them. Little Sarah, that was the Negress Big Basket got for me. I don't know why they called her Little Sarah. Wasn't a damn thing about her that was little. As we approached them, Drayton pulled a pistol and told Dunwoody to tie our hands and feet. I knew nothing good was going to come of this. They helped me into the skiff. When they tried to get Little Sarah in, well she outweighed them both. Couldn't really reach around her. If I hadn't been so scared, I would have died laughing. It was just like trying to roll a sack of potatoes, you always are leaving part of it behind. I mean she didn't have no handhold. Dunwoody got a hold of something, and she elbowed him so hard he lost his breath. Finally, they got her into the skiff face down and butt up. That was how she traveled."

"I figured they would head down river and sell her, which is exactly what they did. I had no idea what they were going to do with me. I don't know if the fix was in, or, if they bribed someone, but I woke up in a sanitarium with a knot on my head the size of a goose egg. Worst food in the world. For about a year, I suspect, they kept me chained one arm to the bed. I must've looked dangerous. Hell, I would have been dangerous to those two if I could've gotten loose."

"Finally, there was this little black fellow who brought me my meals. I always tried to talk to him, but for the longest time he wouldn't say squat. Then one day he said, "you don't sound crazy." I said, crazy! I'm not crazy." He said, "why not, everyone else in here was." That's when I learned that Drayton and Dunwoody had spun some yard about me being crazy, living and cohabitating with black women, and inhabiting a swamp. Which was pretty close to the truth. I told Emanuel, that was his name, that if cohabitating with a Negress made you crazy, then they better start adding on some rooms. It might have irritated some church folks, but it did not make you crazy."

"Well, time went by pretty slowly, but I behaved. They started to let me out to walk the grounds. I got familiar with the place, the schedules. I picked the best time and wandered off. To be truthful, I don't think they cared. Either that or this old man was far more elusive than I thought I was."

The morning came way too quickly. Baptiste was made to repeat every tale he had ever told. Those old stories brought back a twinkle to his eye. Soon it was everyone's guess who was enjoying themselves more. After bittersweet goodbyes, Leander and Reams were back in the saddle, knowing that, most likely, they would never see Baptiste again.

"Old man, I can't wait to take you to "the swamp." Reams was bursting with pride. The thought that he might introduce Leander to "the swamp" was just chewing on him.

"Reams, look around you. We are in a swamp."

"Not a swamp, "the swamp", old man. That is where all the bawdy houses are in New Orleans. You know, where sporting men like me go for, shall I say, entertainment."

"Reams, every time you make one of these out-of-town trips, you always find yourself with some fallen Angel named Buffalo Hump, Buffalo Rump, or Buffalo Chest. I can't imagine what someone with that kind of name looks like. Probably just like a bison, I guess."

"Oh hell, Leander, those are just the Mexican ones." Reams shifted his shoulders, like that was explanation enough.

"What about your medicine bill with that old saw bones to get you cured of your last dalliance?"

"I've got a secret helper in New Orleans now."

"A secret helper? I'll bite, who is your secret helper?"

"There is this guy in one of the houses who lets me know who the clean ones are so that I don't bring home anything extra."

"What's his name?"

"Nimrod."

"Nimrod what?"

"Jesus Christ! Does a guy named Nimrod employed at a whorehouse have to have a last name? Jesus!"

"I guess not, but you fellas seemed so close."

Reams only muttered.

Riding in to New Orleans was certainly different from riding into Monaville. Horse hooves hitting dirty, muddy streets made no sound. Here, against brick or cobblestone, when combined with all of the other horses, they made a noisy clatter the likes of which Leander had never heard before. Building after building lined the streets. These were much older, and far more permanent in nature, than the frontier construction of Texas. Reams directed them to a livery stable, one that he had used on prior trips. This gave Leander some comfort. While they had hardly attracted even a sideways glance, the horse they brought in tow attracted a good deal of attention.

As they walked towards their hotel, Leander now noticed that they were the ones that made the noise. The jingle of their spurs was a stark contrast to the quiet cadence of town people. They

wore brogans not boots. These folks were pedestrians, not eques-
trians. Their universe was New Orleans proper. It provided all their
needs. They had no cause to enter the countryside.

Reams was anxious to head to "the swamp." Leander wanted a
good meal and a bath. Towards the late evening, Leander thought
it best to check the horses. Reams' level of comfort and trust did
not always rise to Leander's level. The evening walk took him past
business establishments of all sorts. Some looked legitimate; others,
made him wonder why Reams had to leave the block for entertainment. Each alley contained a passed out drunk or a drug victim
with his pockets turned inside out. For the first time, Leander felt
totally out of his element. He was not sure whether to feel good or
bad about that.

William Tunstell Lowe was of medium height, and extremely
clean. His shoes were polished to a high shine. He was attired in an
expensive suit of gray wool. Without question, he was a gentleman
of the town. Leander could not discern any unusual characteristics,
but one. His two front teeth crossed slightly, thus producing a slight
whistle when he spoke the letter "S". It did not seem fair to hold
that against him.

Lowe sponsored horse races every Wednesday and Saturday. He
directed them to move the horse to the track's stables. It gave the
public a chance to compare horseflesh. The services of a jockey
were offered, but, to his surprise, Leander said he preferred to ride
his horse. Even as thin as he was, this still meant that he was spot-
ting the competition 30 to 40 pounds.

Wednesday was soon upon them. Butterflies and nerves curtailed
any early-morning appetite. Leander and Reams headed directly
to the track; Reams was to handle the betting. Initially, there did
not seem to be much interest in Leander's horse. When they were
brought to the starting line, the interest increased, probably for the

wrong reason. There was a fully grown white man among black jockeys of the most diminutive size. Reams took every bet he could make. Leander's horses had speed and stamina, the kind you bred for the frontier. The town folks were about to be educated.

The crack of the starter's pistol did not surprise Leander or his mount. Texas horses and riders mixed with fire arms all the time. They say you can fire a pistol off the back of any horse . . . . at least once. What did surprise Leander was how quickly his competition reacted. He was now eating dirt thrown up by the other horses, all of them. Spurring his horse, he dropped the reins and gave it its head. His mount was a quick learner. Reams, standing on the sidelines, was about to faint. The two horses directly in front of Leander were now running side by side. If there was a proper etiquette to the process, neither Leander nor his horse knew it. They hit the slight crack of daylight between the two with all the force their increasing speed could produce. Once past these two, the field opened slightly. His horse was beginning to enjoy it, whatever it was his rider had involved him in. Leander kept his head down, leaning over the horse's neck. The horse was not laboring; in fact, he seemed to now pace himself with the other horses. Leander gave him a slight gig which moved him quickly past the rest of the crowd, save one.

The final turn was fast approaching. Hopefully, his horse would not swing too wide. Leander quickly realized there was more technique to the process than he had imagined. Finish line in sight, one more slight spur might get it done. His horse sensed his heals upward movement. There was no need. Whatever energy his horse had left, he reached down and grabbed it, pulling away from the last of the competition.

Leander sat back in the saddle, the signal to the horse that he could slow down. The signal was ignored, and he quickly rounded the track once more before the horse got the point. Reams was grinning ear to ear when he finally rode up to him.

"Damn near scared me to death, old man! You are supposed to start with the rest of the crowd and you don't get any points for that extra lap."

A crowd gathered around horse and rider. Congratulations mostly, but many remarked how effortless it had been. The horse wasn't even winded. Leander said little. It was a quick spin around a small circle for this horse. These folks didn't appreciate how much distance there was between any two points in Texas.

Leander dismounted and he and Reams walked slowly through the crowd towards the stables. Once clear of the main group, Reams spoke to Leander, almost under his breath.

"Oh man, we need to drop this horse off at the stables and get to your bank."

Leander was confused, "Bank? What for? I don't have a bank, Reams."

"The hell you don't. Have you forgotten? My father and I set it up so old Fuchs' note payments would go to New Orleans."

"I recall something of the sort, but I never made any contact. I mean I have never had any cause . . ." Reams stopped, "Leander, you never met Mr. Cleburn, never corresponded with him?"

"No."

"How have you managed Catalpa all these years?"

"I just paid the bills out of the money the cotton, cattle and horses brought in." Leander was confused and embarrassed. After his parents died, he just went forward totally overlooking the fact that Fuchs was paying installments for the purchase of his parent's Louisiana homestead.

"Well, you must be a frugal bastard. I should let you manage my affairs. I'll introduce you to James Cleburn. He'll be happy to meet you, particularly since you are such a big depositor and getting ready to be bigger."

"How so?"

"Leander, you won that race or have you forgotten? You also took about 10 years off my life expectancy with that slow ass start, but I may have gained it back at the finish. I cannot tell you how much for certain. Hell, down here they bet in dollars, French guineas, doubloons, and piasters around here. I am not certain what a piaster is, but I took the bet and you won. I am guessing, and it is just a guess, but you'll be depositing about $3000, plus or minus."

"What! How did . . . What? I mean together we could not have covered . . ."

"Hell, I know that. But, you know, heat of the battle old man. Everyone was making fun of that lanky hayseed in amongst those tiny black jockeys. I admit you are the dullest man in the universe, but you are my dull friend. So I got a little riled. I told them to put up or shut up. I got some great odds."

"Reams, odds, yes, but they don't mean much if we lost. We didn't have the money to cover."

"If we lost, I figured we had at least the second fastest horse in town and we could have left in a very big hurry."

Leander finally got it and a grin broke out from ear to ear. "So how much did you say?"

"At least $3000, but don't hold me to it. I don't know the exchange rates for all these currencies. What I do know is that we don't want these coins jiggling in your saddlebags all the way back to Texas. Plus, there is one more thing. You won a slave, fella is supposed to be a pretty good farrier for racehorses." Reams nodded slightly to the black man that had been following them. Leander had not noticed him. They were now at the stables.

"Leander," taking the reins from him, "this fellow they call

Rack." Leander stared into the blank countenance of a very power-fully built Negro. There was no softness in his expression. In fact, there was no expression at all. If there was any feeling, it was a slight sourness. Leander got no real sense of who this person was, or how he would fit into his household.

"Rack, take the horse and put it up. You stay with him here until we return."

Rack said nothing. He took the reins and led the horse as instructed. As they left for the bank, Leander asked, "how did this happen?"

"Well, I told you a lot of folks were funning you . . . Hayseed and all."

"Yeah, I got that part, Reams."

"The one with the biggest mouth was a fellow named F. Grant Simmons."

"Who is he and how many bales can he pick?"

"Personally, I doubt any, but he owns about 200 slaves and has a big operation just east of New Orleans. This slave, Rack, was his and he made a big show about the bet. So you got a new hand. I wasn't kidding about him shoeing racehorses. Simmons owns quite a few. Maybe you could pick up some tips."

"Seems a little sullen to me, Reams."

"Well, I don't know his background. Probably just uneasy."

"I hadn't given much thought to horse racing, but there does seem to be a little money in it. I agreed to make the trip to make you happy that you got your old dull friend off of Catalpa. Maybe we should build our own racetrack back in Texas."

"That's a good idea, as far as horse racing goes, but let's finish with the banking business. It will give me time for some whore chasing."

CHAPTER 13

Rack and Romance

CATALPA WAS NO LONGER A HAPPY PLACE. Discomfort and tension hung about the plantation like Spanish moss. The usual "good morning" was now an obligatory salutation begrudgingly extended. The random, almost accidental introduction of Rack into the Catalpa household had changed everything. Nothing in his childhood, or in his background, provided Leander with even the slightest hint of what to do, or how to do it.

When his parents died, Leander just kept doing what they had always done. It seemed to work. Catalpa was certainly more prosperous than any venture his father had ever undertaken. To that end, Leander accepted no credit. He was simply following a pattern that he had observed since birth.

True enough, Rack knew something about shoeing racehorses. Blue had no difficulty picking up the technique; although, he could not fathom the utility of thin shoes with toe clips. His life had been about wear and tear, endurance, and the need to gut it out through a season. Discarding a pair of thin shoes after every race was downright wasteful to Blue.

If Rack understood horse shoes, his talent ended right there. Most farriers could size up a horse and its temperament before they lifted the first hoof. Horses are individuals. Some would sprint for the far end of a pasture at the first glance of a farrier. Others wanted to see how much of their weight they could transfer to the sore back of the horse shoer bent under their hindquarters. Occasionally, but rarely, there were those horses who actually seemed to enjoy the process. Rack was tone deaf to the temperament of horses and mules, a huge disadvantage to all concerned.

The fact that he had little to no aptitude for horses and mules was not the crux of the problem. He was that irritating personality that kept everyone on edge. He remained the same sullen individual that Leander met in New Orleans. In fact, things got worse. Soon he revealed a violent side that, at least initially, was confined to the quarters.

Leander had never employed an overseer or any kind of task master. The seasons controlled the workflow. Mother Nature had more to say about what was done and when. If it was time to chop or pick cotton, every man, woman and child capable of providing assistance, any assistance, were quickly committed to the common purpose. From his childhood, Leander had worked the fields alongside his people. It had never occurred to him to change the process. Each person knew the strengths and weaknesses of the other. As a unit, they proceeded to do what was expected.

Rack was a bully who abused the residents of the quarters. Leander was not quick to pick up on the new hierarchy that Rack was trying to establish. He did sense a new distance between himself and his people. But his own reserved nature, coupled with the unspoken chasm between master and slave, provided no real means to communicate the increasing frustration felt by both. This day, Leander saddled the Roan. He had not ridden the mare for some time. She was barely three. While broke, the young horse still had some rough spots that would only be worked out if he spent some time with her. Midmorning found him checking calves. He was so absorbed in the task at hand he did not see Elisabeth and Ulysses. If you saw one you were most certain to see the other. Ulysses was supposed to be penned when he wasn't being used. That said, the reality was that the donkey could unhook most of the latches around the barn. If he could not work his way free, he would bray and bray whenever he saw Elisabeth. For the peace of everyone, Ulysses was permitted to just follow Elisabeth, much like a pet dog. He was happy. Elisabeth did not mind. Everyone seemed to enjoy the peace and quiet.

Elisabeth cleared her throat, and then did it again, trying to break Leander's concentration. It finally worked.

"Elisabeth, I did not see you come up." Leander was even more reserved than usual. He felt the growing distance but had no idea of the true cause, and no guess at the solution.

"Dey toll me to come get chu." "Dey" wasn't defined and Leander had no idea who "dey" could be or what provoked the errand to retrieve him.

"Who sent you? Is there a problem?"

"Just about eber' body. Ink pinched his toes off."

This was not terribly enlightening. Every other person on Catalpa was a slave, and Ink, the largest mule on the plantation, did not have toes.

"Elisabeth, I am confused, I thought . . ."

"Rack . . . . Gots his toes pinched off. Course he deserves lots more dan dat." Elisabeth punctuated the last statement with a quick nod of her head.

"How did this happen?"

"Not sure. He probably just bein' mean. Dat man is bad true and true." They had started towards the house as Elizabeth spoke.

Leander's mare was a good bit taller than Ulysses, so Leander and Elisabeth were not eye to eye. This gave her the chance to speak without having to make eye contact.

"I take it you don't care for Rack?"

"Wid' chu bring him here?" The directness and utter boldness of the question surprised Leander. They had known each other since childhood, but it was unusual to question his decisions in any fashion.

"Elisabeth, I never had any intention of bringing him here. I did not really buy him. I won him at that horse race." While slaves always knew what was going on at a plantation. They did not always know the reasons. Leander could tell the question was not personal to just Elisabeth. It was probably being asked by all his people.

"Who'd bet a slave? You wouldn't . . . . Not if he'd be any kind of hand."

Elisabeth had a great grasp for the obvious. When Reams told him of the bet, it nagged at him. True enough, there were those who thought little of their people. Probably every plantation had a different approach to the care and management of their Negroes. Even so, who would wager one, particularly, a young, healthy male slave who had a trade. When you asked the question, the same answer kept popping up. Leander suppressed it every time. You would only wager one that was more trouble than he was worth.

The wager could have just been a convenient way to rid a plantation of a problem. Leander had grown to respect and to rely on Elisabeth's judgment concerning the remuda. He would have to give some value to her opinion of Rack.

"So you don't care for Rack."

"Care for . . . Dat man's heart is as black as he is . . . He'd du' devil himself. How can da' man shoe a horse? Dey know, you know dey know a bad man and he'd a bad man. Dat mule Ink, when he let dat back hoof down, Ink put dat shoe right on his foot and pinched off two toes, didn't eben bleed."

"What!"

"Didn't eben bleed, da' little one and da' one next to it."

"Jesus!"

"Dat mule knows. Ebery one in da' quarters knows. Dats' a bad man. Thinks he's somethin'! We neber had no task master. He goin' to run da show. Neber needed him, not dat Negro, no sur."

Ink was still in his stall when they arrived, but Blue was now doing the shoeing. Several of the men were still there. Rack was sitting in a corner with a poorly bandaged foot. With a nod of his head he indicated he was all right. No conversation, the nod was all he wanted to say. Apparently, it took several men to push Ink over enough to move the mule's hoof. Curiosity begged to ask what happened to the toes; however, with Ted and about six Ted Junior's hanging around the barn, it was best to leave the question unasked.

* * *

Leander had grown tired of reading the good book. He had now read it several times. He did not feel any better after each subsequent reading. This confused him. The only book his mother ever read was the Bible, and she read it continuously. Couldn't she remember the stories? Reams had loaned him some books. A few were way over his head, but there were several husbandry books that rang a bell for him. He tried to use the late evenings to study them.

The heat from the fireplace had about driven all the air out of the room. His home had been well chinked. There were no drafts. Before heading upstairs, he stepped out onto the porch for a little fresh air. The moon was full, but frequently hidden by clouds moving in from the north. The air had a bite to it caused by the amount of moisture that it carried. He recognized the makings of a true blue norther. It would be here by morning.

The barn door was slightly cracked. A dull flicker of light shone through. It could be a lantern. Probably was a candle. He did not recall any sick animal, but it was best to check anyway. He retrieved his heavy coat and walked to the barn.

The light came from the far corner stall. Through the stalls boards he could see Elisabeth, and next to her a young mare laying on her side. She seemed perfectly still. She was not agitated. Leander quietly called to Elisabeth.

"Are you all right Elisabeth? Something with the horse?"

The mare was bred. The birth would be her first. If there were going to be problems, they most often occurred with the first pregnancy.

"She's fine. She's was spottin' a little today. I thought it best to stay wid' her."

He thought about leaving it at that. Elisabeth would come and get him if there were any problems. But his evenings had become little more than quiet hours alone. He sat down and leaned against the wall. The floor was cold. The barn was pretty drafty. It made him appreciate his house.

He and Elisabeth reviewed and discussed every potential birth that was expected. Leander kept a journal, but Elisabeth could recall all the breeding pairs, and the approximate date of the expected births. The horses had to appreciate her attention to detail. Leander certainly did.

The candlelight now flickered more frequently. The wind had increased sending more cold air through the boards that Abram and old Squire had brought to Catalpa now so long ago. Leander looked at Elisabeth and noticed a shudder. Her bare arms extending from her thin cotton dress were covered with chill bumps.

"Elisabeth, you are freezing. Here take my coat."

"I can't do dat."

"Well, here we'll use it as a blanket."

Leander took off the coat. Only then did he realize how truly cold it was. He spread it across Elizabeth and himself, putting his arm around her to make sure it covered her. She shivered again, exhaling a frosty breath. Things did not feel as he had expected. She was no longer the bony little girl in an oversized bonnet. There was a softness and a roundness to her. At first, they both seemed tense. Then, they relaxed. He drew her closer. He wanted the same peace, the same tranquility and comfort that she gave to these horses. He just never realized how badly he needed it.

Morning brought a whole new set of emotions. Leander's life partner had been only feet from him all his life. She knew it. He knew it. Together, they were quietly excited about it. At the same time, something nagged at him. He was so embarrassed.

"Elisabeth, I am truly sorry. I am so embarrassed. I cannot believe I have been so neglectful."

Elisabeth thought he might be referring to what they had shared, but had no idea what Leander had neglected.

"What chu sayin'?"

"It is so cold. You are still in a summer dress."

"So, it ain't Christmas." Elisabeth and every other Catalpa slave got their winter clothes at Christmas.

"That's the point. I can't believe I have been so blind, so ignorant. Why Christmas? I have just done what my father did. I am so sorry, I didn't think. I never thought. There is a whole lot of cold before Christmas."

"You ain't tellin' me nothun!"

The door opened to the round form of Blue, who wasn't sure why he was not the first person in the barn this morning. And why the first two were Leander and his sister.

"Morning Blue, I want you to head to town and get winter clothes for everybody."

"Winter clothes? It ain't Christmas!"

"It's cold isn't it?"

"Well, yes sur."

"Then, get everyone their winter clothes."

"But, what about Christmas?"

Leander had to laugh. No one enjoyed Christmas more than Blue. Even now, it held some special delight for him.

"Blue, we are not canceling Christmas. We're just trying to get warm. I'll send Momma Mae with you." With that Leander headed towards the kitchen. He spoke as he entered.

"Momma Mae, I want you to go to town with Blue and get everyone their winter clothes."

"What? It ain't Christmas."

Leander smiled. "You're right, it isn't Christmas. It is just cold. Last night, Elisabeth and I sat up with a young mare. She almost froze."

"Da mare?"

"No, Elisabeth. It was only then that I realized how stupid I have been. There is a whole lot of cold before we get to Christmas. Momma Mae, you must tell me when you need something; otherwise, I am just doing what we have always done. Is there anything else you need?"

"Blankets, would be a big help."

"Then get them. I'll give you a note. Blue is hitching the wagon. I am so sorry. I truly am."

Leander finished breakfast and headed out to the fields regretful, embarrassed, confused and excited.

The quarters soon picked up on the subtle change in the relationship between Leander and Elisabeth. It had the beneficial side effect of marginalizing Rack, to some extent. He was not going to bully his way into a superior position while one member of the quarters had such a close connection to the master. Catalpa became slightly more contented, except for Rack. Blue had mastered any skill Rack had. Thus, Rack was rapidly becoming just another field hand. Rack was not happy.

*　*　*

The day had been a long one. It was well past dark when Leander finally entered the kitchen. He was tired, hungry and dirty. Momma Mae's dinner might revive him, at least a little. He sat down at the table. The fatigue dulled his senses, but the rich aroma of her cooking revived him somewhat.

"I's gots to talk which chu."

Leander looked up. Momma Mae was quite a chatterbox in her own way, but it was odd that she would announce her need to speak to him. He had spent more time in her kitchen than anywhere else on earth. If home had to be a single room, it would be right where he sat.

"Fine, have a seat."

"No, I can't sit, gots to stand. Gots to say somethin' and if you sell me down the riber, den go 'n do it. I gots to say somethin'."

Leander laughed. "Momma Mae, there is a greater chance of me selling myself down the river, than me selling you down the river." She stood very still, but seemed nervous. Leander stopped eating. She had his attention.

"Son, you are a grown man. I knows it, but hab you thought it out?"

"Thought it out? What?"

"Son, your uncles took dat man, what's his name Baptiste, dey took him away for doin' what you doin'."

Leander quickly realized her concern. It was a conversation he did not really want to have. Oh, he had turned things over in his own mind from sun up to sun down. He had not forgotten Baptiste. He certainly had not forgotten his own mother's embarrassment. As Momma Mae stood before him, he knew he had to answer her.

"Momma Mae, no one is going to take me away, or Elisabeth either, for that matter."

"Son, I knows you both are happy. We all do. You likes da same things. You trusts each other. But, you can't forget da color. I means it will be nuttin' but trouble for you."

"Momma Mae, I am the only white person on this plantation. Who did the world expect me to fall in love with?"

Momma Mae nodded. "Leander, what will you do? You can't lib in da quarter. Where do da baby lib?"

Leander sat up straight. "What are you saying Momma Mae? Is Elisabeth pregnant?"

"Spec so, 'bout four months or dere abouts. I node da signs. 'Bout four months, could be four and a little bit."

"Momma Mae, my children will be my children. I will not run from them. They will be raised in my house. Elisabeth could have moved into it, but she cooks for Blue and didn't feel right about leaving the quarters. I appreciate your concern, I truly do. And, yes, I have thought a lot about everything. I am prepared to face any problems. You don't need to worry. Now give me a smile and you go relax. I suspect you have been carrying this around for some time. Four months you say?"

"Dat be right."

Go to bed and rest. I will see you in the morning. Good night Momma Mae."

* * *

Luther Wilhite arrived late at night. This surprised no one. Every foal, every calf, and every other critter born at Catalpa arrived late at night and usually during a storm. Elisabeth saved everyone the storm. He was a long, skinny baby, light complexion with wavy black hair. The parents were delighted. At dawn Momma Mae rang the big bell. Reams and the folks at Oak Ridge could probably have heard it. They would be pleased. The rest of Monaville was less pleased. Color made a difference to most folks. Their opinion was of little import to Leander. He had his plantation, his livestock, his wife and his son. He was quite prepared to face the future. Elisabeth seemed to give him a quiet confidence that he may have lacked before their union.

Cotton growing has a schedule that must be followed. Deadlines had to be met; births, deaths and marriages could not alter the steady monotony of the growing season. Midmorning found Leander on his big saddle bred gelding riding the fields that were to be plowed. The east field was then being worked. For reasons of habit only, they always started in the east field and then moved west along the bottom of the Brazos River. The fresh, pungent aroma of newly broke ground shouted the fact that this land was made to grow cotton. It had the whole package, fertility, water and a river to deliver the bales to market.

"If it isn't Susannah's and Abram's onliest boy." Reams was loping along the fence line. It was getting close to noon. Leander knew that he would welcome some of Momma Mae's cooking. There was no need to tease his friend.

"I am headed in for a bite. Might I interest you in some of Momma Mae's cooking?"

"Leander, you are a dog! Of course you can. I've been riding as hard as could to possibly happen upon you."

"Good, let's cut across the east field. It should be pretty well finished." They eased up the incline, horses nodding their heads as they climbed to the summit. Reams asked about the baby and said he had a present in his saddlebag. At the crest, you could see the entire field. Men and women both were at work. No one seemed to notice them. Reams glanced over at Leander and gulped.

He had seen the look before; he did not like it then. He did not like it now. Leander's face was taunt, his neck a royal Crimson. But his eyes gave it all away. The pupils were mere needle points focused in the distance. Reams was almost scared to look, but look he had to. He turned in the direction of his friends stare. He had barely completed his turn when Leander spurred the large saddle bred horse. Reams had no choice but to follow.

In the middle of the field stood Ink, the biggest mule he had ever seen. He looked absolutely frozen, but all around him were bent and broken switches that had been worn out by Rack. This animal was not going to move for Rack, switch or no switch. Rack's broad shoulders and back were wet with sweat. He had now retrieved a bois d'arc limb about the size of a fence post. Leander was several lengths ahead coming down the rise like a shot. The rest of the field hands had now heard the rolling cadence of the horses. Many just stood in shock.

Rack moved to the front of the mule. With a single swing, he raised that limb and brought it down on the head of the mule, which dropped dead in his harness. Rack took a slight step back. Whether it was the deadly silence of his fellow slaves, or the thunderous roar of the saddle bred horse and rider is anyone's guess. He caught sight of his destiny about a single moment before the chest of the saddle bred hit him dead center.

The noise was a combination of a thud, a crack and thunder. Rack was knocked out cold. It took Leander about 50 yards to slow the horse and turn him. In the process, he looped his lariat. On his second pass he roped the feet of Rack and took off for the far end of the field. Rack's body bounced over each plowed furrow. When it did, his right arm, obviously broken, bounced almost separate and apart from his body. Reams stayed with the mule. He fully expected Leander to hang Rack from the nearest tree. He did not. He left him at the river, returned and drug the dead carcass of the mule from the field. He did not speak of the event ever again.

Months passed. No one knew where Rack was, or whether he was still alive. Frankly, no one cared. Elisabeth had to argue with Momma Mae each morning. Momma Mae wanted to keep Luther in the kitchen. Elisabeth liked to carry him papoose style, as she made her rounds. If anyone could have two mothers, it was going to be Luther Wilhite.

During the day, Elisabeth returned to the quarters to babysit the young children. She felt some comfort in her former surroundings. The big house was nice, but given her background, material things did not mean all that much to her. She liked creatures, critters and folks. It was their individual uniqueness that gave her delight. Babysitting children was as natural as training a young colt. It just took patience.

The quarters were quiet. All of the children were settled down for a nap in Momma Mae's cabin. Elisabeth left them for a moment to get something out of Blue's cabin. She had barely entered it, when, a huge course black hand covered her mouth. He bent her backwards, lifting her feet off the ground. His strength engulfed her. There was nothing she could move. With a quick twist, her neck broke like a twig. She was dropped at the threshold of Blue's door.

The clang broke the silence. The light breeze carried it across the bottom. But it was repeated so rapidly everyone knew something was wrong. Leander raced ahead. In the pit of his stomach, he knew something dreadful awaited him; but he could not imagine what it was. He was still at a gallop when he passed the house and saw Momma Mae, breathless and exhausted, still ringing the bell. He jumped from the horse and ran to her. She was crying, chest heaving.

"What is it? What is it?"

Momma Mae could only whisper, "Elisabeth" and pointed towards the quarters.

Leander turned and looked only to see Blue coming towards him, his eyes red and filled with tears carrying the body of Elisabeth.

CHAPTER 14

Indians Again

TEXAS CONTINUED TO GROW. "GTT", meaning "gone to Texas" was carved on the doors of ruffians, deadbeats, business failures and every other reprobate one could imagine. Occasionally, a fairly normal upright Christian sort would head out to seek their future and perhaps their fortune in Texas. If these pioneers had a common trait, it was an individual boldness. The timid stayed at home.

They sought land, and there was still plenty of it. Some imported the cotton culture of the Deep South and found themselves, like Leander, near the Brazos River. The wheat farmers of the northern states took a shine to the upper plains. Whatever they knew, or had done in the states, was readily transplanted to Texas. No one seemed to mind, no one except the government of Mexico. The North Americans were invited and tolerated because they were to protect and buffer Mexico from the Comanche. The Spaniards had run headlong into the Comanches for years, and always come out on the short end.

They really had no one to blame but themselves. Before the arrival of the Spaniards, the Comanches, a short, stocky people, did not travel well or far. When they saw the horse, their culture, their traditions, their entire way of life changed. They became the most mobile, fastest moving band of guerrilla fighters the world had ever seen. It was the insatiable desire of the colonists for free land that justified the risk.

The Mexican prohibition against slavery was now largely ignored. Most recent settlers did not even bother to have lifelong indentures signed. The Catholic Church never had enough priests to service the colonies. It was not terribly interested in forced conversions in the first place. Thus, the colonists pretty much pursued whatever faith they wanted, if they wanted one. The second decade of Austin's colony saw the Mexicans hopelessly outnumbered in Texas. The disconnect between citizens and their Mexican government would continue to grow.

Leander's son, Luther, was quietly becoming a product of Catalpa. All of the warmth and affection that everyone felt for his mother seemed to be transferred to him. Nursed by Momma Mae, he became a vigorous child who knew no bounds, but who carried his mother's tranquility with him in whatever he did. Like all the children, he took his naps in the quarters. The quiet humming of Momma Mae induced a deep sleep in the most restless child.

As one would expect, Luther could ride almost as soon as he could walk. His easy gait disturbed no one and no animal. He moved around, behind and under every horse and mule on the plantation. Ulysses had brayed for Elisabeth for months. It could have been how often Blue placed Luther on the donkey's back, or it could have been something that reminded him of Elisabeth, whatever it was, Ulysses was genuinely fond of the little boy. Still and all, Leander's son was not going to ride a donkey.

The saddle bred gelding that had shattered Rack's arm became his mount. The horse welcomed his new duty. Luther would walk to the barn, climb on a barrel to reach the horse's bridle. Once he had retrieved it, he could be seen dragging it in the dirt. He was not tall enough to hold it so that it would not drag. The saddle bred gelding would see him coming, walked towards Luther and dropped his head low to the ground so that Luther could put on the bridle. It was a whole lot easier to carry Luther around than some full-grown man. Yes, the gelding liked his new job.

For years, Catalpa had been a resting point for colonists. Settlers had enjoyed the hospitality, and certainly, the meals of Momma Mae. The visitors no longer came. Leander thought it curious; word does travel fast. He seldom went into Monaville. When he did, he noticed the change in people, particularly, the women. There are things you cannot fight. Fortunately, Catalpa was big enough and isolated enough that he could raise his son as he wished.

When Luther started talking, Leander noticed a very familiar dialect. It quietly bemused him; he had to admit he should have expected it. The boy certainly heard more black people during the day than white. As a result, each evening, Leander would hold Luther in his lap, and read to him from one of the books Reams had selected. To his surprise, Luther did not fall asleep. The gentle motion of Poppy's rocker, whether on the porch or next to the fireplace, did not make him sleepy. As long as Leander was willing to read, Luther was willing to listen. The boy was a quick study and would often question Leander during the day about something that they had read nights before.

Still and all, Leander's universe was Catalpa. He did not seek Monaville, but when he was needed, Monaville sought him. For the most part, Austin's colony never had a lot of serious Indian problems. There was the occasional theft of a horse or two. Indians were frequently to blame; but, Leander had his doubts. There were a good many more white horse thieves in Texas that red ones. Mathematically, the odds seem to move in that direction despite the common accusation directed towards the Indians.

Austin had organized a group of Rangers to assist with any Indian deprivations. Many young men were keen on becoming a part of a ranging company. Each had their own personal motivation. For Leander, it afforded a reprieve from the monotony of the plantation. His lifelong buddy, Reams, would provide the entertainment. Avery McElroy, a neighbor, would not miss a chance to roam the colony. Redheaded, red bearded with crystal blue eyes, the Scotsman, as he was called, was a most accurate marksman, who could always be depended upon in any confrontation. Old man Buck Brown had been a part of the local ranging company. Of late, he had been including his son, M. E. One could only hope that their offspring would never grow up to resemble M. E. Brown. He was now in his late teens. As a young boy, he could string together enough cuss words to make a sailor blush. This part of his vocabulary grew continuously. You almost thought he was on a personal quest to learn a new swearword every day. No other aspect of his personal development was pursued with such intensity.

Leander did not care for him. M.E. was brash, impulsive and devious. A young man came through Monaville some time back. He was low on funds and sought work at Brown's plantation. After a month of labor, he requested his wages with the intent of moving on to another part of the colony. He was found the next day dead, shot in the back, with no money on his person. The crime remained unsolved, like so many. Leander had a nagging suspicion that M.E. may have played a part.

Out of respect for his dad, M.E. was permitted to accompany the Rangers. Leander was and had almost always been in charge. Uncle

Baptiste taught him how to track men and game. If you could track someone or something through a Louisiana swamp covered with floating duckweed, you could follow the signs left on the Texas landscape. Simply stated, if someone passed through a place, they changed it. You must look for the changes, a pace at a time. Most folks get impatient and look too far down the trail. In doing so, they almost always miss something. Leander had the skill and the patience. Plus, he could think like a horse. More often than not, the horse was the one that was actually making the way through the unmarked Texas frontier.

They had been moving through the northern part of the colony for almost a week. They had nine men this time, if you counted M. E. Most of them did not. Leander could not help but think of Luther. Acceptance was going to be hard for Luther. Maybe Leander could do something to get M.E. back on the straight and narrow. Old Buck had given up or was no longer up to the challenge. If Luther did not pan out under his tutelage, he hoped someone would take an interest in him. So M.E. was tolerated by Leander, but barely.

After dinner, Leander spread his bed roll out on a flat spot, or what he had thought was a flat spot. The men continued to spin their tales and yarns. Leander enjoyed the stories even though he knew most were lies or hopeless exaggerations. Weary, he drifted off and did not even move for the longest time. A nice breeze blew across the field. The grass was not high enough to impede it. It reminded him of his childhood, napping in the dog trot and cooled by the gentlest breeze the good Lord could provide.

It wasn't quite dawn when he realized that the flat spot he had selected wasn't completely flat. In fact, there was a hard ridge that went right across his back. He had slept so hard that it had left a bruise. Leander rolled on his side hoping the ache would go away if he stayed in a new position for a while.

The nocturnal creatures of the area were moving back towards their home. A mother coon was ushering her offspring towards a tree. It probably had a hollow spot that gave them shelter. Looking across the prairie on his side, he could not identify the distant figure. It was thin. Probably a deer, but its gait was irregular. Side to side sometimes, then it would not move at all. It was a good ways off. Leander continued to scan the area. Soon they would be back in the saddle completing their most northerly loop of the colony.

He returned to the distant figure. It was closer, but still an odd, unrecognized form. Its movements were so erratic. He rose up on one elbow. Perhaps changing his perspective would help. The form was human! He nudged Reams and told him to wake up. The comment roused Avery, the lightest sleeper of the group.

"Reams, cover me. I want to see who that is." Leander grabbed his rifle and moved towards the figure. As he got closer, he knew the form was female, but her eyes shouted that her soul had left her. Her dress was tattered, barely covering her. Her face was caked with mud, dirt and blood. She was so dazed that she did not notice Leander as he walked directly towards her.

"Ma'am, ma'am, are you all right?"

The shock of a person's voice scared her and broke her daze all at the same time. She collapsed into Leander's arms, sobbing. She could barely talk. Whatever she had gone through had reduced her to human wreckage. Reams and Avery were right behind him. Leander handed his rifle to Reams and carried the woman to their camp.

Once she had some water she could not tell her story fast enough. She, her husband, her brother, a young son and an infant child had been returning home from a visit to see her family. They were traveling by oxcart and had camped for the evening when they were attacked by a dozen or more Comanches. The two men were killed outright. After the Indians finished their looting, they took the two scalps of the dead man and put her, with her baby and her son, on the backs of horses and headed west.

During the day, they traveled without stopping. The cries of the infant irritated one of the braves; he grabbed it from her and dashed its brains out against a tree. That evening they made camp. After all fell asleep, she made the agonizing decision to try and escape and seek help. She had no idea if this would anger the Indians such that they would kill her son. He was now the only remaining member of her family. She believed she had walked for a day and a night. However, Leander knew better than to rely upon that estimate. She begged them to find her son.

They left her and any extra equipment with one of the Rangers. If they were going to be successful, they needed to travel light and move quickly. Retracing her steps was easy. It could be done at a gentle lope. Moving through a long depression, the men noticed a group of Indians riding parallel to them on a low ridge.

Before Leander could stop him, M.E. pulled his rifle from his scabbard and fired at the Indians.

"What the hell are you doing?"

"Going to kill some injuns." M.E. was truly proud of his behavior.

"We are looking for Comanches. Those are not Comanches!" shouted Leander, pointing in the direction of the Indians.

"Well they're injuns."

Leander had dismounted, handed his reins to Reams. He walked over to M.E., pulled him off his horse and slapped him across his face. Taking his rifle, he tossed it to Avery.

"Scotsman, disarm him and I mean completely."

M.E., full of more vinegar than need be, bounced up to resist.

Leander turned to him. "Surrender your weapons and I will let you remain with us. If you do not, you and your dad are going to be left here alone."

"Dammit son, do as he says." Shaking his head, Buck Brown could not imagine how the fruit could fall so far from the tree.

Leander handed his pistol and knife to Reams and made it very clear to the Indians on the ridge that he was approaching them on foot and unarmed.

About halfway up the ridge, one of the Indians turned his horse towards him. Leander stopped and waited his arrival. He rode his horse directly towards him. Leander did not move. Rider and horse stopped within an arms length of Leander.

Leander started to speak, but to his surprise, the Indians spoke first.

"I never expected to meet you again."

Leander looked up at the brave. He had no immediate recollection of having ever seen the man before, but his look must have revealed his puzzlement.

"The last time we met you sent me home without my moccasins." While the Indian was as stoic as they all could be, Leander thought he saw the slight hint of a smile.

"Oh, I do recall now. Your name had something to do with a feather."

"Yes, it had been Long Feather. My people had great fun with my story of our encounter. They renamed me Broken Feather."

"I hope you like it." Leander wondered if some retribution was forthcoming as a result of the change.

"Hum, a name is just a name. I will probably have a few more before I die." The Indian's gaze moved in the direction of the Ranger Company. Leander thought it best to try and apologize for M.E.'s behavior.

"The young man who fired that shot at you . . . . well, he is a very young man. I am sorry."

"He cannot tell one Indian from another?"

"Yes, that would be one explanation." Leander wanted to say more, but the man before him had matured a great deal since their first encounter. He probably could fill-in the gaps.

"We are looking for some Comanches. About a dozen I suspect. They attacked a family. They killed two men and an infant. They still have a young boy with them, we hope."

"Comanches, ah, if you follow the sun you will run into the river. Slightly north, it makes a bend. If they intend to cross the river they will cross up there. The young man will be fine if he is strong enough to travel. Comanches make things very hard for us. I hope your young man learns how to tell one tribe from another." Broken Feather was looking right at M.E. as he as he spoke.

"I appreciate your help." Leander extended his hand and they shook.

"That is a handsome horse, Broken Feather."

"I know where there are better ones." He smiled.

"Yes, yes, I suspect you do. Come see me when you want to trade."

They parted. Broken Feather loped back to his people. Leander turned and shook his head. What were the chances? Leander retold the story, with embellishments from Reams. Both hoped that M.E. might learn at least a couple of lessons, but that remained to be seen.

Near the river, they picked up the trail of the Comanches. They were not that far ahead. Most likely, they had spent a good bit of the time trying to locate the woman. Timing became very important. Leander hastened the Rangers along, moving as swiftly as they possibly could.

Towards dusk, perhaps a little later, they happened upon the Indian camp. They had just turned out their horses. Both Indians and Rangers were surprised to see one another. The Indians broke for a thicket. Leander sent four Rangers with Reams to cut off their path. If they reached the brambles, they would be impossible to capture. Leander and the rest charged them from the rear.

In no time, they had passed through the camp. Leander saw a brave raise his rifle and point it directly at him. He turned his horse, dismounted, when he felt the shot pass through the open flap of his coat, hitting his horse in the neck. His shot having been fired, Leander took steady aim and killed the brave.

The Indians were now caught between two lines of fire. Reams charged one as he was trying to reload. The impact of Ream's shot threw him into another brave causing his shot to go wide of any mark. The Scotsman's aim was as accurate as it always had been. By now only two Comanches were left. Both ran for the thicket and made their escape.

A quick search of the camp found the young boy. He was tired and worn, but a survivor of a terrible nightmare. Leander ordered the men to gather up all of the Comanche horses. To leave them would only assist the two that escaped. Rather than try and find them, the Rangers thought it best to reunite the two surviving family members as soon as possible. There was not a dry eye in the camp when they returned.

CHAPTER 15

A Change in the Air

THE RAIN BEGAN IN LATE OCTOBER. IT WAS WEL-
COMED. The crops were in; the fields could use the moisture. By
mid December, it was starting to wear on you, like an obnoxious
house guest who stayed too long. Yet, it did not let up; it just kept
raining. On the rare day that it did not rain, the cloud cover still
blacked out any chance for sunlight. Folks were starting to turn a
little green around the edges.

Every road, path and trail now had the consistency of pudding.
You could not get away from the mud. It covered you, your clothes,
your horse and every tool and implement a man could handle. By
late December, the mud and stick chimneys were collapsing. They
were reverting to what they originally were, just mud.

Wet winters are one thing. Cold winters are another. But this was
to be the coldest and wettest in memory. The first truly blue norther
hit in early December. You could see the clouds build, a deep gray
against a light gray sky. Their size alone gave you pause. There
was nothing you could do but watch and wait. Then, in a single

moment, an invisible curtain of cold air arrived and moved past you without even a thought. Joints began to ache, ears felt brittle, and hands moved for pockets. You knew in your soul this wasn't some ordinary cold front.

This winter the temperature dropped and stayed there. No breaks, no respites. Just a freezing wetness, that tested the strength, and the will of man and beast. It was not a good year to start a revolution; but, no one told the Texians that.

Reams arrived about dinner time. Everyone knew why. He always pretended that it was to bring Leander a new book to read to Luther. It had more to do with dinner than literature, but no one called him on it. Plus, he had truly developed a fondness for the boy. You could tell that Luther was delighted to see Reams, who was a good deal more animated and a great deal funnier than his dad.

Leander welcomed the company, the books and the help in raising his son. He worried about Luther and whether he was providing him with all that he needed. He seemed to be a happy child, easy-going and inquisitive about everything. If the truth were known, Leander had few options. Monaville was not going to be a receptive place for a mulatto child, even one that so resembled his father.

"Storm clouds are gathering Leander." Reams was leaning back from the table scratching his very full belly.

"That shouldn't be much of a surprise Reams. We have had nothing but one blue norther after another."

"Ain't talkin' about that kind of storm, old man. I'm talking about politics, the kind that leads to a fight. You had better get ready." Reams examined his old friend closely. If things went the wrong way, there would be a real fight to be had. He had never been in one without his friend and certainly wanted him in this one.

"You're talking about all that revolution talk, I guess." Leander wasn't terribly excited about the talk or the concept.

"Well, you're damn right. Lots of folks are up in arms."

Leander moved back from the table and sat down in Poppy's rocker. "Reams, you say a lot of folks. It appears to me that most of these folks are newcomers. Land grabbers are what I would call them. They get everything stirred up in a tizzy and hope to latch onto as much land as they can. Think about it. We left Louisiana for Texas and, after some work I'll grant you, we have ended up fixed pretty well. Now what is it that I'm revolting against?"

"Old man, we were land grabbers too. We just got here first."

"Perhaps, but we came here under a set of rules that we agreed to; and under a government that has pretty much left us alone."

Reams went back to massaging his belly. "Ha, some of those Mexican folks should have read a little of our history. The English left us alone too and that didn't work out so well for them. Anyway, the rules are changing and I don't think you're going to like them much at all."

Leander cast a glance in the direction of Luther. Having a son changed so much. If he only had to worry about himself, things would be so much simpler. Hell, if he lost everything, he could still survive somewhere. But it wasn't about his survival or his future anymore. It was about Luther's.

"What is going to change, Reams?"

"Just about everything. You and I are now considered pirates."

"Pirates!"

"I didn't stutter old man. Pirates. That is what Santa Anna calls us. You know who Santa Anna is?"

Leander found himself rocking a little faster for no apparent reason. "The so-called Napoleon of the West, the president of Mexico."

"Yulp that's him. Although I've sensed the presidency of Mexico is not the same as the American presidency. More akin to a dictator, I should say. This guy is not someone to mess with. He seized power by annihilating his fellow citizens. Now, he has us pirates in his sights. He is moving his army in this direction for the expressed purpose of driving all of us out of Mexico."

"Reams, the Napoleon of the West is going to start his campaign in the middle of the coldest and wettest winter ever?" Leander was growing a little heated. He had never been called a pirate by anyone.

"He has divided his army. He intends to encourage the slaves to rebel, particularly those along the Brazos. Plus, he plans on forming an alliance with the injuns. That way, black, brown and red will remove us whites from Texas."

"Yes, and afterwards, the Comanches would just take the place back again."

"Leander, I am not here to critique his battle plan. I am here to tell you a war is coming and it is going to end up in our laps, whether we want it or not."

Leander did not like anything that he was hearing. Slave insurrections had been cussed and discussed across the South forever. Without a doubt, there were slave owners who had every right to fear them. It seemed to ignore the basic fact that most slaves he knew, his own included, were fairly law-abiding. They conform to the rules every single day. If the entire slave labor system went away tomorrow, Leander could not imagine that it would result in wholesale bloodshed. True enough, every race has its Rack, but he had lived among Negroes all his life. Could he have misjudged them so? Would they really fight and kill every white they could if given the chance? Regarding the Indians, the issue became more complex. The young braves of just about any tribe could be motivated to prove their manhood. If so moved, it could result in a good bit of bloodshed. Worse yet, it would be guerrilla warfare and that was hard to defend. As for the Comanches, if Santa Anna formed an alliance he would be the first, and it would be of little point. Even now the Comanches killed whoever and whenever they wanted.

"Reams, where does Austin stand?"

"Our good Empresario's attitude seems to have undergone a metamorphosis in that Mexican prison. He is for rebellion and separation from Mexico. A group of Texians have named him General of our forces . . . ."

"Austin isn't a military man, Reams."

"Hell, I know it, you know and he knows it. They will soon be meeting at Washington on the Brazos. I suspect Sam Houston will take over the military. In the meantime, Colonel Travis is organizing a cavalry company and headed to the Alamo."

"Buck Travis?"

"Yes, headed to the Alamo . . . ."

"Buck Travis!"

"Yes, I said headed to the . . . ."

"Buck Travis!"

Reams stopped, threw his hands down to his side and said, "Leander, let me whisper this real soft and slow. Colonel William Travis, sometimes known as Buck Travis. Now your point is what?"

"This is the same Buck Travis that got into that hair pulling contest down in Anahuac and demanded the immediate surrender of some minor Mexican official, or he would put them to the sword?"

"Well, yes, I seem to recall some little ruckus to that effect."

"Well, Reams, I am sure Mr. Santa Anna will be quick to remind old Buck of it. He is nothing but a whoremonger."

"Leander, you are hitting close to home now. I would hope that a fondness for whores does not disqualify a man from very much."

Leander smiled, "and just how did he get from whoremongering, to protector of Anahuac and Colonel of something?"

"He raised a cavalry company and he's headed to the Alamo, you know in San Antonio de Bexar."

"And, Reams, if I raised a battalion, can I be a General?"

"Hell, I don't know. What are you getting at Leander?"

"Ignoring my personal disregard for Buck Travis, isn't the Alamo that old abandoned mission we saw?"

"Yes."

"What is he going to do with a cavalry company at the Alamo? Ride around in circles in the courtyard? Why does anyone care about the Alamo? If Santa Anna wants to drive the white folks out of Texas, he can skip the trip to San Antonio. I did not see five of 'em when we were there and we were two of the five!"

"Colonel James McNeill is fortifying the mission. He has brought in a bunch of cannon; some were at New Orleans with Jackson."

"McNeill is an artillery officer, I take it?"

"Yelp."

"There are two things I know about artillery officers. I have never seen one who ever saw a cannon that he did not fall in love with."

"And the second thing is . . . .?"

"You start putting a bunch of cannons in one place, they tend to draw a crowd. What worries me is that General Cos surrendered the Alamo to a bunch of Texians a short time back."

"Yeah, they kicked his butt!"

"Did they? Or did Cos not want to get hemmed in an old mission that either he couldn't defend, or wasn't worth fighting for."

Reams was clearly frustrated. "I tell you this Leander Wilhite, if I ever want to start a war, I am not going to even invite you to it."

"Reams, you have got to know that you have truly hurt my feelings." Reams knew his buddy was jerking his string.

"All I am saying is that I haven't liked anything you have said so far. If we are presented with a fight, we don't have the right bodies in the right spots. What do some of the other men think about the situation?"

"They are waiting on you, Leander."

Leander nodded. Glancing at the fireplace, he saw that all the war talk had put Luther to sleep. Reams moved quietly to the door. Leander carried his son upstairs to bed.

The next morning Leander called for Blue to come to Momma Mae's kitchen. Slave communities are much like a pine forest. Even a slight breeze would cause one tree to touch another, then another and then another. While it was true enough that some slave owners might have reason to fear a slavery revolt, Leander did not believe that was the general rule. He put the chance of war into its simplest terms, knowing that what he said would get repeated up and down the Brazos River. Cotton, goods and gossip moved on the river every day. If the slaves were approached by Santa Anna, at least they would know his motive. It would not be some grand act of charity. Leander believed that they would stay put, or at least remain neutral. The devil you know is sometimes better than the devil you don't. The biggest puzzle remained, why go to the Alamo?

Leander rode down the lane towards the river. Calving season had started. It was best to check on new arrivals as soon as possible. It was not raining, but you would not have known that under the canopy of oaks and elms. Each motion of a branch or limb sent large droplets of very cold water earthward. Once in the open Leander could see that the day brought just a very fine mist. It moved in unison with the wind, like a school of fish changing direction every so often. Why do females always pick the worst weather to give birth? Leander was trying to recall a birth of anyone or anything at Catalpa that occurred in the middle of a sunny day. He could not recall a single instance.

Two horsemen came riding towards him, not in a gallop but they were not wasting time either. He recognized the familiar forms of Reams and Avery. Their hats drooped with the wetness. This could not be good news.

Reams spoke first. No good morning. No howdy. "Leander, the Alamo has fallen. The entire garrison was put to the sword."

Leander had rolled this revolution idea around and around. He still was not certain this was a fight he wanted to join. It infuriated him that civilized men would treat each other this way. He understood why the Comanches fought the way they did. It was their culture. It was who they are, but we weren't Comanches and neither were the Santanistas. Why the Alamo no longer mattered. Dead was dead, and it should not have happened.

"Let's head to the barn. I'm sure you have more to discuss." Leander took the lead. Soon they were in the barn and warming themselves by the fire of Blue's blacksmith shop. They tossed their rain slickers over a stall. At least their clothes were dry from the knees up. Reams filled in the details that were then known about the Alamo.

Most of Texas was making tracks towards the Sabine, apparently in the lead were the political authorities of the new Republic. Sam Houston, his army and whatever volunteers he could find were to cross the Brazos near Jared Groce's plantation. The whereabouts of Santa Anna was anyone's guess. Reams suspected that there were 20 to 25 able-bodied men from the Monaville area ready to volunteer, if Leander would take the lead. Leander made no immediate response. There were still so many unknowns. Reams was rapidly growing impatient.

"Dammit! Leander we have got to go. We can't just sit here."

Leander sat down on a barrel. He looked at Blue, who had stopped when Reams raised his voice.

"So you propose that we volunteer?"

"Well, yes, we have to."

"And what is it we are volunteering for, Reams?"

"Dammit, don't start with all these questions now. The war, the war. That's what we're volunteering for."

Leander nodded. "Yes, Reams, the war. I understand that. But so far all we have ever done was rangering. Are you prepared to join an infantry company and waddle your fat butt off all over Texas?"

"Ha, hardly. I'm not built for infantry."

"That's my point. What is it that the men are prepared to do? And don't say fight. I know they will fight, or at least, our regular Rangers will. But I also know they are a very independent group. Just because someone carries the rank of General, doesn't mean they will follow him or anyone else."

"I see. Look, let's volunteer as a Ranger Company. That is what we know. If they don't need us, those that want to take a stroll around Texas can. Those that don't can follow me to my porch."

Leander was more upset about the massacre at the Alamo than he let on to Reams and Avery. They had their blood up and the slightest bit of encouragement would go a long way. Plus, he knew this talk would be unsettling for Blue. He moved the discussion to timing and preparations. Each man would bring two extra horses. If they were to be effective, they would need to be able to cover a lot of ground. Fresh horses were a must. Given the fact that the new government would just barely be out of its infancy, they would expect no support from it. They would carry their own provisions for themselves and their horses. They would leave at daylight from Catalpa the day after tomorrow. Reams and Avery donned their slickers and made for their horses.

"Gentlemen, there is one more thing." Leander's tone told it all. Whatever it was both Reams and Avery knew it was not going to be negotiable.

"If I am to lead this group and be responsible for it, then M.E. Brown is not to be a part." They both knew why. Leander's position was no surprise to either man.

"Odd that you should mention him, old man. He has shown no interest in becoming part of this fight. We understand your point, Leander. We will see you at daylight the day after tomorrow," said Reams.

Leander had not left his seat on the barrel. The gravity of the situation started to hang on him like the morning dampness. To just be able to guess what lay ahead would provide him with some direction. He could not imagine what the future would bring. Leading a Company of Rangers, men that he knew, was one thing. To become part of an army was downright strange. The notion was just odd. Yes, they would be Texians or Americans, but really who would make up this so-called Army? Would we fight big battles, skirmishes or what? Leander had no answers. It was a puzzle. So far it was all pieces, no pattern.

Blue's hammer hit the hard surface of a horseshoe, bouncing once like it always does, sort of its own echo. The noise brought Leander back to the present.

"Blue, what do you think?" They had known each other forever. They shared childhood memories and the tragic loss of Elisabeth. Of course, time and slavery made things all the more convoluted; yet, Blue had often been a sounding board. Blue's own simplicity provided some naked honesty.

"White folks gets demselves in a lots of fights."

"Does appear so doesn't it? I am not sure I would have started this one; but, it seems to be headed our way. Blue, this isn't your fight, but I need you. We all need you and I suspect the grand and noble Republic of Texas is most assuredly going to need you."

Blues stood quietly by the horse he was shoeing. He knew he

would do whatever Leander needed or requested. But Leander had a way of making sense of things that made no sense to him. He hoped an explanation would be offered.

"I suspect this fellow Santa Anna is an ambitious sort. Ambition can get you killed. He is already president of Mexico. Most people would leave it at that; but, if he runs us all out of Texas . . . . . . Well, it would be quite a feather in his bonnet. He regains control over a lot of land, and his country would be in position to rival the United States. He probably doesn't feel we will be much of an opponent. I imagine a lot of us don't have much respect for him either. That is a recipe for a whole lot of bad luck for someone. Blue, I will do my best to keep you out of harm's way. But I need you to keep us in fresh horses, shod and fitted out."

"I can do dat."

"I know you can. Let's take two wagons, and use four Percherons to pull each wagon."

"Four?"

"Yes. The mud is going to be our biggest test. It will wear on the horses. An extra team might be what gets us there. I better go visit with Momma Mae."

Leander stood up shook his head. "Lord, does life ever get easy?" He walked towards the kitchen.

CHAPTER 16

Panic and Preparation

THE DOLL TROUBLED HIM. For miles they had seen nothing but panic and fear. Houses and homesteads were completely abandoned. Meals were left cold on the table. Doors hung wide open as if to say, they weren't coming back. Livestock grazed gardens and milk cows bellowed from pain, their bags stretched tight from inattention. But Leander could not forget the doll.

They rode right passed it. It was hardly recognizable from the mud and manure splatter. No little girl abandons her doll, unless she is overcome by the fear of an invading army. It wasn't much of a toy. Buttons for eyes, and a small piece of calico, probably a dress remnant, fashioned as an apron. Its value wasn't as a toy; there were better toys. Its import was as a companion. Leander knew that at the bottom of his mother's Hope chest, there was a similar homespun doll. His mother had treasured and protected it her entire life. But his mother never ran from invaders. Leander now knew they were riding to something that had created a mass exodus of people, strong, pioneering folk. You did not need to be a scout to track the panic, so visible, so obvious.

The closer they got to Alta Mira, the more refugees they encountered. They were mostly women and children. In fact, there were an alarming number of wagons and ox carts with no men at all. Those males that did accompany the fleeing Texians were elderly or slaves. Leander could only guess and hope that the other men were moving towards Bernardo, Groce's plantation, to join Houston's army.

Henry Fanthorpe's Inn was almost unrecognizable. It had once started as little more than a covered corn crib. Henry, frugal beyond description, had built his business into a very successful stagecoach inn. It now sat on a slight bluff. It was a handsome two-story building with a substantial cellar. The dining room was a large rectangle with tables and benches running its length. More importantly, the food was excellent. Leander and Reams never failed to stop when they were in the area.

Today the Inn no longer resembled the quiet oasis that it had been. The handsome lawn was trampled by horse and man. For a circumference of about a half a mile, there was a mixture of tents, lean-tos, and camps randomly scattered around the grounds. The disheveled appearance of all concerned told the story.

Reams and Leander made their way to the center dog trot of the Inn. Henry Fanthorpe's office was adjacent to the staircase leading to the second floor. He was seated at his desk, but turned slightly in his chair as they approached.

"Leander, Reams, good to see you."

Both men looked at each other. Reams responded and said what they both were thinking.

"Good to see us hell. Looks to me you don't need to see another soul ever again."

Henry laughed. "Yes, we are a little crowded."

"What have we ridin into, Henry?" Reams leaned his rifle against the wall.

"Oh, they're calling it the Runaway Scrape. Houston has been steadily moving east, away from the Mexican army. They burnt Gonzales so Santa Anna could not use anything, like Gonzales hasn't given enough. There is a two week wait to cross the Brazos at old Washington. Got the same wait to cross the Sabine. I'm right here in the middle of it all. We ran out of everything days ago. Right now all that is going on is disease and pestilence. These folks need to spread out. Every new ox cart or wagon brings someone else sick with something someone else hasn't got yet. It's sad. I booted everyone out of the Inn two days ago. Turned all the beds over to the Gonzales widows and their children."

Leander interrupted, "Henry, who are the Gonzales widows?"

Henry shook his head. "Travis sent out a letter asking for help. About 30 some odd men from Gonzales rode through the Mexican lines and into the Alamo, and to their death. I haven't counted, but we have a couple of dozen of their widows and children here. They came by oxcart mostly. They can stay as long as they want."

"How long are you going to stay, Henry?"

"Reams, I can't leave. If Santa Anna wants to string me up, I guess he can do it here as easy as anywhere else."

"Ha, if you cook him dinner, I don't think he'll kill you."

Henry enjoyed the joke, rubbing his chin he had something he had to say. "I haven't been much help to you fellas. No bed, no food, I'm not much of an innkeeper, but I need to ask a favor of you and I reckon this isn't the best time."

Reams was quick to respond. "Henry, when this is all over we will give you a chance to make amends. What troubles you?"

"Captain Bennett is gathering volunteers. He is down at the base of the hill. His camp looks a good deal more orderly than my Inn. There's a boy down there, William Zuber. I have known him forever. He is about 15, I suspect, and is hell-bent on being part of this war. His mom is bent in the exact opposite direction. You'll see her. She stays at the edge of the camp. Never lets the boy out of her sight. I fear he is going to die of embarrassment before any Mexican ever has a chance to kill'em. Could you take him under your wing? If you don't, she will follow that boy to the gates of hell."

"I hope he is not an only child," cracked Reams.

Leander turned to his friend, "and what are you suggesting?"

"Hell, Leander, we all know Susannah Wilhite would not let her onliest boy, Leander, runoff to do battle without her being in the vanguard . . . Oh no!"

"Let's go find the camp and Mr. Zuber. Henry, we will see you again." Reams and Leander stepped out of the office and into the dog trot. They were just about to step onto the well trodden grounds when a small woman approached them. She was worn. The exhaustion could be seen in her face. She had the same hollow look that they had seen before in the eyes of so many other refugees. She showed no fear, but her sorrow was immense, consuming her very existence.

"Are you with the men that just arrived?"

Leander nodded. "I suspect so ma'am."

"Are you going to join General Houston's army?"

"That is our intention, yes ma'am."

"My husband was one of the men from Gonzales." Her voice cracked but you could see that she was not going to let her emotions stop her from saying what she wanted to say. "You must not let that army forget our men. They must remember the Alamo." She grabbed Leander's forearm and now held it with a grip that had to muster what remaining strength she had.

Leander looked down at the woman. Her eyes, once vacant, were filled with an intense anger. "Ma'am, I know we won't, and I do not think anyone will ever forget the brave men of the Alamo and the noble sacrifice that they made." She released her grip, her eyes filled with tears.

They rode slowly downhill still taking in the mixture of humanity that was being pushed by the invasion. As they approached the camp, Leander pointed towards a tree.

"I suspect that is the mother of our Mr. Zuber."

"Jesus, Leander, that is the homeliest camp follower I have ever seen."

"Oh and I guess you are now a connoisseur of camp followers?"

"No, well, I mean . . ."

"Your knowledge and expertise of the fairer sex makes you particularly suited to handle this little chore. I trust you will be successful and young Mr. Zuber will no longer be mortified by the maternal instincts of his mama."

By this time, the other members of the group had been filled in on the so-called mission. Each enjoyed the opportunity to return some of the kidding that Reams so often directed at them.

"Well, go find the boy." Leander spurred his horse on to put a little distance between himself, and more importantly, Zuber's mother.

*   *   *

They had noticed the buzzards in the distance. The birds were now circling, forming a moving column. Their instincts had brought them here. When the men crested the hill, the bottom of that rotating cylinder of ugly black birds was directly over a small homestead. The fear of Santa Anna had not been around long enough for anything to die of starvation. To the contrary, some of the livestock was down right fat, now that they had access to the family garden. When they got even with the house, Leander asked Reams and the Scotsman to take a look around. As they approached the door, the flies and the stench gave it away. Reams called to Leander.

"Old man, looks like we have another reason to join the fight."

The interior was barebones. Just another cabin of another farmer, but clean and neat. Everything was in order. Nothing was out of place. In the corner was a bed, the same rope bed you would find in every other homestead. The woman's face was tranquil, almost serene. Sadness etched the man's face. They were elderly. This was their last effort at life; another couple with a make or break chance they called Texas. They did not have it in them to run. The men wrapped their bodies in the bloodstained bed linens.

"Reams, find a spot to bury them; but, let all of the men help dig their graves. We shall not forget the Alamo, but we should not forget these folks either. Santa Anna killed these people. He surely did."

Leander left a note on the small table in the cabin. The same table the old folks sat around contemplating what options they had. The note was weighed down by the derringer that killed them.

"Leander, it is always darkest before the dawn," Reams shook his head.

"Yes, it is. These folks were old enough to know that. Sad, very sad."

* * *

If first impressions count for anything, Leander was pleased with the appearance of Houston's army. Now, there was not a single matching uniform in the bunch; but, none of his Rangers ever matched.

It did not seem to have much of an impact on their effectiveness. The camp was in an open, flat plain at Bernardo. It was not hidden in some woods. Houston's experiences with the Indians held him in good stead. The tents were uniformly placed. Some troops were being drilled. To his amazement, there actually was a latrine. At least superficially, it gave the correct appearance of an army camp.

Leander spotted Jared Groce just about the same time Jared spotted him. Groce had aged a good bit. He was as affable as ever, but rheumatism had curtailed the use of his arms. He could still move them, but he had no strength.

Jared scurried towards them.

"Leander, I knew you would come!"

"Well, Jared, that makes exactly one of us. A while back, I thought you were on the fence?"

"'I was, I was, but Leonard and others changed my mind. You know it is easy for us old farts to make big war talk. We ain't goin'."

"Can you direct us to General Houston?"

"I would be honored to make the introductions, just follow me."

Groce proceeded down the middle of the camp towards his blacksmith shop. Leander knew the plantation well. As always, it was in fine order. As they approached the building, he took notice of the only man in camp that looked like what Sam Houston should look like. He was a big man, thick with broad shoulders and a barrel chest. He wore a hunting shirt. His footwear was leggings and moccasins. Initially, you could not judge his height. He was bent over what was trying to become a cannon carriage. When Groce hollered for him, he stood up. He had to be well over 6 feet tall. His size was just his size. What impressed you was his head. Perfectly proportioned, it was broad across the cheekbones, with the most intelligent eyes in the camp. This was General Sam Houston alright.

Groce made the introductions. Houston never dropped the mallet that he had been using. He looked over each and every man, and their mounts.

"You fellas here to volunteer? Houston continued to scan the group.

"Sir, we have been a Ranger Company. That is what we know and probably what we would do best."

"Mr. Wilhite, I appreciate your honesty. Now let me be honest with you. I can't feed your horses. We can just barely feed ourselves. Cavalry is a luxury I just can't have."

Leander had anticipated the objection. "General, each man has his mount and two extra horses. We have brought our own forage. We can stay in the field for 30 to 40 days. By that time, we ought to be growing some spring grass. We will not be a burden Sir."

Groce could hardly wait to speak. "General, you'll go down a long piece of road before your find men of this character."

"Dammit Jared, I don't question their character. I question whether I can feed them."

Leander had noticed the frustration building in the men around the cannon carriage. "General, what are they working on?" Leander pointed to the huddle of cussing and swearing men.

"Oh, the good citizens of Cincinnati have given us two cannons. Unfortunately, we have not figured out the best way to mount them."

Leander turned in his saddle, "Blue, could you give these folks a hand."

Blue had never seen this many people in his life. Shy by nature, he was happy to be put to some chore that he knew something about.

"General, Blue can get your cannons mounted, just let him be."

"We call them the Twin Sisters, Mr. Wilhite. Have your men dismount next to the blacksmith shop. Let's go visit a moment."

Houston smiled and handed the mallet to Blue and headed towards his tent.

Houston took a seat on his cot, picked up a piece of wood and opened his pocket knife. Judging from the shavings on the ground, the good General was a consummate whittler. "So what does it look like to you, Mr. Wilhite?" The question was so out of context; Leander hardly knew what the General meant.

"Sir?"

"The state of our fine Republic. What does it look like to you?"

"An unholy mess, if you want to know the truth."

"Ha, I knew you were an honest man. Go on Mr. Wilhite."

"I hardly know who is left at home to defend. There are refugees on all of the roads headed east to the Sabine."

"Yes sir, and being led by Burnet and all the political windbags this country can muster. I'll say one thing for old Burnet; he can run a whole lot faster in this mud than I can. Doesn't stop him from issuing orders to me to stop and protect his rather broad backside."

"It does seem that the people want you to fight."

"No question Mr. Wilhite. No question. But at best, this so-called Army has one and maybe only one fight in them. I don't question their bravery and courage. Most of these men have never had a shot fired at them, and the Santanistas are more experienced than we are. They should not be underestimated. Hopefully, I will have a little more time to drill our companies so that we can fight with some degree of order." Houston continued his whittling.

"So you do intend to attack?"

Houston smiled, "attack or get attacked." He was actually a very good whittler. A long curled piece of wood dropped to the ground, much like the skin of an apple. "You will find that I seldom call councils of war. No point in them. So keep this conversation to yourself. This much I know. The generalissimo has divided his army. I suspect he has no respect for us or our abilities. Every step I make eastward just extends his supply lines that much further. There are countless possible battlefields between here and Louisiana. He is getting stretched pretty good while we are increasing our numbers."

"The flap of the tent opened quickly and entered Pamela Mann.

"Oh Sam, I didn't know you were with someone." She retrieved a bucket and left as quickly as she had entered. She was not a young woman, but not old either. Experienced would probably fit. It was apparent that she and Sam were well acquainted. Houston was bivouacking with his army, but he was not denying himself all of life's pleasures. He was placing the final touches on what now appeared to be a perfectly carved heart. He gave it a final once over and tossed it into a basket in the corner of the tent. The basket was filled with at least a couple of dozen similarly carved hearts..

"That's a lot of hearts, General."

"Yes, perhaps, I always want to have one handy so that I can tell a lady that I have given her my heart." Houston grinned and pointed his knife in the direction of the tent flap recently vacated by the widow Mann.

"Mr. Wilhite, I do want to correct an impression I have made. I do need your men and I need them on horseback. I just haven't been able to afford cavalry. We will fight our fights out in the open. Infantry had to be my focus. Although, we do have the Twin Sisters now. They will give Colonel James McNeill something to do."

The name shocked Leander. "Wasn't he at the Alamo?"

"The answer to that is yes and no. He was the commander that tried to fortify that old ruin. He assembled the cannon. Of course, Cos took all the good powder and left that Mexican crap behind. After the yahoos with the Matamoros fiasco rummaged through the balance, about all we had or could even hope for was for the cannons to fall on Santa Anna. McNeil left before the siege."

"Left?"

"Yes, I know, odd isn't it? Supposedly someone got sick at home. If he tries to leave before our fight, I assure you he will not make it home."

"Mr. Wilhite, did you know any of the defenders of the Alamo?"

"Yes sir, a few."

"Brave men, every one of them, but that battle did not have to be fought. I lost an old friend from Tennessee, David Crockett. Some say he came to Texas to restart a political career. I doubt it. Anti-Jackson men are not going to get far here politically. Probably came for a fresh start, just like the rest of us. Mr. Wilhite, one more thing. The Mexican cavalry is formidable. As we move east, the forest and trees will make them less an issue. Our long rifles will start to play a bigger part. That being said, you have got to protect our flanks. If that cavalry gets loose, things will turn from bad to worse real quick."

"I understand sir".

"I like your horses; we may have to talk about them later. You go and rejoin your men. We will be writing history before too long."

"Yes sir."

CHAPTER 17

Destiny San Jacinto

THE EXCITEMENT WAS PALPABLE. The drilling was over or at least for a while. Camp had been broken and the long line of Houston's army was trading the mud of Bernardo plantation for the thick ooze of rain soaked roads. Some men were thrilled with the prospect of having a chance to kill some Mexicans. Others were thrilled, that perhaps for a while, they would not have to hear how thrilled some men were at the prospect of killing Mexicans. All were in better spirits. At least they were on the move. The immediate destination would be the "which a way" tree.

Houston had asked Leander to ride with him in the lead. They shared an interest in horses, although Houston's preferred mount was frequently a mule. Admittedly, appearances now called for a horse. They had not gone but a couple of miles when a commotion started towards the rear and seemed to get louder as it approached the lead. The name "Houston" was being shouted, followed by a string of curse words, that were both colorful and unique. The voice was certainly female.

Leander and Houston both turned to see the form of the widow Pamela Mann galloping towards them. She and her horse were both breathing hard by the time she reached them.

"God damn you Sam Houston, you let me have my oxen right this minute or I will skin you alive."

She had pulled a large Bowie knife from her belt, and gave every indication that she was prepared to use it. Houston started to reply, but thought it best to hold his tongue. She was now quite the spectacle.

"I'll be damned if you take my oxen off to get blown up in some pissant war." She blew a dangling hair strand from her face.

She then waded through the mud to the team of oxen that were attempting to drag one of the Twin Sisters to whatever fame awaited this Army. With a single swipe of her knife, that impressed everyone with its sharpness, she severed the leather strap that tied them to the tongue of the cannon's carriage. Grabbing a switch, she and her oxen were last seen moving away from the Army of the Republic of Texas.

Houston watched for a moment and then started to dismount, when Leander spoke. "General, I guess giving her your heart did not mean you got to keep her oxen."

Houston smiled, "so it would seem, so it would seem."

"Look sir, I'll get one of the big horses. No need for you to get involved."

"Thank you, Leander."

The roads got no better. To the contrary, they seemed to get worse. What few wagons the Texians had, managed to find every hole, every sink and every bog that was in their path. Each time, Houston was off of his horse encouraging every man in the vicinity to lend a shoulder to the effort.

Those from the area knew that the Army was slowly, but

steadily, approaching the "which a way" tree. It was a large, knarly, old oak, with heavy crooked limbs that seem to point in the two directions of the road's fork. One way took you to Nacogdoches. It meant more drilling, more boredom. The other direction went to Harrisburg, a flat spot on the coast that was trying to become the Republic's capital city. This assumed that the current political leaders had stayed there and were not in full flight to somewhere else. To take this path was to place this Army, and this new Nation, on a road to its destiny. Houston would no longer be retreating.

Leander did not know what Houston would do. He knew he would not risk his army if he did not feel it was prepared to fight. He could feel his own nervous tension rise when the tree came into view. Even though he was mounted, the pace was agonizingly slow. Houston said nothing. Good God! This General certainly kept his own counsel. Leander almost wanted to blurt out the question that was on everyone's mind. Houston rode on.

Sam had heard all of the threats of mutiny. Big talk, in his opinion. So-called President Burnet had threatened him with every possible censure known to man. It was hard for a battle tested veteran like Houston to take a roly-poly apple dumpling like David Burnet very seriously. Plus, where was Burnet? He had sent Rusk to meet with Houston, which gave Burnet more time to run towards the East. Houston just rode on. Like him or not, this Army had but one leader and Houston was it.

It was hard to tell if General Houston had seen the tree. Leander sensed he had, but Houston just rode on. The Army kept moving. The steady cadence of the men was mixed with the clanging of metal. For a moment, it seemed that the entire Army inhaled and held its collective breath. His motion was subtle so subtle, Houston's right knee applied just enough pressure to move his horse slightly to the left. He gave no command. He shouted no order.

Houston and his mount simply blocked the road to the left. His following column of soldiers moved on to the road leading to Harrisburg. As if they all exhaled at the same time, a chorus of cheers erupted and continued until the Army of the Republic of Texas had passed its General. All were prepared to fight.

The forced march of the men had brought them to a boggy prairie on the north side of Buffalo Bayou opposite Harrisburg. All day long they had seen a black cloud of smoke rising from the ashes of what would have been Harrisburg. They knew who burnt it. The Army made preparations to cross the bayou. They would then be on the same side as Santa Anna.

Houston ordered the baggage, and all extra equipment left at what had been Harrisburg, to be guarded by a small group of men, mostly the sick or infirmed.

Leander was preparing to mount up, when a commotion started near the baggage area. Glancing quickly in that direction, he caught sight of Reams locked in some kind of discussion with the young William Zuber. Leander sighed. This was not the time or place for discussion. He headed in that direction, to see what was the problem.

In an adolescent voice a good octave higher than the voice of the average Texian, he heard Zuber shout, "I did not walk halfway across Texas to guard some old bags. I am a soldier and I mean to fight by God."

Reams was growing more frustrated as time went on. "Private Zuber, you are not equipped to fight. Your rifle is not in working order."

Zuber was beet red. Kicking the dirt, and every rock and stick within his reach, his voice became even louder and higher. "Not equipped, that's your fault because of that crappy rifle you got me." Leander interrupted, "Reams, May I have a word with you?"

Reams and Leander turned their backs to young Zuber and moved out of earshot.

"Leander, I cannot let that boy go into the fray, I promised his mom. The only way I could keep him out was to give him a busted musket. Hell, he didn't know any better. He's been cleaning and oiling it like it's the only armament we have."

"So you sold him a piece of crap rifle?"

"Leander, I wouldn't . . . . . . Sure, I did. I made a promise."

"We don't have the time to negotiate with a 15-year-old boy. Tell him that he's a soldier and that he will do what General Houston says. You might remind him that we only know where Santa Anna is. At least two other and maybe more, Mexican armies are out in these weeds somewhere. If they show up and get in our rear, it will get plenty hot for our Mr. Zuber. Tell him and then get up here with the rest of the Company."

The Army moved out entertained by the high nasal twang of Zuber's cussing and swearing.

Texas had no natural lakes. It had rivers, streams, bayous and gullies; but, pretty much it was just plain dirt. Santa Anna had traveled across miles and miles of Mexican and Texas desert. He had fought a battle at Bexar, one of the driest and dustiest towns ever created. Now, he found himself camped on a nondescript piece of land surrounded by water on three sides. Given his own attitude towards water, the selection of this place was odd at best. To his officer corps, it was a total folly, but they had long ago given up trying to influence the Napoleon of the West.

A grove of scrub oaks ran along the sloping banks of Buffalo Bayou. Most were small, low trees. They were large enough to hide a horse, and low enough to provide some shade to a foot sore Army. Both armies now had their backs to water.

The Ranger Company from Monaville had alerted Houston that

General Cos was nearby with about 400 additional Mexican soldiers. No doubt he would join Santa Anna soon. They had returned from their latest reconnaissance when Leander got word that Houston wanted to see him. Leander hastened to the General's tent. He hailed the General who welcomed him. This time Houston was examining a map.

"Leander, do you remember me saying that I never held councils of war?"

"Yes sir, I do recall that." Leander was puzzled at the question, but knew it would lead to something more.

"Well, I had one."

"You did."

"Yes, I did. Some of those with a political bent felt that I should. You know, seek out the opinions of my fellow officers so that they might feel that they are a part of the plan. I guess perhaps they will fight harder for Texas. I suspect that when they come face-to-face with some raging Mexican, Texas will be the last thing on their mind. In the heat of battle, you sometimes forget things. Anyway, I have now concluded that if you lined up the entire officer corps, head to toe, they couldn't reach a conclusion. Look here Leander."

Houston turned the map slightly in Leander's direction.

"Our lines run along this bayou. Hopefully, our men are using the time to get a little rest. Santa Anna's camp is here."

"It certainly is an odd place for a man who's afraid of water."

Houston turned quickly. "What? I have never heard this"

"Sir, I cannot vouch for it; but, when my father and I first came to Texas he met a Mexican colonel. I cannot remember his name. The colonel was in Nacogdoches to see how this immigration thing was turning out. I gather he was familiar with Santa Anna. They were both about the same age. He had a long talk with my father.

I probably would have forgotten it, but for the fact that the name Santa Anna sticks with you. The colonel said that Santa Anna was deathly afraid of water. Every time he had to cross a river, he would take some opium and then charge like hell to get to the other side."

"Leander, if that is true, our fair game has a water problem on three sides, as you can see." Houston drug his finger across the map outlining the water boundaries.

"You see this bridge. That bridge needs to catch fire. If we burn it, then we are all here for the duration. We will live or die on this spot. I want you to find Deaf Smith. He knows this very bridge. Take some of your men and burn it. I mean burn it down. Then, come wake me up."

"Sir, wake you up?"

"Why yes, Leander. I'm going to take a nap. Oh, I do have a favor. You know that dappled gray stallion of yours?"

"Saracen."

"Is that his name?"

"Yes sir, before you ask, let me say it would be my honor, and his as well, if you would use him as your mount."

"Thank you, if the Mexicans see that horse, they will know that we are not some ragtag outfit."

"I will find Deaf Smith." Houston had already moved to his cot.

By mid afternoon, the bridge was gone. It was nothing more than smoking timbers. Leander returned to Houston's tent, leading his own horse and Saracen as well. The General could not have been more delighted. He sat down on his cot, pulled off his moccasins and put on his riding boots. They were shined to perfection. The spurs caught enough light in the tent to get your attention. In the Texas sun light, they would be most impressive.

Houston stepped outside his tent, stretched and turned to his aide. Every soldier in view of his tent wondered if Houston was ever going to wake up. His aide awaited his orders. "I suspect the dew is gone off of the grass."

The aide, failing to catch the joke, nodded vigorously, "Oh yes sir, been gone for some time."

Houston smiled. "It is still siesta time for those boys across the way. Why don't we wake them up?"

By now the aide caught on. Houston picked up his saddle and tack. "Tell the officers to form up their men, quietly. I will shoot the first man who makes a noise. Spread the word."

The aide left in a sprint.

"Leander, I have a good feeling about this; but, just in case some of our boys start to doubt themselves, I want you prepared to come to the center quickly; run over anyone who turns. We cannot let them turn their backs on the enemy. You form up with the cavalry. If we surprise them, see if you can run their remuda through their ranks. It will add to the confusion. And, thanks again for the use of Saracen."

Houston took the lead rope from Leander and commenced to saddle the gray stallion. He was an impressive piece of horse flesh. As was his custom, the General lifted every hoof to check the shoes. When he got around to the right front hoof, he noticed a small round stone stuck between the frog and the edge of the shoe. It was smooth, flat, and white in color. He pulled out his knife and popped it loose. It dropped onto the dark gray gumbo that made up the soil of the Texas Gulf Coast. The contrast of its whiteness in the dark soil struck him as curious. Houston slipped the small stone into his pocket.

Houston rose into the saddle. It was only then that he could feel how powerful this horse really was. He rode directly in front of the long thin line of 900 Texians. They were dirty, mud splattered;

wearing the same clothes they had on when they left home weeks ago. There was not a soldier there who even knew if he still had a home. The whereabouts of his family was any ones guess. Kin and neighbors had been massacred by the very men that they were about to meet. When smoke rose from the burnt bridge, they had figured it out. This was a fight to the death, and it wasn't going to be their death. Not today.

"Trail arms forward." Houston had given the order. They moved forward in complete silence. The grass was knee-high. It removed some of the mud that had caked their boots and moccasins. Before them was a slight rise. The left flank had quickly moved through the small oaks that lined the bayou and was slightly ahead of the Texian center. They opened fire on General Cos' newly encamped troops, who tried to return fire, but soon ran.

The center of the line reached the apex of the slope to the sound of the opening fire and the shouts of "Remember the Alamo, Remember Goliad."

Houston ordered "To the charge, to the charge." The Twin Sisters, now loaded with cut up horse shoes, fired into the Mexican breast works. On the right flank, the Texian cavalry charged and quickly reached the Mexican line. Leander and his men made for the remuda, cutting every tie rope they could reach. The Mexican horses now stampeded through the Mexican camp from the rear, giving the impression that the Texians were attacking from two directions. By now, panic had set in. The Texians had breached the Mexican breast works.

What few Mexican cavalry there were tried to make it to the now burnt bridge. The killing became savage. Most Mexicans were now being clubbed to death. "Me no Alamo! Me no LaBahia!" brought no mercy. Those entreaties soon became shouts of "solades God damnes!" Most Texans fired once and made no effort to reload. It was quicker and easier to use their rifles as clubs. The air became foul with the smell of gunpowder, and the stench of urine and feces from the bowels of dead Mexicans.

Eighteen minutes later, the battle was over. The killing continued. What Mexicans were left were corralled behind a makeshift rail and rope stockade. Reams and Leander rode the battlefield at sundown. Looking for the wounded and stragglers, they heard the continuous report of a single soldier. As they neared the marsh, they saw one man and a Negro. The man was firing at Mexicans still trying to flee their death through the water. He would fire and hand the rifle to the Negro who reloaded it. Reams and Leander started to approach the soldier. Then Leander stopped.

"You know who that is don't you, Reams?" Reams shook his head. "Not really."

"That's one of the Holland brothers from Alta Mira. I think his name is Frances. He and his two brothers went to the Alamo. One brother got sick. He brought him home. The other brother, Tapley, died at the Alamo. We best leave him be."

"Leander, he hasn't got enough bullets to fill the hole that has been left in his heart."

CHAPTER 18

Taking Young Zuber Home

REAMS WAS ABSOLUTELY IN HIS ELEMENT. In total, the Texian army had gathered up several hundred horses and mules, over 600 muskets, approximately 300 sabers, a couple of hundred pistols, and an assortment of uniforms. But Reams thought it best to start the auction with the champagne. It seemed Santa Anna liked the stuff, and there were several cases to be sold. It would be just the tonic to get the sale off to a good start.

The defeated General had also traveled with a large wooden chest filled with gold. Houston ordered its contents, estimated to be around $12,000, distributed among the men, reserving some of it for the sailors in the Texas Navy. Each soldier received about $11.

The auction had to be interrupted once for the safety of all concerned. The Texians had commenced to use the 80 barrels of captured black powder as seats. None seem to be willing to curtail their smoking, so Reams ordered the barrels removed to another locale far away from the crowd. Once some distance was placed between the black powder and the lit cigars and pipes, the sale resumed with a fury.

Houston had ordered his cot removed from his tent. He now rested under a large tree at the edge of the bayou. His shattered ankle pained him. It was imperative that he get to some medical facility that was a little more sophisticated than the sawbones that worked their trade in Texas.

The Yellowstone, a McKinney and Williams' ship, had docked nearby. The plan was to get Houston to New Orleans; however, David Burnet, the so-called president, now returned from his escape to Galveston Island, was making every effort to reestablish himself as someone of import. The Rangers of Monaville had their fill of David Burnet and the other now surfacing politicos. The next morning they were heading home.

It was hard to sleep in camp. More out of tune fiddles than were really called for, got unpacked when the baggage was brought up. As soldiers, they may have been amateurs, but when it came to celebrating, the Army contained true professionals. Assembled and mounted, Leander and his Company made their way to Houston's cot. They all wanted to say their goodbyes to the General. His aide assisted Houston to his feet, hobbled by the bandage on his ankle.

Leander spoke first, "General, we all wanted to pay our respects before we head home. I assume you will be leaving soon."

"Not if Burnet has his way. He doesn't want to release the Yellowstone to me." Houston was clearly peeved.

"What? Sir, if you don't get that ankle treated and treated soon you could lose a leg, or worse!"

"I suspect you're right, but he's not . . ."

"No buts, sir. Men follow me." Leander rode directly to Burnet's tent, a short distance away and called for him. A nicely suited clerk exited the tent saying, "I'm sorry, the president is busy and cannot be bothered right now."

Leander turned to Reams and Avery and nodded. They split,

each going around a different side of the tent cutting the ropes that held it erect. As the walls collapsed, outburst Burnet running directly into the chest of Leander's horse.

"What is the meaning of this? You have no right . . ."

Leander drew his saber. The metallic scratch of its blade moving against its scabbard got Burnet's attention. The short, stocky man looked up at Leander, waiting to hear what he wanted, knowing full well he would have to be prepared to comply.

"Sir, I understand you will not release the Yellowstone so that General Houston can get the medical attention he needs and certainly deserves."

"Well, you see . . ."

"No! Mr. Burnett, you see. Sam Houston has a ticket to where ever he wants, whenever he wants. His ticket is called San Jacinto. Avery go tell the captain to make ready to leave; there is no hold on his ship. As for you Mr. Burnet, if General Houston's recovery is not what it should be, if it has been compromised by your delay, we will find you if we have to use dogs."

Leander whirled his horse around, its tail hitting Burnet in the face. The Rangers returned to Houston's camp.

"Better pack up General, you are free to go."

"Leander, I owe you a horse and a whole lot more."

"You owe me nothing. It has been our honor, General."

"It would be my honor if you would call me Sam."

"Then, Sam it will be. We had better gather up our ward, Pvt. William Zuber."

"That's the chunk of a boy that made the ruckus at Harrisburg?"

"Yes sir. That would be the one. We will return him to his mother."

"No worse for wear, and $11 richer. I suspect he will be well received. Good luck to all of you."

Houston turned, only to be handed his hat and coat by his aide. "We have a boat to catch, General."

Zuber was easily found. Blue picked a horse for him out of the extras. He was soon saddled and riding in the middle of the men as comfortable as he could be. He still had the busted musket.

If young Zuber had any talent, and the issue had some doubt, he could at least find the most direct route home. After leaving Harrisburg, or what were the burnt remnants of it, the group almost immediately ran into a steady stream of returning refugees. Houston had sent messengers towards the Sabine River shortly after the battle. There were a few more men with travelers this time. Veterans had made a beeline to the East to try and catch up with family and friends. All were still dirty and unwashed. Most were very gaunt; but, their eyes were no longer hollow and sad. To the contrary, hope had returned. No one had any idea what this new Republic of Texas would bring, but it was theirs, and that was all that was material.

With Zuber leading the way, the men quickly put the heavy gumbo of the Texas Gulf Coast behind them. Each step brought them to a slightly higher elevation, and amongst a good many more pine trees. They were traveling no trail. They were crossing open country at the direction of Pvt. William Zuber, now retired. For some time, they had been traveling within spitting distance of Lake Creek. The excessive winter rains had filled its banks. While it was full, the water was not moving rapidly. Zuber hunted and pecked and finally found the gradual crossing that he had been looking for. The horses could easily swim it. Blue had the wagons hitched to a team of four; however, the feed that they once carried was now gone, eaten long ago. The wagons would float readily.

Towards late afternoon, young Zuber announced that they would soon be approaching his family's homestead. This woke everyone from their slumber. Aching sore muscles were begging for a change of sorts.

Leander turned to Zuber, "you did not tell us you lived with Indians?"

"Oh, sir we don't, not any longer. The two mud houses were built by the Kickapoo. After we settled here, they would come back every once in a while. Don't see them much anymore. We live in the cabin now."

They heard her holler. The whole valley probably did as well.

"Son, you better cover some ground before she runs all the way."

Zuber spurred his horse and was soon clutched in his mother's arms, pressed against her bosom, which was ample to say the least.

Reams trotted over to get the credit that he deserved for returning her precious son to her fit and unharmed. It being close to sundown, all the Rangers were invited to camp near the house. Mrs. Zuber was quick to share whatever foodstuffs they had.

The horses were hobbled and turned out to the creek bottom. They seemed as anxious to shed their riders, as the riders were to dismount. After things settle down, Leander and Reams noticed an older man, probably in his 50s, half reclining on a pallet on the porch. They had seen no other man and assumed this was Abraham Zuber, William's father.

"Reams, we probably should introduce ourselves don't you think?"

Reams and Leander got up from the shady spot they had claimed and headed towards the porch.

"Mr. Zuber, I assume?" Leander extended his hand.

"No, no, I'm just a friend of Zuber's. I am Louis Rose." His speech was slowed by the cracks of his weathered lips.

Rose extended his hand, but did so with much pain. His homespun shirt hung loose. His pants were cut off at the knees. Some kind of grease covered his entire body. His calves were cut and swollen. They no longer had any shape, but were painfully round down to his ankles. His ankles no longer resembled ankles at all. His feet were purple and swollen just like his calves.

"Sir, what has caused you all this hurt?" Reams could hardly contain his curiosity.

"Some of this is mostly just cuts, but the real damage was done from the cactus needles. Got into miles and miles of them. I didn't think I would make it."

"Where were you coming from?" Reams was now studying Rose's anatomy a lot closer.

"The Alamo." Rose said it as casually as you would have said you were coming home from Sunday school.

"The Alamo!" Both Leander and Reams were almost blown off the porch. Reams had a hatful of questions.

"We were told that the entire garrison was put to the sword."

"Would not surprise me, although I feel certain some others tried to escape. Those Mexicans played that song, the one that means they would kill us all. Lots of brave men there. But a fool's errand if there ever was one." Rose shifted his weight to his side with some pain and continued.

"I heard you pretty much wiped out the Santanistas at San Jacinto?"

"We did our best, but when did you go to the Alamo?"

"I didn't really plan to go to the Alamo. I went to Bexar to visit my friend, Jim Bowie. I had known him forever. Well, one thing led to another and up shows Santa Anna. No one was expecting him. Hell, we did not even have any scouts out. It was winter. Most of the men were at a fandango, and Santa Anna and his entire army gets spotted just outside of town. Those of us that were sober enough made it to the fort, if you want to call it that. I fought with

Napoleon, and I don't mean this so-called Napoleon of the West. I never got hemmed up in a fort. No chance to maneuver. Anyway, it was an ungodly mess. Lots of cannon, but few cannonballs of the right size, and even less powder. If you really wanted to hold it, you would have needed five times the men. Travis showed up in a pretty uniform, but he's cavalry. What is cavalry going to do in a fort? He's a lawyer, you know."

"Yes, we knew Travis." Reams shot Leander a glance that said keep quiet and let the man talk.

"He's writing letters, begging for help. Bonham went out a couple of times and returned, the poor bastard. Well, we had been holed up and fighting for about 12 maybe 13 days. Ain't any help coming, we all figured that out. Travis had no military mind. Bowie was sick. So we were making plans on how to best handle the attack. We saw them building the ladders. Late one evening, Travis called us all together. The cannonade had stopped. It had been continuous. We knew it was the quiet before the storm. Travis said he was going to stay and defend the place. He asked for a vote. So, he drew a line in the dirt, just like we voted back in Louisiana. He moved to one side and asked for those who wanted to stay to line up on that side of the line. Those that wanted to try and escape were to line up on the other side. Tapley Holland bounced across the line, then, everyone lined up with Travis. Bowie had his cot carried across. I did not even need to think about it. Hell, didn't have anything else on my mind for almost two weeks. I bid them farewell and stepped over the wall. Just didn't feel like dying yet, certainly not in a no count church."

Leander's curiosity got to him. "Mr. Rose, Why San Antonio? I mean all the Texians lived east of the Alamo. It seemed a waste of time for the Mexicans."

"That's easy, pride. Santa Anna did not like it when old Ben

Milam booted General Cos out of the Alamo. They're related someway, Cos and Santa Anna."

"What are your plans, sir?"

"As soon as I can, I hope to go back in Nacogdoches. I have imposed on these good folks way too long." Rose rubbed his legs with more grease.

"Do you think you're the only survivor?"

"No. Given some of the conversations we all had, I suspect others may have left later that night. I took nothing and chose to ske-daddle while I could. I do not regret my decision. Those that stayed were brave men, but I'm proud that I fought as well as any of them for 13 days. Just not my time to die. You feel those things you know."

"Yes sir, I guess you do."

CHAPTER 19

Suspense, Hurt and Disappointment

LEANDER AND THE RETURNING RANGERS SOON FELL BACK INTO THE USUAL ROUTINES AND PATTERNS. Monaville still remained the sleepy town along the Brazos River that it had come to be. In large measure, those returning from the Runaway Scrape found most things in order. The various animals were reassembled onto the proper farms and ranches. Life got back to normal quickly. For most Texians, formerly citizens of Mexico, now citizens of the Republic, the difference lacked any real distinction. Leander's crops were planted. Reams' father had sent Big Charlie over to supervise the planting. Momma Mae was generally knowledgeable on the when and where of cotton production. However, Big Charlie just had a gift. If he planted it, it would grow. Leander appreciated the help. It wasn't totally out of charity. After years of being shorted downriver, Reams and his father had built a cotton press and cotton gin. Good crops made good money.

Leander's day started with Momma Mae's breakfast, eggs, ham, grits, biscuits and honey. It made you want to wake up in the morning. Usually, she would say good morning. If she were singing, the greeting waited until the song was over. No use interrupting a good song for just a brief salutation. It was a nice, smooth, easy start to the day, generally. If something had been eating on her, things were different.

"Jesus, could this have waited until I, at least, had my breakfast?"

"No Sur, I can't, been eat'nat me for da longest."

Momma Mae had hit him right between the eyes, a direct shot. He never saw it coming, or if he did, he thought it was a good deal further off than it was.

"If'n you goin' to raise dat boy in dis house, he needs to meet his own kind. Can't be know'n just da chillruns in da quarter."

With one swift kick to his gut, Momma Mae had put the entire issue of Luther's upbringing, every aspect of it, right in the front and center of today, not tomorrow, not three months from now. The matter was the focus of today.

"That boy ain't eber been off Catalpa. What he do when da chillruns go to da fields?" She pointed in the direction of the quarters with her favorite wooden spoon.

Leander knew he was caught between a rock and his cook. He was not unmindful of the issues she raised. Luther would soon be seven. He had been teaching him everything that he could from every book Reams brought by. Learning was not difficult for Luther. Explain it to him once and he had it. His introduction to the world had little to do with childhood friendships and a great deal more to do with who his mother was. Better said, what his mother was. Other than some slight wave to his hair, Luther took completely after his dad. But that wouldn't matter to some. Leander promised Momma Mae he would do some serious thinking.

"I's goin' to bring it up ebery breakfast, ebery dinner."

Leander knew she would.

The days were growing longer, and hotter. Luther accompanied his father everywhere. He could ride with the best of them. The saddle bred gelding and he were partners. Each seemed truly delighted to see the other. Leander had always talked to Luther as if he were an adult. He knew he wasn't, but Leander did not know how to talk any other way. His parents died so early, he felt he had been an adult all his life.

He tried not to smother his son. If he showed any interest in something, he would provide the time for him to explore whatever aroused his curiosity. Blue's blacksmith shop seemed to intrigue him, but, it could have just been Blue. He was fond of Luther. The boy could feel it.

Leander had suffered through about a week and a half's worth of Momma Mae's inquiries. He was almost desperate, but, he wanted to bounce a few things off of Reams. The problem was Reams wasn't around. He was able to buy a little time. The Monaville School was not to reconvene until fall. Momma Mae was dubious when told that the children actually had the summer months off, a concept very foreign to her.

As the cotton grew, it was time to visit Oak Ridge and make some preliminary plans concerning getting it ginned, pressed and bailed. The Yellowstone, the same vessel General Houston had needed, still moved most of the cotton from this area down to the Gulf. It would be prudent to at least confirm its availability as well.

Leander left Luther at home. He wanted to be able to talk freely. On his way, he ran into Big Charlie who directed him to the gin. He had just left Reams there. Leander had not seen his friend in sometime. He expected a warm welcome. He got something a good bit less. When he rode up to the gin, Reams and his father were conversing about something. They saw Leander, but they did not waive. Really, they showed all the emotion of a wooden Indian. Leander thought it odd, but rode to the building and dismounted.

"Howdy, Mr. Whitworth." The old man nodded but said nothing. "Reams, you have been making yourself scarce of late. Haven't seen you in ages." There was still no response from either gentleman. "Luther was asking about you the other day."

"Oh well, I've been busy, I guess."

Leander finished tying his horse and moved to the shade of the building. He felt an awkwardness that he had never felt before. It was almost palpable, but he had no clue what might have provoked it.

"Have I interrupted something? Is this a bad time? Maybe I should call another time?" The old man looked down at his feet, then said, "Mind if I sit down. I am a little tired." Mr. Whitworth move towards a box that would function as his seat.

Reams, still unusually quiet for Reams, cleared his throat. "I guess you probably don't know, but I've been doing some courting, serious courting." Leander said nothing. He was trying to remember what females Reams had recently talked about, or had ever talk about that weren't prostitutes. If he planned on marrying one of his favorite fallen Angels, that would explain the sullen look on his father's face. He had better let this unfold at its own pace.

Reams seemed at a loss for words, so Leander primed the well with, "I see." That appeared to remind him that there was more to be told.

"Her name is Rachel . . . . Well, hell, you've probably met her. Rachel Greene, you know her family runs the Inn we stopped at years ago. Sweet lady, a widow woman. Leander remembered the discussion in the stable all too vividly, and with his entire soul prayed that sweet Rachel never discussed it with Reams.

"Yelp," Reams continued, "she converted me!"

"Converted you to what?" Leander, not one gifted in the area of knowledge of females, was having difficulty connecting courting and converting.

"Going to be a Baptist." Reams announced with all the pride of a new owner of orphaned cats.

"Ha, well I guess there are worse things to be converted to. So when is the date?"

"Three weeks from this past Saturday." Reams voice was a good bit softer than usual.

"Three weeks, you don't give the best man much time to get a new suit of clothes." Leander was about to slap Reams on the back.

There was no response. Stillness reigned supreme. Time slowed to a crawl. Reams made no eye contact. Out of the corner of his eye, Leander saw Mr. Whitworth shake his head slightly. Leander's throat got very tight. He wasn't used to making misstatements. Obviously, he had said something that was terribly wrong in every sense.

"Look Reams, I am very sorry. I just assumed, I mean it was presumptuous of me. I never knew much of anything about weddings, how they work. Just tell me the place and Luther and I will be there." The silence got worse, if that was possible. Leander glanced from Reams to his dad and back to Reams.

"Well, what is it Reams?"

"I don't know where to start. You know women are funny. They aren't like you and me. They have some . . ."

"Just what is it? Spit it out Reams."

"Rachel's first husband ran a goodly number of slaves over on the Trinity. You know how people talk." A slow fire was building in Leander, but complete disbelief was holding it back.

"He seemed to visit the quarters every so often. Rachel has heard about Luther." Whatever control disbelief had over Leander was now gone. A rage was building within him at the mention of his son's name.

"She doesn't want to repeat the embarrassment . . ."

"Embarrassed of what, Reams? Embarrassed of what?" Leander was now in front of his childhood friend speaking in a voice that he did not even know he had. "Embarrassed that the only woman I ever loved, I owned, and could not marry. Embarrassed that I have raised one of the best boys you can find anywhere. I don't understand it, Reams. I don't know what she is embarrassed about. What about you? What are you embarrassed about? Don't want to admit how much time you have spent with him. Would not want him at your wedding! How embarrassing would that be?"

Reams, as large and rotund as he was, seemed to shrink in size. His eyes had no life, no fire, and no courage. They were weak and he knew he was no match for Leander.

"You go have your wedding. We will not attend. We would be an embarrassment. Goodbye gentlemen." Leander turned on his boot heel, tossed the reins over his horse's neck and left in a gallop.

Mr. Whitworth raised his head to see the shell shocked face of his son. For the first time in his life he was disgusted with him. It is not easy, late in life, to realize that your child has a character flaw, and that it is too late for you to correct it.

"Son, I suspect that you have just made the biggest mistake of your life." He rose and walked to his house.

Leander could not share the event with anyone. He had no closer friend than Reams. So he rode, and rode, and rode some more. Each day, he stayed in the saddle longer and longer. The excuse was that he needed to see this part, or that thing. Catalpa had been enlarged again with the 640 acres he got for fighting at San Jacinto. But that was all a fabrication. It was just an excuse. The days Luther did not accompany him, he stayed out even longer, but he never left Catalpa. He seldom spoke. He did not want to visit with anyone except Luther. He rolled things over in his head until he was exhausted. Catalpa was taking on the atmosphere of a monastery.

Then at breakfast, he told Luther to change into one of his dress shirts. He had them, but had never worn them. They never went anywhere. Today he would need to wear a dress shirt.

"Son, we're going to try out that schoolhouse in Monaville."

"We are! You and me?" Luther seemed keen on the idea.

"Yes you, no, not me. I am too old."

Momma Mae smiled but said nothing. On the ride into town, Luther asked one question after another. Leander was not sure how things were going to go. Personally he had never attended school. Riding passed the schoolhouse was as close as he had ever gotten to one.

There were children of all ages and sorts playing around in the schoolyard. The older ones seem to be more engaged in some form of serious flirtation. The door was open and a few students were inside. Luther had never seen so many children. They studied him real hard. He studied them back. Once up the stairs, there was no turning back, although even Leander now had his doubts.

In the back of the room, at a small desk was a large woman named Isabel Henderson, a femme sol if there ever was one. She stood. Leander told Luther to take a seat, which he did closest to the children that were inside. Miss Henderson was everything you expected a school marm to be. She carried herself well; maybe too well. Queens should have had her bearing. She protruded up front as far as she did in the rear. In profile she would have made a perfect letter "S". Her clothes were clean, her collar high and starched.

"May I help you" the voice wasn't as bad as a nail file on a blackboard, but Leander wasn't interested in hearing it forever.

"I am Leander Wilhite and this is my son, Luther. I would like to enroll him, if that is what you do?"

"She shifted on her feet, cleared her throat, and then said, "Wilhite of the Catalpa plantation?" To Leander, it seemed an odd question.

"Yes ma'am that is our home."

Miss Henderson studied Luther. "I suppose I will have to clear your son's enrollment with the school board."

Leander smelled a problem. "And why would that be?"

She shifted again. "You can see we have a limited amount of space. Plus, the current students have been here before and are at certain levels in their studies. How old is he?

"'bout seven. What levels are seven year olds at? I know nothing of these things."

"Most are starting to read, and count . . ."

"Oh, Luther can read probably as well as I do and he can count as high as you would want to go. Do you think he would be behind?"

"Behind, no not if he can do that. Still and all, the board would want to pass on this I am sure." Leander was getting tense. He did not want to make a scene, but judging from some of the inbred, knot heads on the playground, he was pretty sure that Luther would not be wearing a dunce cap.

"And just why would the board want to pass on my son's admission to the only school in the community?"

Even Ms. Henderson could see the reddening around Leander's collar.

"Well, I suspect . . ." Which, Leander interrupted. "Just who is on the board?" She named the local Baptist preacher, and about four women that he did not know, but may have heard of. "I suspect there may be some less than noble reason for your hesitancy. Let me explain my position. I have answered the call of this community each and every time it has been in need. I have spent more time ranging than anyone and have killed more Comanches than I personally can count. I funded the Company that fought with Houston at San Jacinto. When I came in, I noticed that over half of the horses outside were bred, born and trained at Catalpa. If my livestock is good enough for this town, then my son is good enough to attend school here. You visit with your board. If they have a problem, tell them to be at my house this evening. In the meantime, I trust you will make Luther feel right at home."

Leander turned and said, "Luther, I'll see you this evening."

Once again Leander left in a quiet rage.

* * *

Avery could barely stay in the saddle. He was so covered in dust, when he dismounted plumes of dirt were released with every step. He waved slightly to Leander, but headed to the water trough. Dropping his hat to his side, he totally immersed his head. Still blistered and sunburned, he was now a good bit lighter in color than his hands still caked with sweat and dirt.

He slowly turned and walked to the stable. Blue and Leander had been repairing a wagon wheel. It was not a difficult chore, but it went quicker with four hands instead of two.

"Leander, you can't abandon us, you just can't." Avery's eyes were so bloodshot it hurt to look at them.

"How did it go?" Leander kind of wanted to know and yet he kind of didn't.

"It was a mess from the very start. Reams took the lead. He can organize things, but he cannot track. Hell, no one can track like you. We finally found their trail. One helluva massacre. They killed all of the men and women. They were just after the young'uns. That made it all the more desperate. There was no messing around with this group of Comanches. They headed due West like a house afire. Maybe you could've kept up with them. We did not plan our day's right. Ran out of water. Found the body of one little girl, neck broken. She probably could not keep up; the horses started going lame. We had posted men away from the camp, just like you always did. Woke up one morning and found two of them dead. Their throats were slashed. Pretty demoralizing. Hell, I haven't even been home. The others went to tell the widows. Leander, we never lost a man like that. Those Comanches, they wanted to tell us something. If you don't lead us, I don't see these men going back out again."

"Avery, I have done my share for this community. I don't plan on doing any more."

Avery shook his head, "Leander, we all feel bad about the falling out you and Reams had. It's sad. You have been friends forever. You can't stay holed up at Catalpa."

"Don't you think its best? I seem to make a lot of folks uncomfortable when I'm around. It does force me to do some things differently, but, it looks like that may be to my advantage." "Leander, they say you're not selling horses anymore. You have the best ones around. Most every family in these parts has bought from you."

"I'm still selling livestock, horses, mules and cattle. I am just not selling them locally. They seem to bring a good deal more elsewhere."

"Leander, there isn't a man in the company that doesn't want you back. They will follow you to the gates of hell. I know what you're going through, but we're all married men. Women just get things in their bonnets. We have to adjust, you know, to deal with them."

"Avery, I keep hearing about women this, and women that. It amazes me that any of you have fathered any children. It appears that when you got married, you left your gonads at the door."

"It's nothing against you or Luther. I truly don't believe it's personal; it's just principle with them."

"Avery, I can't see how anyone could have a problem with Luther. Even Miss Henderson admits he is as bright as anyone in the school. He shows a whole lot more manners than some. Do you have any idea what he's doing right now?"

"No."

"Every evening, after his chores, he teaches his lessons to the children in my quarters."

"You let him do that!"

"Hell yes. I would much rather be surrounded by smart folks than dumb ones. Since the wonderful folks of Monaville don't seem to be very accepting of me, I might as well raise the caliber of the Catalpa community."

"You do know some would disagree?"

"Avery, do you really expect me to care?"

"This thing with Reams has really hardened your heart. You know there are others who feel differently. We really need you."

"Need and want are two different things. You have a son about Luther's age, maybe a touch older. Does he get invited to the homes of other children?"

"Oh yes, it is pretty much a regular occurrence. Can't keep him home long enough to do his chores."

"Does he get invited to birthday parties?"

"Sure."

"Has he ever had a birthday party?"

The Scotsman got quiet. He knew he had walked right into the crosshairs. He was ashamed that his conduct was no better than anyone else's; yet, here he stood asking for help.

Leander watched his reaction. "I see you got my point."

"Yes sir, I did."

CHAPTER 20

Houston at Houston

THE TOWN HAD REACHED THAT CLUMSY, AWKWARD, ADOLESCENT STAGE OF DEVELOPMENT. It was still generally referred to as Houston town, but the more intelligent folks were doing everything to shorten the name to Houston. Of course, Sam himself preferred the shorter version. The Allen brothers, two imaginative New Yorkers, were doing everything possible to promote their new development, including adding cool, rolling mountains in the background of their sales brochures. Texas had mountains somewhere, but they were hundreds of miles distant from the current capital of the Republic of Texas.

By the end of 1837, Houston had a population of 1200 people. The male sex was well represented; but, females were in short supply. The citizenry enjoyed one theatre, 30 saloons, 50 gambling halls, and over 100 grog shops. There were no houses of worship, absolutely none. Rumor had it that the Episcopalians and the Catholics were about to take a stab at introducing some level of spirituality to the town. The thought did not seem to excite anyone.

1838 was the last year Sam Houston could be president. The Republic's Constitution prohibited him from succeeding himself. Mirabeau Lamar had been elected to the high office. David Burnet, the "pious politician" was to be his vice president. Houston detested both men. Still, the government, young as it was, made plans to continue under new, and certainly, different leadership. More than likely, the capital would be relocated, a suggestion that the hero of San Jacinto considered to be a personal affront.

Leander had been selling a fair number of his horses through brokers in Houston. Customarily, he had taken them to the town by himself. However, this time, he thought Luther might enjoy the trip. Now eight years old, he was a tall boy for his age, and would be a great deal of help if he were to accompany his dad. It had never failed that if he had orders for four horses, he could have sold six. Luther would give him the opportunity to take a few extras.

They arrived at Ben Fort Smith's City Hotel. It wasn't much of a hotel, but it was frequented by those who had business in the capital city. It was a rough hewed log building. One long room had a bar and gaming tables. It smelled exactly like you would think a frontier bar would smell. Walking across the room, you would move from the tobacco smoke of pipes and cigars, to the smell of sweaty cowboys and old leather, and on to rot gut alcohol and stale beer. If you still had an appetite, meals would be heeped on a plate, oozing into one pile of hash. That was what it all ultimately became, hash.

There was a long shed that adjoined this room. It had a dirt floor and was generally used for dining during the day. In the evening, they raked the trash out, and covered it with beds, which were nothing more than a blanket over a moss mattress. The cost was $1.50 per night.

Leander and Luther had made it to the livery stable just about the time the afternoon stagecoach arrived. It literally splashed into town, throwing more mud and manure up on the boardwalks, scattering dogs, cats, and not a few hogs that were trying to rid themselves of lice and ticks in the pools that made up Main Street. Houston was one large mud puddle, and it was a deep one at that.

The coach pulled up to the Capitol building. It was an imposing structure for this town. It was over 70 feet wide and 140 feet deep. The size alone would have called your attention to it, given that everything else was pretty primitive. However, what really set it off, was that the finished boards that covered it, had been painted peach blossom. No one could explain why. It was not what you expected. Most likely, somewhere there was a female who got her way, and was smart enough to keep her victory to herself.

Eighteen men disembarked from the stagecoach. You could pick out the nine that paid for inside seats, from the 9 that rode up top by the amount of dirt and mud on their clothes. All were pleased to be standing on the ground, albeit soft muddy ground.

Luther was speechless. Being an intelligent boy, he, at least, knew to keep his mouth closed so that he would not appear to be another gawking bumpkin. Leander enjoyed introducing his son to the novelty of city life, although, he did not want to spend any more time there than necessary. As they moved away from the stable, Leander caught sight of a familiar form, limping slightly, but as recognizable as ever. He turned to Luther, "son, you are about to meet the hero of San Jacinto himself."

Luther gulped, now looking at a tall, powerfully built man, smiling at his father.

"Mr. President, it has been some time."

"Leander, it is good to see you. Is this your boy?"

"Yes sir, this is my son, Luther."

Houston stuck out his hand engulfing Luther's.

"I am headed back to my office. If you have a moment to visit, follow me."

Leander would not have refused the offer for the world. Houston's office was right down from the Capitol. It was a small two room affair. One room was floored and one was not. Fortunately, they must have run out of peach blossom paint. It was white. Houston seemed quite content with his official surroundings.

Now seated, Houston stretched out his leg. You could tell his ankle still hurt him.

"What brings you to Houston?"

"Selling some horses, sir."

"Leander, I have not forgot that I owe you a horse. However, you seemed to have forgotten that you are to call me Sam." Houston winked at Luther and pulled out his whittling knife.

"Yes sir . . . I mean Sam."

"I guess you have heard that tomorrow we will inaugurate Lamar and Burnet. By the way, they told me how you convinced Burnet to release the Yellowstone. I wish I had been there. The guy is the biggest jackass in the country. I suspect they will move the capital, if, for no other reason to spite me. Lamar wants to break all my treaties with the Indians, and, then move the capital right into their backyard. Sounds like a smart plan to me!"

"Sam, he never seemed that bright to me, and Burnet, well, he showed his colors long ago."

"I will be a state representative while Lamar is president. He won't get everything that he wants I assure you."

Houston's door was always left ajar, so the knock was really unnecessary. Still, Leander turned when he heard it.

Pamela Mann was no longer dressed in homespun. To the contrary, her hooped skirt barely made it through the door. Her hair was combed and everything a woman could accent was well accented.

"Sam, excuse me. I have to run, everything is coming so quickly. Dr. Smith has been slightly delayed. We have moved the ceremony back to 7:30 PM, if that is fine with you?"

"Oh fine, Pamela. You may know this man from our time at Groce's. This is Leander Wilhite and his son, Luther."

"Yes, I do recall. You both are welcome to attend my son's wedding tonight. We would be honored to have you. It will be at my hotel, the Mansion Hotel. Sam can direct you. I have many more errands to run. I hope to see you tonight." She left as quickly as she came.

"Uh, Sam?"

Sam was now looking down at his whittling, with a sly smile on his face.

"Yes, odd that our paths cross again."

"I guess odd would be a good word. Isn't she the one . . ."

"That took her oxen. Yes, thank heaven you got the Twin Sisters to San Jacinto. Pamela has actually done quite well for herself. She is now on her third or fourth husband. I've lost count. She does own that hotel and is discrete with her girls, shall we say. Unfortunately, she is the most litigious woman in town. If it weren't for her, our courthouse would probably close. The local district attorney has charged her with forgery and fornication; or, it might be fornication and forgery. Before you think it, I had nothing to do with either charge. Needless to say, she is notorious, but well-liked. You will have to come tonight."

"This is her son's wedding?"

"Oh yes, Flourney, but everyone calls him Nimrod. I am the best man, for reasons that escape me. Old Dr. Ashbel Smith will be there as well. You may recall him from San Jacinto."

"Yes sir, I guess we should go find us some new duds. We did not plan on attending a wedding."

"By the way, you might want to hang around for Mr. Lamar's inauguration. You may enjoy it." He winked, and then placed the final touches on the knife he had whittled for Luther.

"Here son, you can use this one until your dad thinks you're old enough for a real one."

* * *

The Mansion Hotel was an impressive two-story building that was actually well painted. Candles were lit in every window. A steady line of carriages dropped people off at the door. Additional planking extended the boardwalk so that the dancing slippers of the attendees remained unsoiled. Neither Leander nor Luther had ever seen so many hooped skirted women in their lives. However, even bedecked in the finest fashions of the day, the dames of the ball were all eclipsed by the soon to be outgoing president of the Republic.

Houston made the short walk to the hotel, arriving exactly on time, a family motto. He wore a ruffled shirt, a scarlet cashmere waistcoat and a suit of black velvet corded in gold. The bride did not command such attention. Because his ankle was still weak, he wore boots instead of his dancing slippers. This would not deter him from the dance floor, but it did encourage his partners to move a little more quickly. In the main dining room, the host had tied wax candles to barrel hoops which hung lighted from the rafters. The soft light gave a magical quality to the event. Even some of the more coarse guests looked a little more genteel.

After the ceremony, brief and to the point, three men brought out their fiddles and those inclined took to the dance floor. The hungry moved into the hotel's dining room. The table was decorated with magnolia leaves and pine boughs. Duck, rabbit and flounder was offered, along with candied yams and champagne. Even political enemies were soon friends, at least for the evening.

Luther was less than pleased with the sleeping arrangements of the City Hotel. At home, he had his own bed, multiple blankets, all clean, and his own pillow. He had none of that here. More importantly, he had his own room. Any nocturnal noises made were his; that was not the case at the City Hotel. When Leander woke, he looked towards his son who was already awake. He had a frown on his face. Luther, the most good-natured child in the world was frowning. Leander could do nothing but laugh. He did not need to ask why.

After breakfast, they made their way to the Capitol. Folks had arrived early. All of the seats down front were taken. This suited Leander. He had no idea how long these things would last. If they went on too long, he could exit quietly. Luther continued to observe the people. Leander could only guess what questions he would have to field on the way home. Houston had its share of colorful people dressed in the most unique attire.

The audience was abuzz about Lamar's speech. They were intimate with Houston. They knew him. They lived with him and many had fought with him. Lamar was a bit standoffish. He wrote poetry, a talent universally lacking among the attendees. He considered himself an educated man, a man of letters. This was to be his supreme chance to raise the political dialogue to a new level. Lamar could hardly wait for the opportunity to give his inaugural address.

The audience quieted. Someone, unknown to Leander, approached the podium. He obviously knew many in attendance. He raised the resting gavel, and brought it down on a block of wood. His welcoming remarks were brief and direct. Before Lamar's address, he thought it proper to give the outgoing president a moment to make a few remarks. Judging by the outburst of applause, Houston remained a favorite. But for a constitutional provision, he would have been easily reelected.

From behind a curtain, out stepped General Sam Houston, dressed in a powdered wig and knee breeches. The crowd was on their feet. Yells and whoops echoed off the walls. Lamar was aghast. Burnet was red-faced. Then, just as the noise started to abate, but barely, Houston smiled and drew his sword, the same sword he drew at San Jacinto. Pandemonium broke loose. So many recognized the sword. All were clapping, feet were stopping. Burnet was almost faint. The only thing the moment lacked was an enemy force to destroy.

Houston started his speech with his humble personal beginnings. He took everyone through his years with the Indians. He held up his ring finger, the one that wore the ring his mother gave him. The ring inscribed with the word "honor". He retraced his journey to Texas, the miles of mud, the sweat of camp; and he ended at San Jacinto and the founding of a great Republic. By this time, the audience was limp. The emotion had been wrung out of them. Houston sat down and slightly turned towards Lamar.

Lamar had watched, minute by minute, second by second, as Houston chewed up every possibility that he had to impress, to inspire, to lead. He was speechless. He could not utter a word. He handed his text to a clerk for him to read. No one cared. No one stayed.

CHAPTER 21

War Again

LEANDER AND LUTHER RETURNED TO HOUSTON REG-
ULARLY. The reputation of their horses was well established. The
demand was there, and the prices were far better there than anywhere else. Houston continued to grow. It became a little more civilized with each trip. The wild element did not leave; it just became
a smaller sum of the whole. The total population did ebb and
flow depending on the severity of the last yellow fever epidemic.
They seemed to hit the town about every other year. The notorious
Pamela Mann was taken with the fever of 1840.

Houston stepped right back into the presidency, the very moment
Lamar's term expired. This surprised no one. Houston continued to
seek the annexation of Texas by the United States. Unfortunately,
the entire issue got entangled with the slavery debate, thus, freezing both sides to a position of inaction. Houston flirted with Eng-
land and with France in a vain hope that the United States might
see Texas as a more attractive prize. It did not work. The strategy
might have worked between members of the opposite sex; but it
had little impact between countries.

In the process, Houston married Margaret Lea, gave up swearing and drink, and became a 40 gallon Baptist, much to the amazement of the entire Republic. But the frustrating courtship between Texas and the United States would not be consummated on Houston's watch. No one could deny his great effort. Some of his detractors suggested that Houston came to Texas to create a nation for himself to lead. Without question, he became a leader of a Republic, but his massive effort to join Texas to the United States revealed his true intentions. Still the effort to reunite Texians with their homeland continued.

The home of the Republic was now Austin, just as Houston had predicted. Indian attacks were common, also as predicted. President Anson Jones, like most politicians, was very capable of exaggerating his own importance and the impact he had on every event that he touched. When word came that the annexation of Texas had finally been approved, he fashioned a suitable ceremony that was to enshrine himself, his words, and his deeds into the pages of history forever. He dressed in his finest suit. Friends, colleagues and every person of import, and a good many without any import, gathered at the flagpole on the Capitol grounds.

As he reached the end of his monologue, President Jones took hold of the rope that held the Lone Star flag of the Republic of Texas aloft. As it descended, slowly for effect, Jones announced that the curtain had fallen on the drama known as the Republic of Texas. A slight breeze still caught the Texas flag. Quietly, without notice, Sam Houston, the hero of San Jacinto, stepped from the crowd. The breeze stopped. The last flag of the Republic of Texas went limp in his arms. Anson Jones was peeved. Houston, again!

Jones would take that grudge with him as he left office. His efforts, such that they were, to join Texas to the United States, were largely ignored. At least, they did not get the attention that he felt they deserved, and, more importantly, he deserved. The slight, the hurt, the neglect were nurtured by Jones every day and every evening. He could not step out of Sam Houston's shadow. Finally, on a trip to Houston, the former capital, he took a room at what was now the Capital Hotel. It was the original Capitol building reconfigured as an Inn. It was a most suitable locale, for Anson Jones, the last president of the Republic, to send a bullet through his brain. He was no longer in Houston's shadow.

* * *

Rachel Whitworth could hardly contain herself. This Sunday, even she felt that the preacher had gone on a little too long. That was the unanimous consensus of all of the male attendees every Sunday. Rachel could not wait to gather up the gaggle of church women and show them what presently rested in her purse. Dressed up, bonnet wearing, churchgoing ladies, are hard to pull away from any church ground, on any Sunday. She knew she would have an audience if she would simply make her way to the shade of the big live oak. She wanted everything to appear normal, but within her, her soul was afire. It would not be long. He could not go on forever. Finally the service was over.

The women started with their usual greetings and inquiries. Comments were made about each other's hair, dress, shoes, etc. None were terribly sincere. The older damsels were starting to inventory their latest ailments. Rachel did not have the patience to defer too much longer to descriptions of gout and bunions. She feigned to be looking for something in her purse. It was a complete fabrication. What she desired was and had been right on the top where she had carefully placed it. When she took it out, the women quieted. "Ladies, have you seen this?" She continued to unfold the

now worn newspaper. In her hands, they could all see the name,
"The Liberator."

"What is it, Rachel?" One of the more curious women asked.

"This is one of those abolitionists' newspapers. This one is published by William Lloyd Garrison up in Boston."

"Oh, that doesn't concern me. We don't have any slaves and
probably never will." The comment came from one of the older
women who would have preferred to return to the subject of gout.

"Ladies, it most certainly does concern you, and each of you.
We all know that only 5% of Southern households own any slaves
at all. Apparently, our abolitionist brethren up north don't care to
make a distinction. Ladies, our honor is at stake. Let me show you
the headline." Rachel unfolded the paper. In bold black ink, the
headline read "South Repent."

Some of the assembled ladies gasped. Rachel had their attention.
"It would seem that all of us Southerners are now considered sinners in the eyes of our fellow man. For those of you who believe
we are predestined for heaven or hell, you can readily see that Mr.
Garrison has an opinion, doesn't he?"

Some of the younger congregants were not nearly as moved as
the older women. The elders had grown up with the doctrine of
predestination. The only comfort they had in this life was doing the
best they could. The opinion others had of them gave them some
assurance that they would be saved. Still, their own Baptist faith
had voted at their last convention to prohibit slave-owners from
becoming missionaries. This resulted in the immediate formation of
the Southern Baptist Convention. Still, when members of the same
faith started drawing hard lines in the sand it was upsetting.

"What does it mean?"

"The abolitionists are a small but dedicated group. Garrison wants to free the slaves immediately, without compensation to the slave owner."

"But they were paid for, they are expensive," said one of the ladies.

The conversation fractured among the women with each talking to every other lady.

"I don't own any slaves, but I don't want you just releasing them on us. Where would they live? What would they do?"

Rachel regained their attention. "Ladies, you can see that the North isn't too concerned with us sinners. We count for pitifully little, I'm afraid. I resent someone who has never met me calling me a sinner. If Mr. Garrison was so foolish to make such a statement in front of my husband, he would quickly regret it."

The ladies adjourned to their carriages. Their husbands would hear about it later. Under that tree and under churchyard trees all across the South, a fracture occurred. It was quiet, even subtle. The North never sensed it. Politicians would continue their debates. Compromises would be sought, rejected, and renegotiated. Senators and congressmen would grapple for themselves, and for their regions. It no longer mattered. Their efforts would have no consequence. They could not prevent the inevitable. William Lloyd Garrison's newspaper of 1845, as small as it was, had insulted the churchgoing women of the South. It had united slave-owners and non-slave-owners. From this point, the battle lines were drawn. Washington could play their parlor games. They could think they could defer it. However, only a fool would call the people of the South sinners, and expect that it would be forgotten. Was the North so insensitive to Southern honor?

* * *

By 1852, Leander was a grandfather and a doting one at that. On their many trips to Houston, Luther had met a number of children his age. Each trip would offer a new chance to renew friendships and to expand the number of acquaintances. Soon there were so many that Leander pretty much lost count.

Leander was also tone deaf when it came to affairs of the heart. He frequently saw Luther with others his age. He was not perceptive enough to notice that a petite, redheaded girl seemed to have taken a shine to his son. Devon and Luther were married in Houston. It was a small affair. Her parents had been taken in the yellow fever epidemic of 1849.

Leander made a quick trip to New Orleans. Catalpa needed to be made more fashionable if there was going to be a woman around the house. The outside of the home would be finished. The boards came from Groce's sawmill. Blue showed every bit the skill his father had. But there had to be more. New Orleans was the place to find what was needed.

New Orleans had grown into a very cosmopolitan town. By the time any news reached Catalpa, it was pretty old news. What Leander learned in New Orleans was a shock, a disturbing shock. The future, his future and his grandson's future did not even resemble the past. In New Orleans, there were many editions of papers published by abolitionists. Garrison was but one. The tone of those papers was rabid, as if written by people from another country. The hate and the vitriolic were almost abnormal. Leander, so long a citizen of Catalpa only, could see that his very existence was threatened. North and South might as well have been different planets.

Still, he had come for a purpose. He found what he wanted. The furnishings would greatly improve the downstairs rooms. Those rooms would be Luther's and Devon's. The upstairs would be his and eventually his grandson's, John Ross. Leander had lived in a sleeping loft his entire life. He did not need much more than that as his true home was outdoors.

The hotel's dining room was crowded. In fact, everything about New Orleans was crowded. An older, well-dressed gentleman approached his table and asked if he could share it. He was balding and bespectacled. He introduced himself as Richard Henry Dana Jr. of Boston. He did not need to add the last part. The accent was obvious. Leander welcomed the company. Perhaps, the conversation might enlighten him as to what the average Northerner was thinking.

Dana was anything but the average Northerner. He was a published author. Regrettably, Leander was not familiar with "Two Years before the Mast", but thought it might be worth reading. More importantly, Dana was a lawyer, one that was frequently hired to assist in the defense of runaway slaves.

Leander paused. He did not know if his question would offend Dana; however, he decided to ask it as politely as he could.

"So Mr. Dana, I take it you are an abolitionist?"

Dana finished the bite in his mouth, wiped his mouth with his napkin and said, "Hardly, probably the farthest thing from it."

"But, . . ."

"But, I represent fugitive slaves. Yes, that is true. My involvement came by a circuitous route. I have several friends who are ardent abolitionists. They are probably well intended, but they have absolutely no business sense. They have become obsessed with the emancipation of the Negro. After all, we do live in a practical world and they are ardent, if they are anything at all."

"But you said that you are not one of them."

"I am not. You see, friends of lawyers frequently expect lawyers to share their same interests. Emancipation is only one of a thousand causes that my friends would love for me to take up, pro bono, of course."

"Pro what?"

"That is pro bono. It means that I am to work without pay. Mr. Wilhite, I hope people consider me a charitable person; however, I do have to feed my family. The Bar, in general, grew a little weary of constantly being collared to fight someone else's cause. The abolitionists were successful in getting a personal liberty law passed in Massachusetts. Other Northern states have done the same. By their terms, if I agree to defend a runaway slave, Massachusetts pays my bills."

Leander now realized the depths of the commitment some folks had to abolition. Dana was certainly well informed and Leander wanted to continue.

"You say you are not an abolitionist, yet you work for them?"

"I am not a bank robber either, and I've been hired by a few of them. Mr. Wilhite, let me explain. No, I'm not an abolitionist. I do not agree with slavery. I think it wrong. That being said, I can read the Constitution. It is a contract. It permits slavery. It commands the return of runaway slave. You hear a lot talk about Fugitive Slave laws. Totally unnecessary, except that a lot of northern states are not doing what the Constitution requires."

"It appears worse than that to me. My slaves have been bought and paid for. I maintained them. Despite what I read, I take care of them. They are a sizable investment. Yet, if one were to accompany me to Massachusetts, your state would provide them with an attorney, at no cost, to fight me for his freedom without compensation to me. It doesn't sound like we're in the same country, or for that matter reading same Constitution."

"Oh, it gets worse, Mr. Willhite. While in Massachusetts, if you interfere with the case, or make any effort to retrieve your slave; you will be charged with a felony."

"Felony !"

"Yes, it is ridiculous. Look, Mr. Wilhite, the slavery issue is really a very simple one. Any lawyer could argue all sides to it, but the Constitution provides the answer. It is legal. And, to anticipate your next question, if it is legal here, it is legal in any of the current or future territories of the country. All that talk about Popular Sovereignty is nothing but a bunch of politicians pandering to a base of support. New York State got it right. They bought the slaves from their owners. It took quite a while, but they got it done. It was tantamount to a condemnation case. The slave owners got fair market value . . . Mr. Wilhite, I understand your talk of secession. My state talked about it years ago regarding another issue. If the truth be known, if you folks tried to crawl into the pockets of my northern friends as far as they want to crawl into yours, they would howl louder than you are."

"Mr. Dana, where does it end?"

"War, I am afraid. The abolitionists are taking their marching orders from the Lord. For them, the Supreme Law of the land is carved on clay tablets not written on parchment. At least, that is how they see it. It is hard to negotiate with folks like that. I personally find it sad. You Southerners are a warm, hospitable people, much more so than the people up North, You, as a group, are being castigated for a system that is used by very few of you, what 5% of the households? Plus no one ever talks about what happens after the slaves are freed. It will be a tragedy if it comes to war; but, I see no alternative, Mr. Wilhite. I have enjoyed meeting you. I do hope our paths cross again."

Dana rose, leaving Leander alone and very much depressed. He could not believe that anyone had the right to so alter his life. Disturbing, very disturbing.

* * *

Leander's back was to the barn door. He looked up at Blue, who nodded in the direction of the door. He turned to see Luther, but not just Luther. There was a crowd of men behind him.

"Dad, there are some men here that want to speak to you."

Leander stepped forward. He acknowledged them all. They were part of his old Ranger Company, only like himself; they had their sons with him. Time had passed so quickly. In a glance, he was looking at his men as they appeared now, and in the forms of their sons, as they had appeared at San Jacinto.

"Gentlemen." Leander tipped his hat and said no more.

"Avery McElroy, the Scotsman, spoke for the men." Leander, we do not need to educate you on the facts. We all know that the South will soon be forced out of the union. As much as the North hates us, our way of life, our culture, they seem committed to tying us to them, under their rules, at their whim. Myself, and these men with me, recognize a fight when we see it. We know it is upon us. You also know that there is not a coward among us. We have fought together before with courage. None of us have ever given anything less than our all. But we need a leader. We want you to be that leader. And, Leander, we will not take no for an answer."

Leander rubbed his forehead. There was no need to discuss causes, reasons or provocations. The South had heard them for 40 years. You can only be treated like a redheaded stepchild for so long. Pretty soon, even the slowest dullard gathers that they are not wanted. Looking into the faces of these good men, Leander wondered why the North wouldn't just let us go. We spoke the same language as the North. For the most part, we shared the same culture. We wouldn't, we couldn't be enemies! We would only be enemies if they would not let us go. Such an odd predicament. Unwanted and wanted at the same time. Leander knew he had no choice. The yoke was already around his neck. It would not be removed until it was over, for once and for all.

"Gentlemen." He was slow to gather his thoughts. "What we're about to do is as serious as rejecting a king, something we did long ago. I am not declining your request; however, I think we should visit with Governor Houston before we get too far afield. Maybe a few of you who know him, might want to accompany me, to see what our old General has to say."

Avery, Reams, Buck and a few others agreed to go. They would leave at dawn. After dinner, Leander returned to the barn. He really did not have any specific chore to do. It was what he knew and where he knew it best. The future he did not know. Just guessing made it all the more foreboding. It was almost twilight on a quiet, peaceful evening. She slipped through the door to look for him. Leander saw her.

"Momma Mae, is there anything wrong? He knew she had heard the talk. They always do.

"Leander, what dis war 'bout?"

"Momma Mae, it's about you, yes about you."

"Me! I ain't dun nuttin'." She was almost defiant in her response.

"No, Momma Mae, not you personally. You have never done anything, but to do everything that was expected and more. If you asked 20 people why this war is upon us, you would get 20 different answers. Most will say things like the tariff, or state's rights. I have never seen anyone stand up and take a bullet over a tariff. As far as state's rights go, that is a legal argument best left to lawyers. Hell, most folks can't even read. It is a little hard to get exercised over a piece of paper, when you can't read what's on it in the first place. No, the basis will be slavery, on that there can be no doubt. Momma Mae, it is wrong for someone to own another person. I think all of us who do, have known that for quite some time. That's the easy part. The hard part is unraveling the system. How to get from here to there."

Leander moved his hand from one point to another.

"The very sad part is that a few reasonable men could have figured out a way, a process. It would have taken some thought, some time, but, it could have been done. You would have your freedom. Perhaps another system of labor would work these cotton fields. I just don't know."

"Duz freedom means I got's to leave Catalpa?"

"Momma Mae, neither you, nor any of my people will ever have to leave Catalpa unless you want to. Momma Mae, a lot of men are going to die. They are not dying for slavery, or for freedom for that matter. They are going to die because of a very small group of haters. People so obsessed with hate that their whole goal is to get as many other haters involved in their movement as possible. There is no reason left, just hate. You can only insult someone for so long. Once you nick someone's pride, their honor will take over. This war will be fought for pride and honor. All other reasons are secondary."

* * *

They ascended the steps of the Governor's mansion. Leander touched the smoothness of one of the Doric columns. He turned to his men, "Sam is certainly living in a nicer house as governor than he did when he was president." He told the doorman who they were. He recognized him, Joshua Houston, Sam's former slave.

They were ushered into a small parlor right off the center hall. Those still feeling the chill of the ride moved closer to the fireplace.

Houston entered shortly thereafter. He could not have been more pleased to see them. He remembered them all from San Jacinto. He invited them to sit.

"Gentlemen, in the past I would have offered you something a little stronger than coffee. As you probably know, my wife has turned me into a Baptist."

Reams seized the moment. "How funny sir, my wife did the same to me. I guess it's the dancing you missed most."

You could see the twinkle in his eye. Houston got the joke and it reminded him of the camaraderie shared around so many campfires years ago.

"Yes Reams, the dancing, that's the hard part. I must say it is a delight to see you fellas, on what is most likely my next to last day in office. So if you need anything done, we had better get about it quickly. Margaret is packing as we speak."

Leander spoke up. "General, I would like to come back to that point in a minute. We came here to get your ideas on secession. If Texas leaves we are prepared to join the fight, but we really can't tell what is likely to happen."

Houston nodded. "Gentlemen, I suspect that tomorrow Texas will leave the union. The secessionists have the votes in both state houses. I have already told their leaders that I will not take an oath of loyalty to the Confederacy. They will probably vote to declare the office of Governor vacant. Obviously it isn't and the vote is hopelessly illegal. However, I will not fight it. I disagree with the decision, but I have never stood in the way of Texas and will not now."

Avery was taking the discussion a little off course but there was something that he had to know. "Sir, why has it come to this?"

"A very small motivated group of agitators. Most folks up north pay little attention to these debates that have gone on, for what, forty years. They are busy with their own lives. They do not own any slaves. Most have never seen one. The fact that some Southerners have them is of no concern to them. But, to the abolitionists, it consumes their very existence. For a multitude of reasons, and not all of them as lofty as they would have you believe, they hate you. So they push and pull and pretty much keep Congress stirred up, when it ought to be working."

Avery still wanted more from Houston.

"Sir, do you know Thaddeus Stevens and that senator, Charles Sumner. I hear they are the ringleaders."

"Oh, do I know them. Let me give you some insight into those two. It may explain what sometimes defies explanation. The last time I saw Stevens, he had begun wearing a woman's wig; he's bald, slick as can be. If he wanted to hide his baldness he could have gotten a man's wig. Not Thaddeus. His wig has long tresses just like a girl. Thaddeus is not someone you would really want to spend any time with if you could help it. He was born in poverty with club foot. He has never had a good day. He is quick to hate people at the slightest provocation. I suspect that his real venom is for the rich planter. However, he might as well hate the entire South while he is at it, or so it seems."

"Now, Sumner is a very odd duck. He is a man that has had a lifelong love affair with himself and his own brilliance. Knowledge he has, but he is the most unbalanced person I have ever known. Do you know of Henry Wadsworth Longfellow?"

"You mean the poet, Reams answered."

"Poet, yes he may be a poet, but in my view he is quite a salesman. Sumner and Longfellow were bosom buddies. Longfellow announced that he intended to marry. Sumner became distraught, almost suicidal. Longfellow became so concerned that he went to his bride. I can only imagine the conversation. Honey, you know that trip, our honeymoon that you are looking forward to. I have a great idea! Let's invite old Chuck Sumner to come along."

After swallowing their astonishment, the men burst out in laughter.

Houston grinned, "he may be a poet, but he is quite a salesman."

"What I am trying to say is that these folks are not well balanced. Some are obsessed to the point of madness. Anyone who holds up a cold blooded murderer like Brown as a hero is not exactly quite right. However, they have the moral high ground. I've owned slaves. Margaret and I freed what few we had left. They would not leave! After tomorrow, when I no longer have a job, they may think better of their decision. However, they are still part of the family. I disagree with slavery; yet, I've bought slaves that I felt were being abused. That said, you know I would defend your right to have them."

"Where do you come down sir?" Leander had to know.

"You see that fireplace there? Last night I burnt a letter from Abraham Lincoln in that very fireplace. He offered me all the troops I could want or need to hold Texas in the union. I refused his offer. I do not want to see Texas leave. It is a mistake. The South cannot defeat the North. We don't have the population or the resources. The war will be ungodly bloody. But I will not stand in the way of Texas. Texas will regret its decision, but if that is the way Texas wants it, I will always support Texas. Margaret does not know it, but our oldest son is on his way to New Orleans to enlist in the Confederate ranks. No, it never should have come to this. I know how you men can fight. By the time the war wakes up our unfocused northern brethren you will have already killed a lot of their sons, brothers and grandsons. There will not be any chance to reason then. It will be a blood feud for sure. I understand all the arguments. I have a grasp of all the facts. I will support you and Texas, if that is the way you want to go."

Leander rose, followed by the rest of the men. "Sir, we had to come."

"I appreciate that, as always you have honored me by your presence. Here let me walk you out." The men made their way to the door. Leander and Houston followed behind them. Leander had taken one step off the grand porch that was the entrance to the mansion when Houston grabbed his shoulder.

"Leander, when I saddled Saracen, Good Grief, so many years ago, I noticed he was limping slightly. I lifted his hoof." Houston reached deep into his pocket. "This small rock was stuck in his hoof. Wasn't anything to pop it out. For whatever reason, I put it in my pocket. I have carried it ever since. You can see I have rubbed it pretty smooth. It got me through San Jacinto with just a leg wound. Let's hope it does the same for you. Here, it's yours." He handed Leander the small white stone. The sunlight hit it; the whiteness had quite a luster. It surely was smooth.

"Thank you sir, I am so very grateful."

"It's Sam, Leander, just Sam." They shook hands, neither one totally comfortable with their parting or their future.

* * *

It was just barely dawn. Leander was mounted on his blooded bay stallion. Of all his horses, he felt this one was the one that could get him through a war. His deep mahogany coat always shined, no matter what time of the year. He had a solid, quiet temperament. However, he was a proud horse. He knew what he was and he wasn't bashful about showing it.

Leander and his Company, now considerably enlarged beyond

his former group of Rangers, were positioned in a grove of trees on the right front of Beauregard's Army. He could see the North's lines opposite a no count creek called Bull Run. There was a gentle slope to the battlefield. Before lost to the slope, he could count at least 20 enemy field pieces. Any one of them melted down would have made four of the Twin Sisters. They were not loaded with cutup horseshoes. Not quite.

Their rifled barrels would spin canister grapeshot into the opposite lines, cutting men to pieces. It would be sheer butchery. At his side hung his sword, the same one he wore at San Jacinto. This time, it was purely ceremonial. His pistols would do his killing. Now, one gun could kill six men. He had two more stuck in his belt and had two more in his saddlebags. The weaponry was staggering. Yet, his orders were to slam into the exposed flank of the Yankees. This was pretty much the plan back at San Jacinto.

The North's camp was mostly hidden by the terrain. The part that could be seen was an endless, uniform pattern of tents. He had been told that each side would have in the neighborhood of 30,000 men when the show started. Jackson's brigade was coming in by train. Leander could not comprehend it. 60,000 men who all looked alike, spoke the same language, and until a couple of months ago, saluted the same flag. Leander no longer questioned it. His focus now was to get his men home safely, his son included. This was not going to be an 18 minute battle. Not this time.

He saw it first. Then, he heard the infantry come to attention. He cast a glance at Luther. He had turned out far better than any father could have ever hoped for. He looked handsome in his uniform. More importantly, he looked brave. He had his mother's quiet peace. It just never left him. The bugle broke the silence. He heard the order, "To the charge." It was the same one he had heard at San Jacinto so long ago. It had now begun.

www.ingramcontent.com/pod-product-compliance
Lightning Source LLC
Chambersburg PA
CBHW032022240626
47154CB00003B/749